Those That Remain

Rob Ashman

For Don

Chapter 1

Lucas wanted to shoot his visitors. The gun lay in his desk drawer and he was itching to pull it out and blast away. He had to stop them from torturing him with kindness, but wasting two FBI agents on his first week back was such bad form. So, in the absence of being able to kill them, he chose instead to only half listen.

The two guys in FBI regulation suits were talking, but all he heard was the faint mumbling of soft, understanding voices. They were being ever so gentle and considerate, which would be good, if it wasn't for the fact that they had been ever so gentle and considerate for the past three goddam days.

They were well trained to deal with people being rehabilitated back into work after they had suffered significant trauma. But how many times did he have to go over and over the same damn stuff? It was always the same story, always the same chronology, always the same people, and always the same outcome.

Monday 21 March was a significant date in the Lucas household calendar. It was the day he finally returned to work. He had been back now for three days. Not that anyone would have known because he had been holed up in his office talking to the FBI suits for the entire duration.

Lucas harboured a dark thought which he kept to himself. *Let them bring a new guy in to run the show, and I'll drive a desk in a back office somewhere.* It was once the job he loved, but now the role of Police Lieutenant appeared like a giant nettle which he had no intention of grasping.

After everything that had happened, Lucas couldn't move on. How could he? There was no resolution to what had taken place, just one giant loose end.

One big, fat, ugly loose end.

He was aware that the talking had stopped, and the FBI agents were staring at him with a look of expectation that said, 'It's your turn to talk now.'

He looked up and didn't even bother to pretend. 'Sorry, guys, I wasn't listening. You need anything else?'

'It's been a long few days, but I think we have all we need,' the taller of the two men replied, nodding his head. Lucas still couldn't remember their names.

You had what you needed two damn months ago, Lucas thought, keeping his mouth shut.

They rose from the circular conference table and shook hands across it. There was a palpable sense of relief that the gentle tones and soft questions had at last come to an end.

'Thanks guys.' Even Lucas had to admit his words sounded hollow and disingenuous. He just wanted them both to piss off.

Lucas ushered them to the door, limping without his stick, and showed them out. He flopped down in his chair and shook his head. There was a knock on the door and his mail arrived.

The plain white document-sized envelope with the handwritten address stood out from the rest. Lucas pulled it from the stack and held it in his hand, turning it first this way then the next, as if examining a piece of evidence. It was addressed to him with a date stamp of Monday 21 March and, from the postmark, he could just about make out Baton Rouge, Louisiana.

It was written in an ornate copperplate script with flurries of expert swirls around his name: Lieutenant Edmund Lucas. He frowned and edged his finger into the corner of the flap, and then slid it along the top, ripping it open.

The envelope felt empty.

He peered inside.

It certainly didn't contain a letter or a document, but Lucas knew there was something at the bottom. He tipped the envelope sideways to extract whatever was inside.

The first grains of white sugar rolled from the confines of the envelope and onto the polished surface of the desk. Lucas was stunned, unable to comprehend what was happening.

He tilted it further. More grains of sugar spilled out and pooled in concentric circles on the table top. The more Lucas tilted the envelope, the more sugar cascaded down, along with what looked like squares of white paper. Lucas upended it and allowed the complete contents to empty onto the desk. He stared at the mess of sugar and paper, holding his breath.

It took a few moments for the cogs to turn and for realization to dawn. Then tears welled in his eyes and he exploded, slamming his fist into the table.

'No!' he yelled at the top of his voice.

As he punched the desk a second time, the door burst open.

'Are you alright, boss?'

'No, I am not!' Lucas spat the words across the office. 'Get those FBI bastards back here now.'

He was ready to grasp the nettle, spoiling for a fight.

Chapter 2

Screams raged inside Mechanic's head, while the rest of the room remained deathly silent. The air was sultry hot as the ceiling fan struggled to make headway against the Florida night. A pale yellow glow from the sodium street lights penetrated the thin cotton window drapes. The figure on the bed scanned the silhouettes of bedroom furniture and ornaments. Tears of exertion pooled into bloodshot eyes, giving a blurred and watery view of the emptiness.

There was no one to help.

The attacks were becoming more frequent now. They were more intense. The inevitable was not far away.

Bathed in sweat, with bedsheets sticking to trembling limbs and torso, Mechanic's head shook from side to side, with a face contorted by the intense effort of trying to maintain control.

Had it been there? Was it real?

Mechanic's imagination ran a roller-coaster ride of exaggeration with the sounds of a neighbourhood asleep. Afraid to swallow. Afraid to breathe. Listening.

Mechanic's chest heaved with the need to suck air into bursting lungs. Lying rigid on the bed, listening, silent screams resonating deep inside to drown out the terror.

There it was again. A gnawing whisper, so deep in the mind it could be forgotten. Then it was gone.

Was it real? Or was this just another night of shredded emotions based on a false alarm?

Mechanic's body convulsed and another torrent of air rushed into the lungs and out again. Then silence. Listening.

Then came the faint, but unmistakable, sound of someone murmuring in the whispering gallery of Mechanic's mind. Like the sound of a warm breeze through long, dry grass, gently building in volume, only to fall away to nothing.

No mistake, it was there.

No need to bury the scream now. Mechanic let it out, full blast.

Mechanic bound from the bed, tearing the sodden sheets from flailing arms and legs, careering through the bedroom door, smashing first into one wall and then the next, running helter-skelter down the hallway to the room at the end.

The door provided little resistance as Mechanic crashed through, plaster crumbling from the wall as the handle slammed into it. Falling flat to the floor with arms fully extended in the push-up position. Head arched backwards at a neck-breaking angle, baying to a non-existent moon.

Staring at the ceiling, Mechanic listened. The only sound was the crack of vertebrae as the pressure and contortion increased.

Mouth gaping open. Sucking in air.

Listening.

Nothing came.

The seconds ticked by. Nothing. Just silence.

Mechanic's body sent pain signals to the brain. Eventually the effort proved too much and the powerful figure crumpled to the floor, forehead banging down hard on the matting.

Lying there exhausted, the steady pattern of breathing gradually returned. The tension ebbed away. The attack was over. The pain had done its job.

Then, with a sound like the death swing of a sword, it was back. No false alarm this time, positive proof.

The gnawing, scratching whisper grew in clarity and volume. Like someone talking at the back of a great hall and slowly getting closer.

Then the footsteps started.

The sound of heavy boots on wood block floor echoed around the walls and vaulted ceilings of Mechanic's mind, with doors opening and slamming shut.

The footsteps got louder. Daddy was approaching.

Moving to a crouched position, Mechanic grasped the heavy dumbbell weights on the floor, stood up and started driving the bars up and down. Muscles bulged and veins stood out, the sweat of fear replaced by the sweat of exertion.

Must burn it out. We're not ready, Mechanic's thoughts tumbled together. *Kill the bastard through pain. Focus on the pain.*

The gnawing whisper and the heavy boots came ever closer, forcing themselves to be heard.

The pain came quickly and with it Mechanic's body began to shake. Arm and shoulder muscles burned with lactic acid.

'Must force it out. It's too soon. Focus on the pain,' Mechanic snarled into the full length mirror on the wall. Blowing air in and out through clenched teeth with the rhythm of the pumping weights, the mirror was soon awash with saliva.

The footsteps stopped and the gnawing whisper spoke in soft, gentle tones, as if coaxing a child.

'Put the weights down.' Daddy was here.

This served only to galvanize Mechanic into a frenzy of renewed effort. Blood engorged the neck and face. Arms and shoulders were now distended with swollen flesh and sinews. But the constant repetition of pumping iron grew slower as muscles lost their ability to function.

'It's too soon, it's too soon. I'm not ready.' Mechanic spat the words at the reflection in the mirror as the weights took their toll.

'Put the weights down. It's time to go to work.' Daddy's voice was clear and confident, less coaxing, more demanding.

By now the bars hardly reached the horizontal lift position. The effort involved contorted Mechanic's face into a grotesque picture of pain and fear. Head to one side, body arching backwards, the force of gravity winning the battle. Spit ran down the mirror in rivulets.

'Put the fucking weights down now!' The voice boomed around Mechanic's head.

The grip gave way and the weights fell to the floor with a clanking thud. Mechanic stood naked in front of the mirror, arms hanging down, pumped and useless.

Pain still surging.

Staring straight ahead, Mechanic didn't move. As the minutes passed, the face relaxed, hyperventilated breathing slowly returned to normal, anxiety levels dropped.

Mechanic's reflection stared back, its contours distorted by the clinging fluid. All evidence of effort faded away. All evidence of control faded away.

The lips parted with a faint smile.

'That's better. You're ready when I say you're ready. Now let's go and please Daddy.'

Chapter 3

The air in the bedroom was as still and warm as its sleeping occupants. The darkness of 3am worked its way into every corner as if to muffle any sound that might wake the sleeping beauties. The quilt covering the two of them rose and fell in the gentle rhythm of deep sleep.

A bathrobe lay tossed into a heap at the foot of the bed. Footprints in the thick pile carpet, where heavy wet feet had crushed it flat, were slowly drying and returning to their original position. Books lay casually discarded on either side of the bed, books designed to exercise the eyes to sleep rather than the mind to action.

Edmund Lucas was a sound sleeper.

He was calm and collected at all times or, at least, that's what he told himself. He was cool under fire or, at least, that's what he told his staff. And he was a great husband, though not even he had the gall to tell his wife that. In addition to this glowing self-assessment, Lucas had a rather unusual trait. Since the age of twenty-six he had never been startled by anything.

As a highly strung young patrolman he'd pulled over a car which had unexpectedly exploded in front of him as he questioned the driver. The guy turned out to be a religious maniac, intent on bringing some unfortunate individuals closer to their maker. The explosion turned out to be a homemade bomb which went off prematurely due to the hot weather. Something to do with sugar, fertilizer and plastic bags sweating in the heat.

Lucas was blown a good ten feet through the air, but miraculously landed in one piece. The driver, however, was blown into what could only be described as bite-sized chunks. Lucas was in a bad way following his sudden flight, and it remained a remarkable stroke of luck that he survived. Fortunately for him, he did.

Ed Lucas had never been startled or jumped at anything since that day. He figured the blast had blown away all his nerves.

Ironically, the two weeks spent in the hospital high dependency unit did more for his career in the police force than anything he'd done before, not to mention the improvement it brought to his fictitious love life. After six years of working as an unremarkable uniformed officer who drove a patrol car around his beat, he became a local hero. Overnight he was transformed into the guy who tackled the terrorist single handed. The papers and news channels had a field day. The force milked it for all they could – it was good PR at a time when they badly needed it.

Regaining consciousness five days later, Lucas didn't have the heart to tell them he'd had no idea that the man was a religious nutcase, even less that the mad bastard had a bomb in his car. All he knew was the guy had a brake light out.

The media circus paraded around him, and Lucas just lay back in his intensive care bed and let it happen. Later, he'd often reflect that, in all the interviews he gave, no one once asked the obvious question: 'So, Officer Lucas, how did you know the guy had a bomb?' It wasn't important to them, so Lucas considered it shouldn't be important to him either.

His hospital-acquired love life now slept beside him. Somewhat larger than the one-hundred-and-thirty pound nurse who'd blanket bathed him as he lay unable to move, but still possessing the same caustic wit and magic eyes.

Mrs Lucas was now almost the same size as Mr Lucas. He often said she only grew fat to piss him off, saying that making love was now like trying to balance two ball bearings on top of one another. She'd reply that if he was larger in the men's department, the ball bearings wouldn't have to try so hard to balance. Of their many marital jibes, they enjoyed this one the most.

Lucas, like his wife, was an only child and, also like his wife, his parents were dead. As they moved from place to place over the years, they'd accumulated a wide circle of friends and were known as a sociable couple.

She always said their friends liked her but tolerated him. Lucas countered this one day by saying, 'If that was true, they'd visit when I'm not here.' She smiled and replied, 'They do, honey, I just don't tell you.'

For whatever reason, kids never came along. They tried hard for several years when they were younger and did all the tests. Nothing wrong with him, nothing wrong with her. However, life changed dramatically when they were both aged forty-two and what she thought was the onset of early menopause turned out to be a most unexpected pregnancy. For the next six weeks the news put their well-structured and well-ordered lives in a blender, switched on with the lid off.

The mental turmoil stopped when she miscarried. The pregnancy was ectopic and she lost an ovary in the process. They were both devastated. Lucas shut his emotions in a box and locked them away for good, while she too never got over it.

Not once did they consider it a sign that they could at last become parents. They simply both slipped back into their 'let's just forget it ever happened' lives and threw themselves into their work. Since that day, they always thought of themselves as happy but not really complete.

The phone rang, its synthetic warble demanding attention. Neither of them stirred.

It rang again, as if annoyed at being ignored. Still no response.

On the third ring, the bulk next to the phone moved. A large black hand oozed from under the quilt, like mud from beneath a sneaker, lifted the receiver and took it under the covers.

'Lucas.' The voice was deep, slow and sleepy.

'Sorry to wake you at this hour, sir, but there's been a burglary at the home of Celia Mason.' The voice paused for a response. None came.

'Sir, this is Metcalf from the station. There's been a burglary.' He paused again. Lucas emerged from beneath the bedding and tried to focus on the luminous green digits of the clock.

Metcalf had thirty years' service. He'd been there and done it all. He was in his late forties with his sights set on early retirement, but he looked much older. He'd risen to the dizzy heights of desk sergeant at the pace of an injured snail. Maintaining an easy life was now his main objective. Metcalf feared this call was going to be anything but easy and could put a sizeable dent in his comfortable existence.

'Sir?' This didn't sound good. The continued silence was the sign of an unhappy Lieutenant. Lucas was renowned for his silence before the storm.

'Sergeant,' Lucas spoke at last. 'There are around two thousand burglaries in our area every year. Why am I being told about this one? And why at three o'clock in the morning?' His voice was still slow, but not as sleepy.

'Sorry, sir, but it's Celia Mason's home.' There was another long silence. The sergeant was beginning to believe his colleagues who'd said that he'd be 'dead meat' for calling so late.

'You said that once, Sergeant. Unless you make sense with the next sentence you utter, I'm going to kick your ass around the station. And that will happen in around five hours when I normally get in.' Metcalf gulped.

'Sir, Celia Mason is the daughter of Judith Somerville, the congresswoman. The one you called slayer. The one you called the law and order dragon, the one you called ...'

'Okay, okay, I know what I called her.' It was Lucas's turn to pause. 'I'll be in within the hour. When I arrive I want a full briefing and I want Bassano there as well.'

'Yes, sir. I'll call him.'

'I'll see you in an hour,' said Lucas. 'Oh, and Metcalf, who told you to call me?'

'No one, sir. I thought it important enough to call myself. Why do you ask?'

'No big reason. I just wanted to know how many asses to kick when I get in.' Metcalf swallowed hard as Lucas hung up.

Lucas sat up in bed and absorbed the conversation. As he stared into the gloom, the vision of Judith Somerville invaded his mind. Whenever that happened the picture was always the same. His thoughts drifted back to two years ago when she'd been running for Congress on an aggressive law and order ticket, the ferocity of which the state hadn't witnessed before. She'd portrayed herself as a woman who was supremely well equipped to manage a crisis. Unfortunately, it was almost always one of her own making.

She and Lucas had been guests on a television news programme following the brutal murder of a young man in a park. She'd chewed him up and spat him out. Every which way he turned in the debate, she demolished him with a ferocity and venom that physically hurt. She tore him and his police force apart in front of shit knows how many millions, dismissing any attempt by Lucas to defend the steps that had been taken to apprehend the killer.

Lucas distinctly remembered the low point was when she labelled him and his force 'limp dicks'. She later issued a public apology but the damage was already done and her votes secured. He still winced at his ritual flaying in front of the cameras and vividly remembered his two overwhelming thoughts on that eventful evening. At first he'd wanted to screw the ass off of her, she was seriously horny. By the end of the show, he wanted to kill her.

She'd promised to kick some police butt if she was elected and stem the obscene level of violent and serious crime. Three months later she did just that and, as promised, Lucas's department endured a significant amount of kicking. She was all over them like a dose of clap. She restructured, rationalized and performance-measured them to death. That was two and a half years ago, and Lucas still had her as his cross to bear and the force still had a bad case of the clap.

Lucas snapped his thoughts back to the present.

He whispered into the darkness, 'May God protect us and may God protect my pension.'

The day had started badly.

Chapter 4

Driving to the station, Lucas was on autopilot. The roads were full of traffic for such an early hour. Beside him on the passenger seat was a brown paper bag containing a selection of fruit and cold meat grabbed from the fridge. He always made a point of ensuring he set off to work with a healthy lunch and then bought food from the deli up the street.

For Lucas, his weight was a constant source of embarrassment. His wife didn't care, his friends didn't care and his colleagues didn't care. However, it engendered in him a feeling of quiet self-loathing. In his mind, he ate little and exercised more than most. In reality, he caught the lift to the first floor and ate for two people – one of whom stuffed himself with chili dogs and the other was a fat bastard.

Lucas fought with his weight like a kid fights with a hosepipe, wrestling to bring it under control but far too much fun to turn off. It wasn't something he wanted to get to grips with or acknowledge. Instead, he was happy to pack healthy food in a bag, drive it to work, put it in the bin and then eat a fast-food lunch.

Lucas tore himself away from the bag–bin–deli conundrum and thought about what lay ahead. Under normal circumstances he drove to work with his brain fixed in catch-the-villain mode. Today it was in damage control mode.

She's gonna go fucking nuts, Lucas thought as he waited at the traffic lights. He was still trying to anticipate just how fucking nuts she could be when the driver behind honked his impatience at being made to wait at a green light. Lucas put his hand up in apology and pulled away.

Walking up the steps to the front office, Lucas concluded that he and his precinct were likely to suffer major collateral damage at the hands of the darling congresswoman, regardless of which action he took. The chances of securing an arrest for the crime were almost nil and he figured there were two options available: deal with it as any other burglary, almost guaranteeing no result and suffering the fire and brimstone treatment from Congresswoman Somerville, or throw everything at it in a vain attempt to get a result and risk accusations of special treatment.

What a screw-up, he thought.

He decided to do what he always did when faced with a difficult decision and that was not to make it, at least not until he'd been fully briefed. He got into the elevator and pushed the first floor button, his head still buzzing with the consequences of the decision he had to make within the next thirty minutes.

Arriving at his office he punched the handle down on the door marked Lieutenant and strode in, flicking on the lights. He picked up the phone and hit one of the buttons.

'Metcalf, it's Lucas. Has Bassano arrived? I want the two of you in my office now and bring all you have on this Mason robbery.'

Minutes passed. Lucas tried to relax with his feet on the desk, his full weight pushing the reclining mechanism of the chair to its limits.

Damned if I do, damned if I don't, he mused. He then snapped out of his daydream and lost patience. 'Where the hell are they?' He lunged forward to grab the phone when there was a knock at the half open door and both officers trooped inside.

'Thanks for coming in at this early hour.' He nodded to Bassano, motioning for them to take a seat.

Bassano was a senior detective who looked like he was straight out of a TV cop show. The son of a second generation Italian American father and a Swedish mother who'd come to America as a tourist, his was a gene pool to die for. Six feet one inch tall with chiselled features and an equally chiselled body. He worked out in the gym to make sure everything was as it should be, but actually didn't need to. It was just the way he was built. As much as he prided himself on his physique, the winning combination every time was his brooding Italian charm and his piercing electric blue eyes.

It didn't matter if he was clean shaven or sporting two-day-old stubble, or if his hair was swept back in a movie star style or a bedraggled mess, Bassano was a magnet to women.

Where women were concerned he didn't have one type but one thing was certain, for just about every woman he met, he was definitely theirs. Age didn't matter, shape didn't matter, social class didn't matter. They threw themselves at him. Bassano didn't understand how it worked, all he knew was it did. He sat opposite Lucas and it was clear that today's look was 'just got out of bed'.

Lucas resumed his briefing. 'I'm sure that Metcalf has told you about the burglary tonight at the home of Celia Mason. Nothing especially traumatic about that, except that this is the daughter of our beloved congresswoman, Judith Somerville. I'm sure you'll agree this puts an entirely different perspective on the amount of shit we could get ourselves into. I also don't need to tell you, gentlemen, that this is very sensitive and could blow our balls off if we screw it up.' Both men nodded, knowing only too well Judith Somerville's penchant for removing balls when it suited her.

'Okay, Metcalf, fill us in.' Lucas reclined his chair once more and the mechanism creaked and groaned in protest.

'Well, sir, we had a phone call from Mr Mason at 2.35am. He said that the house had been broken into and various items stolen while they were asleep. Apparently, he noticed items were missing when he got up to take a leak.'

'What was stolen?' asked Bassano.

'The usual,' Metcalf continued. 'Silverware, trinkets – anything that was small and sparkled.'

'Method of entry?'

'Crow bar under the patio door. It wasn't deadlocked, just lifted clean out of the runners.'

'Alarm system?' Bassano was on a roll.

'When the officer got there, he reported that both Mr and Mrs Mason were drunk as skunks. They'd thrown an all-day party and forgot to prime the alarm.' Metcalf folded his notes away.

'Brilliant, just brilliant. Is there anything at all to go on?' Lucas was on his feet now, prowling around the office.

'Nothing, sir, just a run-of-the-mill burglary.' Metcalf knew this wasn't what the boss wanted to hear.

'What do you think, Bassano? Have you got anyone out there processing the scene?'

'Not yet. By the sound of it there were about a hundred people at this party. We'll collect prints okay, but I'm not sure what they'll tell us. We can run what we find against the database and see what comes up. But other than that ...'

Lucas returned to his long suffering chair, reviewing his options. The three sat in silence as if waiting for a eureka moment, each one conscious of retaining his balls.

The phone rang. Lucas answered it.

'Sorry to disturb you, sir, but I had a Judith Somerville on the line for you.'

Lucas shut his eyes. 'How does she sound?' he asked, not wanting to know the answer.

'Like a pit bull has bit her in the ass.' The caller paused. 'Sir.'

'Tell her I'm busy. Take her number and tell her I'll call her back,' Lucas ordered, determined to show who was the boss.

'No, sir, I had her on the line. She's gone now. She told me to tell you ...' There was a pause while he consulted his notes, '... she's at her daughter's house, she's waiting and she's not happy. In that precise order, sir.'

'Thanks.' Lucas replaced the receiver in its cradle and stared at the expectant faces opposite him.

That damn woman, he thought. *I should've killed her when I had the chance.* Despite Bassano and Metcalf awaiting his pronouncement, his thoughts rambled on. *Any court in the land would have accepted a plea of self-defence. Any court that had seen that fucking TV programme, that is.*

Bassano took his chance and interrupted. 'Sir?' Lucas pulled himself together.

'Okay, I want a forensic team all over that house. I need everything you've got. If there's a fibre or a print that doesn't belong to someone at that party, I want it. Get a team working on the guest list, I want everyone interviewed. I want this case cracked. I want maximum effort. Got it?'

They both nodded, clear about what Lucas wanted from them. Even though he was not directly involved, Metcalf found himself nodding too.

'Let's get to work. I want results fast.' Lucas thumped the desk. He had made his decision.

Across the city, in a quiet well-to-do neighbourhood, another decision was about to be made.

Mechanic was emotionally shredded. The planning had been rushed and the execution at the house a total disaster. Daddy would not be happy.

Lying in the dark, Mechanic tried hard to focus on the ritual. The soft strains of Pachelbel's Canon in D played through the headphones. The fantasy preparation was in full flow but it wasn't working. Mechanic's mind drifted back to the house and replayed the sequence of events over and over again. How could it have gone so wrong?

There was so much catching up to do, the plan was never going to be ready. Worst of all, Mechanic knew that control was ebbing away with each attack. It was just a matter of time.

Eyes closed, Mechanic rehearsed what needed to happen: the method of approach, the forced entry and the precise ceremony of killing the occupants – a procession of grainy images from a low-budget horror movie. Then came the unmistakable sound of footsteps. The thud of heavy boots stomped on wooden floors as Daddy moved from room to room inside Mechanic's head.

Doors opening, doors slamming.

This was getting way out of control.

Mechanic tore the headset off and crashed down the corridor. Jerking the weights off the floor.

'It's too soon,' Mechanic snarled into the mirror as the frenzy of pumping iron did its job. The pain surged and acid coursed through tiring muscles, burning them with every lift.

Footsteps were fast approaching.

Daddy was about to make his decision.

Ready or not.

Chapter 5

Lucas enjoyed driving, but was hating every mile of this trip. The needle hugged sixty-five as he drove the seventy miles down US 98 to Keaton Beach and the home of Celia Mason.

With the cruise control on, he'd little to do except to think of the tactics which he would employ once he met his nemesis. He'd decided back at the station that the personal touch was the way to play it, and had asked Metcalf to telephone ahead to inform Judith Somerville that he was on his way. He didn't want to make the call in case she chewed him out over the phone. Lucas would have to meet the infernal woman sooner or later and it was best to do it face to face.

He made good time to the row of expensive beachfront properties. The house was big and, like its neighbours, overlooked the Gulf. It had beautiful trimmed lawns on each side, an avenue of imported trees and a long sweeping driveway. At the back was a large pool area and two sun terraces with access to a strip of private beach.

I wonder who paid for this lot, Lucas thought as he climbed out of his car, knowing exactly where the money came from. He started up the driveway, gravel crunching under his feet.

It was well known that Judith Somerville's husband was a successful man in his own right and ran his own real estate business. What was not so well known was that he knew jack shit about selling houses and it was Judith who pulled all the strings. Her husband was a world-class socializer who would win gold if brown-nosing ever became an Olympic sport. He was a superb frontman for the company, but was never anything else.

Lucas always suspected that it was set up this way so that Judith could concentrate on her political image without the risk of tarnishing it with the sordid necessity of making money. He also suspected that not all of the business deals wouldn't stand up to close scrutiny since Judith wielded her political influence in the background to ease them through. It would never do for the congresswoman to take a fall if some of the rather more underhand transactions become public. That, Lucas surmised, would be her husband's job.

Looking at the house, framed in the pale glow of the morning sun, Lucas had to admit that the Somervilles were very well off and that Celia Mason was taking handsome advantage of her parents' riches. This house was all about family wealth and an ostentatious wedding gift from Mommy and Daddy.

The big brass knocker thumped hard on the door, echoing around the vaulted ceiling of the entrance hall within. The door opened only to the extent of the thick safety chain connecting it to the frame. A man's face, ashen grey with red-rimmed eyes, peered around the woodwork.

'Yes, who are you?'

'Lieutenant Ed Lucas, Florida State Police Department.' Lucas showed him a card he'd removed from his wallet. An arm snaked out from behind the door and grabbed it. The door slammed shut.

Bit late for the Fort Knox routine, Lucas thought. *Pity you weren't as keen on getting value for money from your alarm system last night.*

Lucas was getting impatient, but tried not to allow himself to get boiled over before he even saw Somerville. The same grey-faced man opened the door and ushered him into the house, giving him his card back.

'Please come through to the lounge, Mr Lucas. We've been expecting you.' The man walked on ahead.

'Thanks.' Lucas grimaced at the exaggerated emphasis given to the word *we*.

The room was spacious, with two four-seater sofas facing each other across a marble coffee table which was big enough to hold a sporting event. Pallet-knife oil paintings hung on the walls, original pictures from a local artist, depicting ocean and beach scenes. The far wall was mostly glass, giving a splendid view of the pool area and beach down to the water's edge. This also housed the derailed patio door.

To the right of the hallway, Lucas could see the dining room. Glass cabinets along the walls housed cut crystal and polished silver which sparkled and glittered while a rich walnut table and eight chairs were positioned in the centre. The same painter whose paintings were featured in the living room had also provided the paintings for this room – he'd done well out of the Somervilles. Lucas was drinking all this in when he realized that the man he'd followed was no longer in the room. A familiar voice greeted him from behind.

'Lieutenant Lucas, so good of you to pay us a personal visit to clear up our little difficulty.' It was Judith Somerville.

Lucas turned to see her emerge from the kitchen, slinking towards him. She was dressed in a tight-fitting top and a long silk wrapover skirt that revealed a generous glimpse of thigh when she walked. Her long black hair was piled up high at the back and held in place with grips. Sunglasses were perched on top of her head. The ensemble was finished off with what Lucas could only describe as a pair of hooker heels. Memories from their first meeting flooded back, the ones about the screwing, that is, not the killing.

She glided around the sofa and sat on the edge of one of the seats, motioning for him to sit in the chair opposite.

When he was seated, she reclined into the soft cushions and crossed her legs. The skirt wrap parted and fell to either side. What Lucas had previously only glimpsed was now firmly on display.

She smiled and looked at Lucas, saying nothing. It was obvious he didn't know whether to meet her gaze or feast his eyes on her expanse of thigh. It was so easy with men like Lucas. The top, the skirt, the whole ensemble was just a technique for disarming them, to make them think more about what was happening in the front of their pants than to concentrate on serious debate. Judith broke the silence when she gauged Lucas was uncomfortable enough.

'I'm unhappy with this situation, Lieutenant,' she said flatly. 'I hope you're receptive to the sensitivity required in handling our …' she paused, '… unfortunate mishap.' She delivered the line like a woman who was telling her boyfriend that penis size didn't matter.

Lucas's mind was still halfway up her skirt. He jolted himself back to reality and grunted a noise that could be interpreted as either yes or no, making a nondescript waving gesture with his hand. He was outmanoeuvered, already struggling.

She continued, 'You, of all people, know my stance on law and order in this state. I've campaigned on it and bettered it. My record is one of achievement.' She stopped, allowing Lucas to catch up.

'Congresswoman—' Lucas started, but was cut off.

'Needless to say, an incident such as this is a godsend to those political elements who have, shall we say, differing views to mine. I have no doubt that they wouldn't hesitate to use my daughter's misfortune to undermine my strong record, which could prove most damaging.' She fixed Lucas with a stare that made him feel about eight years old. 'Damaging, that is, for all concerned, Lucas. Am I making myself clear?'

'I appreciate that this could cause adverse publicity for you and your family,' Lucas replied, finally off the mark, 'and that any coverage could be used against you by your opponents.'

'Well done, Lieutenant. Well thought through.' Her tone of voice ensured Lucas was back to being eight years old again. 'But that's just half the picture.' She pulled her skirt back in place with a flourish and leaned forward. 'This story is bound to break sooner or later, irrespective of how carefully it is handled. We have to consider it inevitable. When that occurs, I want to be able to provide a response that states the incident has been dealt with and that the perpetrator of the crime is already in custody. All of which, of course, is due to the effective law enforcement processes I've implemented since I've been in office.'

She focused her gaze on Lucas across the marble-topped table. Lucas eventually broke the silence.

'Bringing this to a satisfactory conclusion will be in both our interests,' Lucas said.

'That's correct, Lieutenant.' Judith rose to her feet and stared down at Lucas. 'And let's not be under any misunderstanding here. It *will* be brought to a satisfactory conclusion.' She emphasized the 'will' with a foreboding that Lucas painfully recognized.

Lucas nodded his head as if in surrender. 'Everything possible will be done. The team are on their way here now, Congresswoman.'

'Good,' she replied, making her way back into the kitchen. She continued the conversation over her right shoulder. 'To allow your team as much free access as possible, my daughter will move to my residence in Tallahassee until this settles down.' She returned with four envelopes.

Judith waited in the centre of the room with the envelopes in her hand. If Lucas wanted them, he'd have to go and get them. He moved to stand in front of her and she handed them to him, one by one.

'This one contains a statement from Celia, my daughter. This one is a statement from her husband, Charles. This one is a list of all that is missing and approximate valuations. And finally, this one is a list of the guest names at yesterday's party.' Lucas now had all four envelopes. He was about to speak, but Judith raised her hand to stop him.

'Should you require any further information, please contact my attorney as he will be acting on behalf of Celia and Charles. My car is waiting, I must go. Goodbye, Lieutenant.' She offered her hand to Lucas who shook it. 'The house keys are on the dining room table.'

'Thank you, Congresswoman,' was all Lucas could manage before she swept past him and was gone, closing the front door behind her.

Lucas was rooted to the spot, clutching four manila envelopes. He heard the car pull away from the driveway.

'Thank you, Congresswoman,' Lucas said to no one. 'Thank you,' he continued a little louder, pacing around the living room floor, shaking his head in self-berating mode.

'Thank you for a delightful kick in the nuts more like.' Lucas was furious with his performance. 'And why the hell did I shake her hand? Should have been her damn neck. Good job I worked out my tactics beforehand, otherwise I'd have risked screwing it up.'

Lucas was still giving himself a hard time when the sound of heavy tyres on the gravel outside made him stop. There was a sharp rap on the door. He opened it to find Bassano standing in the front porch while the forensics team got out of the van. Lucas glanced at his watch. It had been five and a half hours since Metcalf's call.

It wasn't long before the whole house buzzed with the energy of professional seekers, people who piece together the past from the crumbs left behind. The air tasted of fingerprint powder as white-suited professionals puffed and brushed their way around the house. This was punctuated by the repeated flash of a high-resolution camera, snapping at anything that looked interesting. With so many photographs taken, Lucas was sure the entire interior of the Mason home must be in one shot or another.

One of Bassano's team disappeared back to the station with the envelopes containing the statements and guest names so the process of elimination could begin. Lucas went outside and sat in one of the wickerwork chairs on the pool deck, deep in thought. Silver-gray powder clung to the cuffs and forearms of his jacket, a testament to the chair having already been passed as clean.

The method of entry was straightforward. The burglar had approached the property from the back, walking along the water's edge up the beach to the house, probably dragging something behind him to cover his tracks. Once at the house, he'd cut through the mosquito netting that surrounded the pool and slipped through. He'd secured the netting back in place with black insulation tape, sticking it to the underside of the frame.

From there he walked along the poolside to the patio doors. There were sandy footprints on the decking, but nothing that gave any indication of size or make of shoe. The sea breeze had seen to that. The burglar had slipped a flat-edged tool into the runners and prised one of the doors loose. He'd lifted it out and rested it against the frame to give the impression of it being partially open to anyone who passed by. Then he was in.

Once he'd gathered up the goodies, the burglar had left the same way, again securing the pool netting back in place with tape and covering his tracks along the beach. Metcalf had been right, just a run-of-the-mill, standard burglary.

Lucas sighed, rising from the chair and heading back to the living room. He avoided the squares of carpet that had been marked off in red for special attention. Drifting through each room of the house, his mind was in neutral, soaking up what he saw. Glancing at his watch, he noticed that it had stopped. He shook his wrist and put it to his ear. The metallic tick, tick, tick told him it was still working. Lucas walked back to the living room and looked at the clock on the mantelpiece which read 10.22am. He adjusted his watch.

'I'm going back to the station, there's nothing I can do here. If you find something, call me.'

'The initial sweep should be completed around two o'clock,' replied Bassano. 'We're pushing for results later today or early tomorrow.'

'That's fine,' Lucas said at the front door. 'Just keep me posted.'

Driving back to the station, Lucas's mind once more wandered through the Masons' home, evaluating what he'd seen. Something bothered him.

Lucas believed that all good cops had a sixth sense. It wasn't something that could be taught at the Police Academy, nor was it something that could be gained with experience. You either had it or you didn't. It was what made you look beyond the facts and peel back the veneer to find what lay beneath. Lucas's sixth sense was in overdrive.

He knew what he saw, that was clear, but he had an overwhelming feeling of being taken by the hand and led up the garden path. The more his mind roamed around the house, the stronger the feeling. Something wasn't right.

Back at the office, the afternoon passed into early evening. Lucas spent the remainder of his day dealing with the ever-expanding administrative demands of his in-tray. Several times he caught himself drifting back to the Mason property, its expensive designer decor, and that damn woman in that damn skirt. But there was something that just didn't add up. Something didn't fit the picture.

There was a loud knock at the door and Bassano walked in. Lucas liked Chris Bassano and had a huge amount of respect for him, but there was one thing that drove him crazy. Whereas Lucas always came to work in a sharp suit, with his shoes polished and his shirt ironed to within an inch of its life, Bassano looked as if he'd been dragged through a hedge backwards. Whenever Lucas told him to tidy himself up, he'd respond, 'But, Chief, you're well dressed enough for the both of us.'

Bassano had learned early on that the way he dressed added to the impression he made on a woman. When his shirt looked as though it came straight from the washing basket and a six year old had done his tie, it added a pinch of vulnerability to an already desirable package. It was a dynamite combination and, as long as the women kept coming, he really didn't mind. His wife, on the other hand, had minded a great deal.

Lucas motioned for him to sit down. 'What do you have so far?'

Bassano walked around his desk to join his boss at the conference table. 'Fingerprints and statements have been taken from all the guests we could get hold of.' He consulted a ream of computer printouts. 'That's sixty-five so far with fifteen left to go.

The team has almost completed the forensics so we'll be ready to go first thing in the morning.'

Lucas nodded. 'That's good, let's hope it throws up something quickly. I don't think our delightful congresswoman will wait long before sticking her nose in.'

It was 6.15pm and both men were washed out from their early start. 'Get yourself home,' Lucas said. 'Get a good night's sleep and pray that Celia Mason's burglar left us a calling card.' Bassano smiled, bid Lucas goodnight and left the office.

Lucas stared into space with both of his elbows on the table, supporting his ample chin in his hands. His mind was full of the images of the day, trying to find the piece that didn't fit.

He left the office at 7.30pm, still searching for it.

Chapter 6

Mechanic's face reflected back from the smoked glass cabinet. The glazed eyes and vacant stare told their own story. The battle was almost lost.

Daddy's voice was harsh and insistent. 'I said, do it now.'

'Not ready,' Mechanic replied in a trance. 'Need more time.'

'Damn you,' Daddy's voice reverberated around Mechanic's head. 'You screwed up. I said *now*.'

The weights had not worked. Pumping the barbells had brought excruciating pain, but the attack just kept coming. Mechanic was struggling to stop Daddy taking full control.

The preparations were a long way from complete and the constant attacks didn't help. Daddy was impatient for the next one. The screw-up at the house ensured that.

'Do it. Do it now,' Daddy snarled.

This was bad.

Mechanic swayed and struggled to hold onto the last vestiges of control, the gas ring hissing while the blue flame heated the metal skewer. Mechanic took it from the flame and lifted the T-shirt, exposing an impressive six-pack that was already streaked white where hot metal had burned away the skin pigment. Mechanic's head swam and the room blurred. Control was fading fast.

'Kill the bastard through pain,' Mechanic shouted, trying desperately to drown out Daddy's voice. 'Kill him now.'

The skin sizzled as the red hot skewer scorched and blistered its way across Mechanic's stomach. White smoke rose into the air and the sweet smell of melting flesh filled Mechanic's senses.

Mechanic screamed, falling back against the wall, the skewer clattering to the floor. Searing pain surged through Mechanic's body, making it shake uncontrollably.

The room spun wildly as Daddy's voice faded away.

All was quiet. Daddy was gone, at least for now.

Chapter 7

Lucas rose early. A restless night had not helped him get his thoughts in order and he needed to make a prompt start. On the few occasions he had managed to drift off, his dreams were full of the large beachfront property with its lavish furnishings and Judith Somerville with her lavish legs. Equal portions of both combined to guarantee that Lucas had precious little sleep.

Depositing his bag of food and his briefcase in his office, he made his way down to the incident room on the floor below. In the lift he could feel the familiar knot in the pit of his stomach – the expectation of what today might bring. The hunt for bad guys was bread and butter to Lucas, and he relished it.

Opening the door to the incident room, he turned on the large fluorescent lights. Around the walls were roller shutter covers. Lucas lifted each one in turn to reveal boards covered with pieces of evidence collected from the Mason house the day before. Others were blank, waiting to receive new material.

Desks made up the rest of the room with computers and fax terminals plugged into sockets. Large boxes cluttered the floor with stickers on them to describe their contents along with more pads of paper and sticky notes than Staples.

Lucas raised one of the shutters to reveal photographs taken of the interior of the house. The pictures were arranged in groups, each depicting a different room.

Lucas stepped back and sat on the corner of the desk, staring at the collage of images. His eyes scanned each one in turn: the hallway, the lounge, the kitchen and so on. He mentally checked off items in the photographs with what he'd seen. There was something odd about the lounge, but what the hell was it? It wasn't the furniture, it wasn't the pictures hanging on the wall, and it wasn't the oversized coffee table. What was it?

He snapped back to the present. 'Damn thing,' he said under his breath, shaking his head.

'What is, sir?' Bassano was standing right beside him. Lucas had been so lost in the photographs he hadn't heard him come in.

'Oh nothing,' Lucas replied, 'just a touch of indigestion.' He pushed the knuckles of his right hand into his chest, breathing deeply. 'Ready for a successful day?'

'We've got the lot, sir. Probably have the whole house in one box or another. If there's anything to be found, we'll find it.'

'I've got a good feeling about this one,' Lucas lied. He rose from the desk and walked away from Bassano to avoid eye contact. 'I feel a result coming on,' he lied again.

Lucas always thought it was necessary to talk up an investigation at the start. He firmly believed that people who searched for evidence thinking they'd find it would always be more successful than those who didn't. His nagging doubts he kept firmly to himself.

'What time is your briefing?'

'7.30am, sir,' Bassano replied, breaking out writing pads from their paper binders.

'I'll join you for the beginning and then get out of your hair. Call me if you turn something up.' Bassano nodded while Lucas left to make another assault on the paper mountain in his office.

Bassano watched him go and then he turned to the board that Lucas had been staring at.

'Indigestion, my ass,' he muttered, and continued unwrapping the stationery.

Bassano always considered it an odd coincidence, but crime scene photos always reminded him of his marriage. He was never sure why but thought it had something to do with the remnants of guilt. Like most of the disasters in his life, his marriage had started off with so much promise. One hot afternoon, in the midst of an eye-watering series of female conquests, Bassano had met Isobel on his way home from work.

She was a stunning blonde with wide green eyes and a figure to stop traffic. They met on the underground when her heel broke on the stairs and she toppled over in the rush of busy commuters. Bassano caught her as she fell. He was used to women falling at his feet, but not literally.

It was the end of the day and she took the initiative. She bought him a thank-you drink in a nearby bar and he returned the compliment with a don't-mention-it dinner the next night. They made a fabulous couple and were the envy of their friends. She knew about his past but was confident in her ability to tame his wilder side and within weeks they moved in together.

During their fifteen month courtship he was faithful. Despite the avalanche of female attention, he shunned it all in favour of Isobel but this spell of monogamy didn't survive the ordeal of the wedding ceremony and Bassano broke his vows within three months.

At first Isobel kind of knew but chose not to notice. As time went by, she lost count. Her body clock was ticking and, while she yearned for kids, she wanted them with the guy she fell in love with – not the one she married. She accepted that he was wedded to his job, but not the way he used his dick as a hobby.

She issued him with an ultimatum. After a torrent of tears and apologies, he agreed to change his ways, which held good for precisely seven days. Then the blonde in the sports bar and six bottles of beer ensured that on day eight the ultimatum was enforced.

He returned home from work in the early hours of the morning to find the apartment empty along with his wardrobe. He didn't have the first idea where his wife might be but knew exactly where his clothes were. His cuffs and collars had been cut from his shirts and scattered on the bedroom floor. His underwear lay in a bucket of diluted battery acid, slowly disintegrating. The bath contained his suits and shoes floating in a solution of pink fabric dye. After a frantic search, he later found that the bucket also contained his CD collection. Battery acid and digital storage media didn't mix well.

That had been two years ago and they hadn't spoken since. He hadn't even tried to find her. When he looked back on the whole sorry state of his marriage, that said it all. He was divorced six months later.

There was one unexpected upside. Bassano ended up screwing his ex-wife's lawyer. He was sure there must be a code of conduct somewhere to say that was against the rules. Of course, like all of the others, she didn't stick around. Maybe it had something to do with the fact that Bassano was also banging her PA.

It was clear that women experienced an oestrogen-fuelled fascination for him, a fascination which could only be satisfied with a bout of incendiary sex. But this attraction was only ever based on feminine curiosity. Once this had been gratified, none of them wanted to take him home to meet the family. Isobel had made a valiant attempt to make their relationship work but since she left there had been no significant others.

Bassano snapped his thoughts back to the matter in hand, feeling guilty that crime scene photos were the only things that made him think about Isobel.

His first task was to compare fingerprints taken from the house with those of the party guests. This process of elimination should yield a small group of prints that were not accounted for. These were called 'owner unknown'.

This was a tedious job, but there were eight of them sifting through the print collection matching them to the guests' prints and by 10.30am they had their first hit. This was taken to the records department where the print was compared to those held in the police files. Some were computerized and some were not. To speed up the process, the search was done by category of offender, in this case burglary and theft.

By 11.30am they had a match.

'Sir, we got one!' Bassano sounded ecstatic on the phone. 'It's a guy named Ambrose Wilson. He's 28 years old and lives out near Keaton Beach. He's served four months for burglary and has a stack of previous arrests, all theft related. His prints were found on the patio door, the coffee table and the bedroom.'

'Good work. Let's go pick up Mr Wilson and see what he has to say.' Lucas punched his fist into the air.

'Already underway, sir.'

'Let me know when he's here.' Lucas hung up, returning to his paperwork much happier than when he'd left it.

Ambrose Wilson was extremely pissed off about the cops pulling him from his favourite bar, especially as he had money riding on a pool game that he was about to win. He didn't complain at all about the loss of his hard-earned cash, but he gave full vent to every other social injustice he could think of as two officers led him to the police car.

When Ambrose spoke, he was incapable of keeping both feet on the ground at the same time. He ranted at the top of his voice all the way to the station. After all, as far as Ambrose Wilson was concerned, helping the police with their enquiries was another way of saying 'You're in the frame for it, but we can't pin it on you just yet.'

Ambrose continued to shout his innocence all the way to the interview room. At this stage he had no idea what he was accused of but whatever it was he wasn't guilty. He continued his tirade right up until his lawyer arrived. Then he shut up, not saying a word.

'Ambrose,' Bassano was well practiced in coaxing the reluctant, 'we just want to ask you a few questions.'

'My client understands that he has not been charged and that he may leave at any time,' the lawyer answered for him.

Jefferson Gill, defender of the guilty, was a successful circuit attorney and well known to the officers at the station. He'd defended Ambrose on numerous occasions since his first arrest seven years ago and had demonstrated an impressive record of wins for his client. Even when Ambrose was guilty, he'd always get him off on one technicality or another. That was until his last excursion outside the law when Ambrose lost big time.

Prison had shaken him up to such an extent that he'd been straight ever since. Not even a parking ticket, but then it was doubtful he actually owned a car.

'Ambrose, where were you last night between the hours of 1 and 2am?' Bassano was still in coaxing mode.

Ambrose said nothing. He concentrated hard on the table, not meeting the stare of either officer.

'Ambrose, we need to know where you were. It's important to us to establish your whereabouts.' Bassano was used to questioning unresponsive suspects. He was calm and collected, with a slow, deliberate delivery. Bassano watched Ambrose's face for any change of expression, increased blinking or erratic hand movements, anything that may indicate discomfort or stress. Nothing.

He continued regardless. 'Ambrose, there was a burglary last night at a property in Keaton Beach and certain items were stolen. Do you know anything about it?' Ambrose said nothing, still examining the table top.

'Ambrose, your fingerprints were found inside the house. I can only draw one conclusion from this, that you were there and somehow involved. Now if you weren't, you need to help us.'

'That is completely unsubstantiated, Officer Bassano,' Gill interrupted. 'Those two facts are not necessarily connected.'

'I understand that,' Bassano continued, 'but I am merely trying to establish how Ambrose's fingerprints could have been found inside number 1316 Ridgeway Crescent.'

Ambrose Wilson flinched, his mouth dropping open. He looked straight at Bassano.

'Which house?' he asked, managing to regain control of his bottom jaw.

'1316 Ridgeway Crescent.'

Ambrose turned and whispered into the ear of his attorney.

'My client wishes to speak with me in private. Would you please excuse us, officers?' Gill's politeness grated on both of them but they switched off the tape and left the room. Lucas was in the corridor outside.

'Well? What do we have?'

'Bit unusual, sir. Couldn't get a single word out of him to start with, but when I mentioned the address of the house he almost had a seizure. He's talking to Gill now. I'm sure from his reaction he's involved somehow.'

'But if so, why didn't he react when you confronted him about the burglary?' Lucas murmured. Gill came out of the room.

'Would you be so kind as to join us again, officers?' He turned and went back into the interview room. Bassano glanced at Lucas and pushed two fingers into his mouth mimicking a violent bout of vomiting before following Gill into the room.

When everyone was seated, Gill said, 'My client wishes to make a statement to help you to eliminate him from your investigation.' Bassano loved his spirit of public service. There was a long pause, then Ambrose spoke.

'I work at number 1316. I do a lot of houses down Keaton Beach, 'cause there's a lot of money there.' He paused again. 'I sort the pools out and such, you know, doing the dips and clearing the filters. But I never turned the house over. Honest I didn't.' Ambrose started rambling about being straight since he'd come from jail, and how he didn't want to go back, 'cause if he did, then ... Gill placed his hand on Ambrose's arm.

'Start again, Ambrose, just like you told me. Just tell the officers, nice and slow.'

'Well it's like I said, I clean and do the pool and decking areas ...'

An hour and a half later, back in Lucas's office, Bassano sat at the table and went through the Ambrose Wilson interview in his head.

'Fuck it,' he said to no one in particular. 'I thought it was too good to be true.'

'Has he been released?' Lucas asked.

'Yes,' replied Bassano. 'And the cheeky shit asked for one of our patrol cars to drop him off at the same bar we picked him up from.'

Lucas smiled. The irony of the situation appealed to him, bringing a little gentle humour into an otherwise crap day. 'Do you have anything else to go on?'

'A couple of owner-unknowns, but no match yet.' The phone rang. Lucas answered it. 'Yeah.'

'Sir, Congresswoman Somerville is at the front desk and is demanding to see you.'

'Oh good, send her up.' Lucas's smile broadened. Replacing the receiver, he turned to Bassano. 'Our beloved congresswoman is on her way. Would you like to stay for the fireworks?' Bassano got up and walked out without saying another word. Within a matter of seconds there was a sharp rap at the door and in marched Judith Somerville, looking as if that pit bull had taken another bite out of her ass.

'What the hell is going on, Lieutenant? I'm told you arrested a man with a rap sheet as long as my arm and with his fingerprints all over the inside of the house. And for some inexplicable reason you've seen fit to let him go.' Her face glowed an attractive shade of pink.

Lucas ignored the question and ushered her to a seat at the large conference table.

'Congresswoman, thank you for making a personal call.' He was beginning to enjoy himself. 'You are correct. We did bring a man in for questioning who is a known felon and who has his fingerprints all over the inside of your daughter's house. And yes, we have let him go on the basis of a technicality.'

'What damn technicality?' The pink was escalating into red.

'A small matter of innocence, Congresswoman …'

'Lucas, the guy was the pool man. He had his prints all over the inside of the house, but he works outside. It's obvious, any fool can figure it out.' She paused to regain her composure. 'Do I need to remind you of our previous conversation? I thought

I made myself perfectly clear regarding the consequences that would follow if—'

'That's true, Congresswoman, you did,' Lucas interrupted. 'It is also true that Wilson worked at your daughter's home, cleaning and maintaining the pool, and that, despite working outside, his prints were found inside the house. But Wilson did not rob your house.' For Lucas this had been a long time coming. Somerville was fizzing with rage.

'It would appear that when Ambrose went to 1316 Ridgeway Crescent his job was not just to dip the pool.' Lucas fixed his eyes on his prey, waiting for the penny to drop. There was no reaction so he continued. 'Ambrose Wilson serviced more than the pool at your daughter's house.'

'That idiot of a girl.' Judith Somerville flushed angry red. She snapped and sprang from the table, shouting at Lucas, 'Celia was screwing this Ambrose character?'

'I think you're being a little hard on your daughter there, Congresswoman, as well as being a little misdirected.' Lucas was reveling in his victory.

Her face contorted into an unattractive and confused expression.

Lucas continued, 'No it was your son-in-law who was the attraction for Ambrose Wilson, not Celia.'

Lucas sat back and watched Somerville crumble before him. Her mouth gaped open and her face turned grey.

'We will, of course, keep this in the strictest confidence, but if the release of Wilson comes under any scrutiny, we would be duty-bound to release the tapes. Now, ma'am, I'm sure you have more pressing matters to attend to, so I won't keep you. Shall I show you out?'

Somerville slumped into her seat and said nothing. Lucas felt it unnecessary to contribute further to the conversation and she wasn't capable of comment anyway. After a while she rose to her feet and, without turning her head, said, 'Thank you, Lieutenant, I'll see myself out.' She closed the door behind her.

Lucas remained seated for a full fifteen minutes savouring his success. Screw the outcome of the investigation – now that Somerville was off his back he couldn't fail. If his team caught someone, then fine. If not, at least he could demonstrate due diligence in handling such a high profile case. Anyway, Somerville wasn't going to be a force to be reckoned with now that Lucas held this over her. Today's triumph was sweet indeed.

As he soaked up his moments of satisfaction, he glanced at his watch.

'Damn.' It had stopped again. 'I need to get this seen to.' He twisted the tiny gold crown between his thumb and finger, shaking his wrist and holding the watch to his ear. Tick, tick, tick.

Lucas froze, staring at the watch. His mind forced an image into his consciousness. It was the picture of the Masons' lounge. He held his breath and tried to recall what it was that he'd seen. Then it hit him.

'Damn it,' he exploded, jumping from his chair. As he strode along the corridor from his office, he cursed himself for being so blind, for not seeing what was right in front of his face. He burst through the doors of the incident room and stood in front of the picture board, scanning the images. Bassano was eyeing him with suspicion but knew better than to intervene.

'Get me the inventory of what was stolen.' Bassano retrieved the file and handed it over. Lucas looked at the photographs, then at the list, and back again. 'Shit,' he said, tossing the papers onto the nearest desk.

Bassano looked at the pictures, then at his boss, and back again.

'Someone is taking us for a ride,' Lucas said.

'In what way?'

'This is what we're meant to believe. Someone breaks into an expensive beachfront property with the sole intention of relieving its occupants of their worldly goods. From the list of what's missing, he manages to bag a little over two thousand dollars.' Lucas turned and looked Bassano in the face. 'So why leave a three-thousand-dollar carriage clock on the fucking mantelpiece?' Lucas stabbed a chubby finger at the snapshot showing the clock.

Lucas continued to let off steam. 'It's not big and it's not heavy. It's easily fenced and looks expensive.'

'Maybe he didn't see it?' Bassano ventured an ill-considered opinion.

'Didn't see it? It's gold with revolving crystals at the bottom. It screams, "Take me, I'm expensive." And you could hardly miss the damn thing, it's at eye level. No, if you went into that house to steal one thing, you'd walk away with that.'

'Why would anyone go to the trouble of breaking in and not help themselves to the best stuff?'

'Because it wasn't a burglary,' replied Lucas. 'I just don't buy it. It's been bugging me all day. It's just been engineered to look like one. Whatever the motive for the forced entry, it wasn't robbery. Someone just wants us to think it was.'

Neither of them spoke. Their thoughts were interrupted by the head of the forensics team charging into the room. His name was Curtis.

'Sir, I think you'd better come and see this.' He was breathless and agitated.

'What is it?' Bassano asked.

'I'll explain down at records.'

The two men followed with the same degree of urgency. They arrived at records to find the place empty, the normal hubbub and chatter replaced with the hum of the air conditioning unit.

Curtis spoke first. 'Sir, I've sent everyone on break. I wasn't sure how to handle this.'

'Spit it out, Curtis. What is it?'

'We didn't turn up anything from the prints, so I asked the guys to run the MO through the burglary records – the cut netting, the patio door prised out of its runners – and we came up with a couple of possibilities.'

'That's good then,' said Bassano. But Curtis shook his head, looking less enthusiastic.

'The thing is, sir, we got a new guy on the team who mistakenly ran the data though the homicide files and we got a match there too.' Curtis was being very deliberate in his briefing.

'But this isn't a homicide. It's a burglary, and, anyway, the slit netting and lifted doors is commonplace, I'd have thought,' Lucas said.

'Yeah, I figured that too, but there was something about the homicide match which alarmed me.'

'What was that?' asked Bassano.

'It was a precise match. The others had slight deviations, but this one was a one hundred percent positive match, right down to the details about fixing the netting back in place with black insulation tape.'

'Okay. So what are you telling me?' asked Lucas.

'I ran more details from the case through the system and found something weird. In the homicide case, the killer left a thumbprint in the centre of the TV screen like a calling card.'

Lucas felt suddenly uneasy. 'And?'

'I phoned the house and asked one of the SOCO guys to dust the TV.' Curtis cleared his throat. 'There's a thumbprint in the middle of the screen.'

'That means nothing,' countered Lucas. 'People are allowed to touch their TVs, aren't they?'

'Sir, they rushed it over, I've got the print here.'

'Have you run it?' Bassano felt a knot of anxiety building in his stomach.

'It's a seventeen-point match.' Curtis looked almost apologetic for delivering the news.

'Match to whom?' Bassano asked.

'The print matches a serial killer with twelve kills to his name. There is no positive identity, just the previous investigation code name – Mechanic.'

'Jesus.' Lucas let the word out with a rush of air.

'It gets worse.' Curtis was not looking forward to this. 'Our records show that Mechanic committed suicide by torching himself and his last three victims in a car. He's been dead for three years.'

Chapter 8

Mechanic sat on the floor, exhausted, stripped to the waist with a roll of crepe bandage around the middle with gauze patches placed over the burnt area. It hurt like hell and every movement reminded Mechanic that the situation was getting worse. It was just a matter of time and all control would be lost.

'What are you doing?' Daddy's voice was soft and melodic. Mechanic reeled around to work out where it had come from. This was a complete surprise. No warning, no footsteps, no whispering. Nothing.

'I told you to get it done.' The voice was gentle but insistent. Mechanic was in uncharted territory. This had never happened before.

Mechanic tried to scramble to the weights room but stumbled back against the cupboard, knocking crockery off the worktop. Cups and plates shattered sending china shrapnel skidding across the wooden floor.

'You got it wrong. Now fix it!' This was terrifying. Daddy was taking over.

Mechanic slumped down. 'No, it's too soon, it's too soon.'

'Work out what happened and sort it! I can't wait any longer,' Daddy boomed.

'But, I can't yet.' Mechanic's will was disintegrating fast. Options were limited. This was bad, very bad.

Tearing at the bandages, Mechanic ripped away the gauze, exposing the angry red burn. Seizing a jagged piece of broken plate, Mechanic stabbed the serrated edge into tender flesh and dragged it across the raw wound. Pain tore through Mechanic's body as the shard cut deep into the burnt flesh.

Mechanic screamed in pain as blood pooled onto the floor.

For the second time in two days, Daddy fell quiet. What it would take to silence him a third time?

Chapter 9

Lucas sat in the quiet twilight of his office. A small halogen lamp spilled a cone of light onto his paper-strewn desk and the back wall glowed pale yellow in its reflection. The remainder of the office was dark.

He reclined heavily in his chair, watching the devils of the day dance before him. The station was still alive with the sounds of law enforcement by night, but all Lucas heard was the thumping in his chest and the rushing in his head. It was 7.30pm.

He had made Curtis take him through the matches again and again, but there was no mistake. Mechanic had definitely been in the Mason house. Lucas sent his team home. He needed time to think. He'd called his wife and told her not to expect him until late. This was going to require careful handling.

Lucas was fully aware that, in circumstances such as these, there were protocols to follow, people to inform, wheels to set in motion. But he damn well wasn't going to raise the alarm on a case that he knew nothing about, especially one that involved an allegedly dead serial killer on his patch. He needed to be in control, he needed to be up to speed, he couldn't afford to be behind the game.

He only knew scant details of Mechanic's existence, but anyone who'd picked up a newspaper or turned on the TV in 1979 would know of Mechanic. At that time, Lucas had been in a cushy job, sitting in an office in Chicago and considering himself fortunate that he wasn't the sorry bastard having to bring this sadistic killer to justice. He didn't need to know the details then. How times had changed.

His thoughts raced: *Why the hell was Mechanic there? And why was the break-in staged to look like a burglary?*

Lucas was getting annoyed by his train of thought – it wasn't helping him. His first priority had to be to understand what had happened to Mechanic in the past if he was to stand any chance of unravelling the events of the present. Six boxes sat on the conference table, each one marked with an index number and a large sticker on which was written CODENAME – MECHANIC. He crossed the room and picked up the box with the lowest number on it. He slowly walked back to his desk, pulled up the chair and adjusted the light.

The box was full of thick buff-coloured folders which had been forgotten for the past three years. The daily drudgery of enforcing law in a busy city was a walk in the park in comparison to what was contained in these folders. Each box told its own dreadful tale of how fragile the human mind can become and the damage that can ensue when it falls apart. Lucas took the file, turned the front cover and began to read.

Horror first descended onto the state of Florida when Mechanic's mind snapped at the home of Lillian and Gerald Lang. They lived in a fashionable suburb of Fort Myers in a stylish house that Gerald had designed himself. He was a successful architect and she was a stay-at-home mom, looking after the two children. Tom was eight and Katie was six.

Anything they didn't have, they probably didn't want. Gerald commanded vast fees from his work and Lillian tried her best to spend it. She kitted the home out with every conceivable luxury and clothed herself and the kids in the latest fashion. The more he earned, the more she spent. They were happy that way. They had no debts, no problems to speak of and no enemies. That was until around 4am on 16 June 1979.

The blood patterns on the wall suggested Gerald Lang had been sitting upright when the bullet of the .45 slammed into his forehead. He'd been disturbed from sleep by the intruder who'd entered the bedroom, but evidently not for long. Lillian Lang was in that hazy world of half awake and half asleep when the back of her husband's head splattered her with bone, tissue and blood.

From the wallpaper under her fingernails, she was clawing her way up the bedroom wall to get away from the exploding head when the blunt instrument struck the side of her temple and she lost consciousness. She slumped from the bed and onto the floor, never seeing who'd hit her.

The gun that was used must have been silenced because the children never left their beds or, it can be assumed, ever woke up. They too were shot through the head as they lay sleeping in separate rooms.

The killer returned to the master bedroom and proceeded to bind and gag Lillian Lang with strips cut from her own nightdress. Then began the ritual.

Gerald Lang was pulled from his bed and dragged along the floor by his feet, out of the bedroom and down the stairs. What remained of his head left a trail resembling a butcher's slab, along the carpet and on each of the wooden steps, as it cracked and splintered its way down the stairs. Fragments of bone and brain tissue marked its journey through the house. The killer dragged him into the garage and, judging by the size of the blood pool on the concrete floor, left him there for some time.

The children were next. They were dragged to the garage in the same manner and laid out on the floor. Having found the keys, the killer loaded each body into the family car – Dad in the driver's seat with the two children in the back. The key was placed in the ignition and the doors closed. Each body was held upright by its seatbelt, an absurd safety precaution given the circumstances.

Lillian Lang was left on the bedroom floor, a purple and yellow ridge running down the right side of her face. It would soon fade to nothing more than a small skin blemish. She was otherwise untouched. Her whole life sat seat-belted and bloody in the family car, leaving scars that would never heal. Bloody footprints on the carpet indicated that the killer had left the house by the same way he came in, through the patio doors which were lifted from their runners by a crowbar-type implement. A single thumbprint was placed as a calling card in the centre of the oversized TV screen. From this point on, Mechanic was born.

Lucas's mind raced, each fact firing tiny memory triggers. He recalled the news coverage and the inevitable hysteria-provoking articles in the press. He turned the pages of the file and the scene-of-crime photographs tore at the pit of his stomach. However you pictured such carnage, it never reflected reality. Lucas flipped through the pages in an attempt to avoid for now what he knew he would have to study in detail later.

On 2 August Mechanic snapped again.

This time it was at the modest home of Jeff and Julie Tate. He worked as a sales manager at a paint manufacturer in Tampa, she was a telephone operator for a firm of accountants. They also had two children. Zak was eleven and Luke was nine.

Their fate was a carbon copy of the slaughter of the Lang family. Jeff had been shot in bed, removing most of the left-hand side of his face, and Julie had been clubbed about the head and the nape of her neck. She'd fought with Mechanic, but only briefly until the blows rendered her unconscious. She was bound and gagged on the bedroom floor. Both kids would have been shot through the head too if it hadn't been for Luke's unexpected sleepover at a friend's house. Unfortunately, this after-school treat only included Luke. Zak Tate was belted in the family car along with his father.

When Luke's dad didn't turn up to take him home the following morning, and several phone calls weren't answered, his friend's mom dropped Luke off on her way to the mall. It wasn't far to walk from their house, but the Florida summer was in full heat and the air quality was poor. It wasn't worth the risk. Days like this were never a good thing for Luke. She dropped him off outside the house and waved goodbye.

Luke Tate found the front door bolted from the inside, preventing him from entering with his key. He shouted through the door, but still no response. He went around the side, raised the garage door and walked in. He never made it to the house door at the back wall of the garage. He saw his father and brother sitting bolt upright in the car, gaping cavities where their heads had once been.

This triggered Luke's asthma. The bout was so severe that his hopeless fumbling in his overnight bag for his inhaler was useless. He died on the floor of the garage. Mechanic had achieved a full strike after all, and the calling card thumbprint was testament to the identity of the killer.

Lucas's mind swam in the memories of three years ago. He recalled that when the news had broken that the killings were linked, the police had tried to play down the term 'serial killer'. But with the persistence of the press and the morbid fascination of the general public, it was a lost cause. Fascination quickly escalated into panic. The terror spread like wildfire.

The third set of killings in October sent the emotional temperature rocketing. Fort Lauderdale was the venue, the Andrews family were centre stage.

It was exactly the same ritual as before. A heavy, blunt object left Janet Andrews with a fractured skull, while three bullets fired at point-blank range left her nothing to live for. Dad plus the two kids had been belted into the car, Mom was bound on the bedroom floor with straw-coloured fluid flecked with blood running from her right ear and down her jaw line. The single thumbprint was once again in place, like a stamp of quality.

For four days Janet Andrews lay in a coma, blissfully ignorant of the horrors that awaited her. She had recovered enough by the fifth day to be told of her family's fate and she wished with all her heart that she could slip back into her coma, never to return. On day six, she realized that the ringing sound in her head had been there the day before. On day seven, the doctors told her that her balance would return given time, but the ringing in her right ear would probably remain. Trauma-induced tinnitus, they called it.

Post-traumatic shock set in on the eighth day and her time in a coma seemed to Janet Andrews by far the best option. On day nine, and in a confused state, she put it to the test.

Her fall was not dramatic. A healthy person would have survived, but a single flight of hospital stairs to a woman with a serious head injury proved too much for Janet Andrews. It was never clear whether her failed balance took her over the top step or if it was a desperate need to not face the world without her family. Either way, the outcome was the same. The fall knocked her unconscious and she died hours later of a massive brain hemorrhage.

Lucas read the scribbled file notes. The Andrews family had been devout churchgoers and as she lay in her hospital bed the impact of what happened had convinced Janet there was no God. How could there be?

In the days after the killings, she felt completely betrayed by her faith. All those Sundays, for what? All those prayers and participation in religious pageantry, for what? The loss of her faith became as much of a personal tragedy for Janet Andrews as losing her family. How could such a large part of her life turn out to be a total sham? Now she was armed with stark evidence that God did not exist, she was freed from the onerous process of having to believe in Him.

She had always held the firm belief that suicide was wrong in the eyes of the Lord. However, now that she was unencumbered by that view, her tumble down the stairs was never considered an accident. Rather it had been viewed as the last actions of a sick woman with nothing to live for and no belief in a divine force to keep her from doing it.

A handwritten note had been scribbled at the bottom of the file notes. It read, '*Claim for hospital negligence pending, Dick Harper, 23 Oct 1979*'. Lucas stopped reading and replaced the files. Dick Harper. Now that was a name to conjure with. Lucas knew him well or, at least, he knew the folklore that surrounded him. He was a bull-headed bastard of a man who'd held the position of Lieutenant at the time of the Mechanic murders. He was straight out of the old school. Harper had been promoted through the ranks in his early years, due mainly to his uncompromising style and formidable reputation which exactly fitted with the times.

'Cops make the best villains,' he would boom. 'Just use it wisely.' Double talk for 'Do whatever needs to be done, but don't get caught while doing it.' Harper hadn't been a bent cop. He'd proudly boast that he'd never accepted a bribe in his life, but he wouldn't let the mere technicality of a known scum-bag's innocence get in the way of a good collar. He held the criminal fraternity in a grip of fear, a grip that was as often physical as it was metaphorical.

Unfortunately for Harper, the force's top brass had changed as did their attitudes to such activities. They brought with them a new enlightened style for a modern police force. The problem was that Harper couldn't change and he was increasingly seen as out of step.

His career had suffered, and Harper had felt the control that he'd enjoyed for so long slip away from him. He'd been beside himself with rage and frustration as known criminals walked free from his station after procedures hadn't been followed. Sleight-of-hand lawyers constantly unearthed irregularities in the treatment of suspects.

One explosive disagreement with his superiors had stood out from the rest. It followed a vigorous interview with a street mugger who'd been caught kicking the shit out of an old woman because she wouldn't let go of the bag over her shoulder. Harper was heard to shout at his boss.

'Doesn't anybody care that the bastard did it?'

'That is not the issue here,' was the cold, monotone response.

'Well, sir, I beg to differ, but it's a major fucking issue to me.'

There was no doubt that Harper felt a good deal better for replying as he did, but the resulting suspension from duty took the shine off it. He was reinstated two weeks later when the mugger failed to turn up to corroborate his complaint. In fact, he failed to turn up anywhere at all, not at his apartment, nor his place of work. Nowhere. Without him it was easy for Harper to cry victimization and his pasty-faced boss had to eat lots of very public humble pie. The complaint was quashed.

The other cops at the station never questioned where the mugger had gone nor had his disappearing act come as a great surprise to anyone. Harper hadn't touched him personally, but had leaned on certain members of the criminal fraternity to do themselves a favour. This was food and drink to Harper, his own version of the force's new enlightened techniques.

Lucas looked at his watch. It was nine-thirty. The remaining two boxes contained murders nine, ten, eleven and twelve plus the interview notes, analysis, statements and hypotheses. All based on a nightmare three years old.

Lucas didn't open them. He'd seen and read enough for one day. He lifted the telephone.

'Hi, this is Lucas, get me FBI headquarters Quantico.' He replaced the handset and waited. Within seconds it rang.

'Hello, this is the FBI. Can I help you?'

'Yes, this is Lieutenant Edmund Lucas of the Florida State Police Department. I'd like to talk to Jeff Charmers. And, before you ask, I am aware of how late it is.'

'May I have your identification number please?' asked the operator. Lucas gave his ID.

'Won't keep you a moment.' The line echoed and buzzed as the code was processed. After a while she returned. 'Putting you through, Lieutenant.'

'Jeff Charmers.' The voice was bright and alert despite the hour.

'Jeff, this is Lieutenant Ed Lucas of FPD. I'm sorry to call you so late.'

'That's okay. It must be urgent.'

'Yes it is. We need to reopen an investigation into a serial killer who murdered twelve people three years ago. The case had been closed and the killer presumed dead, but we've found his fingerprints at the scene of a crime. Your department was involved with the previous case, and we need your expertise again.'

'What was the name of the killer?'

'He was given the code name Mechanic,' Lucas replied.

'Okay, I'll get to work on it straight away and someone will be with you first thing in the morning. I'll fax you with timings and arrangements.'

'Thanks.'

The wheels were now in motion. But the more Lucas knew about the case, the less he felt in control.

Chapter 10

Mechanic sat with both hands clutching the steering wheel in a white-knuckle grip. The car was pulled over to the side of the road , its lights and engine turned off. This was the worst place to be, out in the open. Mechanic was a sitting duck.

'Worked it out yet, sucker?' Daddy's voice echoed around Mechanic's head, each word designed to paralyse with fear. The attacks were relentless and came without warning. Mechanic popped the cigarette lighter into the dashboard, heating up the element. It was the only thing to hand which could inflict serious pain.

Mechanic's head shook from side to side, eyes tightly shut. 'It's too early, I'm not ready.'

'Screwed up this time, chump,' the voice mocked. 'It's not good enough, it's really not good enough.'

'Can't go on. It's too soon.' Mechanic's eyes opened, and saw a pale, tortured face reflected in the rear-view mirror. This was desperate. The final morsels of control were slipping away. Mechanic frantically tried to retrieve the lighter from its holder, fingernails digging around the edges.

'I say now. Do it now.' Daddy's voice thundered.

'No. No I can't.' Mechanic pulled the lighter from the dash. The coiled metal glowed red in the dark and Mechanic felt the heat just inches from the soft flesh of the inner arm.

Ready for the searing pain to break Daddy's hold.

It was no use. Mechanic's resolve crumpled and the lighter was replaced in its holder. Mechanic stared straight ahead into the distance. All control was gone.

'I suppose there are loose ends. Work left unfinished.' The words dribbled from Mechanic's mouth, eyelids fluttering as if struggling to stay awake.

'You suppose right, chump. But have you worked it out yet? Have you worked out how you got the wrong fucking house?'

'I wasn't ready. I told you I wasn't ready.'

'It was a shoddy screw-up. Have you worked it out yet, chump?' Daddy was pressing hard, wanting answers.

'Not sure. Need to go back and look. Need to do it right.'

'Then turn the car around and go back to work. Daddy's not pleased. You need to please Daddy.' The voice in Mechanic's head died away into a distant recess.

Slowly a thin smile formed across Mechanic's lips. The gear shift was slammed into drive, the engine gunned into action and the back wheels spun in the gravel. The back of the car slewed around and Mechanic lurched back onto the road, pulling hard on the opposite lock to straighten up. The lights flashed on and the car sped away.

Two hours later Mechanic stood in the lounge of a beachfront property. Any doubts of poor preparation were long gone, this was definitely the right house. It was shrouded in darkness while the occupants slept. Vertical strip blinds swayed back and forth, the night air drifting through them. The patio door was propped up against the frame, allowing the sea breeze to blow in.

Mechanic enjoyed this part the best. Standing breathlessly still, allowing eyes to become accustomed to the greyscale colours of the room at night, listening to the sounds of the house cooling down after a long day baking in the Florida sun. The floorboards were settling, the refrigerator softly humming and the air conditioning unit cutting in. Mechanic soaked up the atmosphere, relishing what was to come next.

Comfortable with the background noises, Mechanic moved through the house. Standing in front of the TV, Mechanic crouched down and removed a black glove to press a naked thumb into the centre of the screen. Mechanic replaced the glove, skirted the leather sofa and stepped through a large archway which led down a long hallway to the bedrooms.

After several paces Mechanic stopped, listening to an unusual noise. What was it? Someone turning over in bed? Someone throwing back the quilt to cool off?

Shit, someone was getting up.

Mechanic moved back through the arch and stepped to the side, pushing hard against the living room wall and dropping to a semi-crouch position. The sound of feet padding on carpet was growing louder. Questions rushed around Mechanic's mind, the training kicking in. Will they turn a light on? Is it a man or woman? Is it a child? Mechanic heard the door knob twist and the noise of the carpet pile brushing under the door as it opened. Someone was coming down the hallway. All questions disappeared as Mechanic focused on the next few seconds. There was no need to think, just to act. Pure instinct.

Mechanic's right hand swung in a fierce upward arc smashing Dave McKee full in the throat. The backhanded strike connected hard, forcing McKee's head up and back. The sound of cracking bones filled the confines of the archway as the vertebrae in his neck jumped out of position.

These were the only noises to be heard from the attack since McKee's smashed larynx failed to work. His head reflexed back to its normal position and his knees buckled. Air rushed from his mouth and he emitted a gargling noise as the blood ran down his windpipe. McKee's hands were wrapped around his shattered throat and his head sagged to one side. Mechanic pivoted on the left foot and stepped back away from him. With gun drawn and levelled at McKee's head, Mechanic waited.

The seconds ticked by. Dave McKee's weight became too much for his lower body to carry and his knees hit the soft pile of the lounge carpet. His eyes protruded from their sockets in a cartoon-like stare, his hands still clutching at his smashed throat. Poised in front of the choking, kneeling figure, Mechanic squeezed the trigger.

The mild spit from the silenced gun was always such an understated announcement of the complete devastation that followed.

A small ridged hole appeared in the centre of McKee's forehead. The back of his head exploded sending splinters of bone along the hallway, hitting the floor, ceiling and both walls. The force of the bullet lifted him from his kneeling position and laid him flat on the soft carpet. Mechanic stepped back against the living room wall, waited and listened. There were no more sounds. No one stirred.

After several minutes, Mechanic stepped around the large red stain on the carpet, holstered the gun and unclipped a fourteen-inch rubber baton. Thanks to her husband's unexpected arrival in the hallway, finding Hannah McKee was a piece of cake. Their bedroom door was still slightly ajar.

Mechanic slipped silently inside.

Chapter 11

The early morning sun splashed leafy shadows across the block stone frontage of the station as Lucas swung his car into the parking lot. While driving to work, he'd pondered the irony that such a blissful, welcoming morning could herald what Lucas was sure would be a blissful bitch of a day. He bounded up the front steps, his mind clear and crisp. He was confident that he could handle whatever the day threw at him. Twice in his career he had seen others in his position fall apart when tasked with such a prominent case. They had both lacked clarity and had consequently drowned in their own confusion. That was not going to happen to him.

Lucas nodded good morning to those he met on his way to his office, passing the main fax machine as he did so and tearing the waxy paper away from the top tray. It read:

From: Jeff Chambers
To: Edmund Lucas
As per our telephone call, expect Special Agent
Dr Jo Sells to arrive am today.
Regards
Jeff
Director of Behavioral Science Unit
FBI Academy, Quantico.

Lucas read it and continued to his office, calling into the incident room first. Bassano was removing the contents of the boxes from the night before and creating incident boards for each of the murders. However bleak the pictures had looked earlier, they were even more harrowing once they'd been pinned to the boards in the first flush of morning sunshine.

'Morning chief,' said Bassano gulping black coffee from an enamel mug. 'This is a right cluster-fuck.' Bassano was renowned for his cheery greetings.

'It sure is.' Lucas couldn't have put it better himself. 'Just a few words before the dogs of war descend on us.' Bassano stopped what he was doing and drew closer to Lucas. 'I hope to God we went wrong somewhere in identifying the print and there's a rational explanation of why a previously dead serial killer pays our state congresswoman's daughter a visit. Because then we can all have our asses kicked for wasting time and resources and get back to the daily shit that we all know and love.' Bassano smiled at the twisted summary of their predicament. Lucas pressed on, his voice no more than a whisper.

'But until that happens, this is real. It's the biggest case we've had to deal with, and it's one where solving the crime is only part of what we have to deliver. Everyone is going to be looking over our shoulders to see how we're progressing, and they'll all know a better way of doing it – the press, the FBI, the politicians, and the public. So when we get the press involved I don't want any own goals, no extra pressure by cocking up. Understand?'

'Yeah boss.'

'We need to cover a lot of ground fast. I want pace and lots of it.' Lucas eyeballed Bassano who nodded his head.

Bassano spoke in a hushed whisper. 'That's what I meant, sir,' he paused, 'about it being a cluster-fuck.'

Lucas shook his head, turned and walked to his office.

Bassano was a good detective with an uncanny ability to join the dots. He had the knack of spotting what others would miss. However, a constant worry for Lucas was Bassano's hopelessness when it came to field training. Despite his physical prowess, he was useless at the rough stuff and found it almost impossible to follow the most basic of training procedures. Bassano couldn't grasp that there was a right way to do things which would help to keep him safe. Several times when they'd been through the basic capability tests, Lucas had despaired as Bassano's report came through marked 'fail'.

Lucas told him on more than one occasion that if he didn't start practising what he learned in training he would end up dead.

Lucas reached his office to find the phone ringing. He picked it up: 'Yes, Lucas here.'

'Hello, sir. I have a Dr Sells to see you.'

'Good. Send our dear doctor up to my office will you?'

'Yes, sir.' With a click, the line went dead.

Lucas shuffled reams of paper together, shoving them in a desk drawer in a vain attempt to tidy his desk. He removed his jacket and tilted his chair back at a dangerous angle. He picked up a report which had failed to make it into the drawer and began reading. There was a knock at the door.

'Come,' Lucas barked. The door swung open and in walked his visitor.

'Good morning, Lieutenant, my name is Dr Jo Sells from the Behavioral Science Unit at Quantico. I thought that an early start was in order under the circumstances.' If it wasn't for the close proximity of the back wall, Lucas would have fallen off his chair. He flailed around searching for words to say, at the same time trying to regain his balance.

'Er, yes. Yes, I had the same thought myself,' he replied. There was a pregnant pause. Lucas was at least in a stable position now, sitting bolt upright, with both hands placed firmly on the top of his desk.

'Weren't you told to expect me, Lieutenant?' Jo eyed him carefully. 'You should have received a fax this morning informing you of my arrival.'

'Yes, we were. I mean, I was. But the fax contained little detail. It just said ...' The words died in his throat.

'Don't tell me it merely said Dr Jo Sells?'

'Yes, it did.' Lucas waved the fax in the air as if submitting evidence.

'Lieutenant, the Jo is short for Josephine.' Lucas could only manage a faint 'Ah'. She continued. 'Isn't it a bitch when that happens?'

'When what does?'

'When you expect one gender and get another.' She punched the words at him across the desk.

Lucas considered the question. He supposed that it very much depended on what you were expecting in the first place. If like him you were expecting a small bookworm of a man in his mid to late forties, wire-rimmed spectacles and hair swept over the top of his head from one temple to the other, then yes, it most certainly was a bitch. If, on the other hand, you were expecting a thirty-something, hazel-eyed, stunning beauty that you're sure you dreamed of as a teenager, then no, it wasn't.

Dr Jo Sells was everything her name and profession suggested she wasn't. She wasn't classically pretty, but her looks were striking. She was around five feet ten inches tall with long auburn hair pulled into a plait which swung between her shoulder blades. Jo always considered her height an advantage because it hid the fact that she was a well-built girl. At college she'd caught the training bug and swam, ran and rowed her way to a first class honours degree in psychology. Her punishing exertions disciplined her mind and shaped her body.

Eight years on she still had the bug and the figure to prove it.

To anyone who asked why she drove herself so hard, she'd look them straight in the eye and reply that she was addicted to the pain. This would have the effect of terminating that line in chat which was inevitably being pursued by a curious male. She stood before Lucas in a well-cut suit, oozing confidence and poise.

She was sure her boss, Jeff Chambers, did the Jo Sells bit on purpose to wind her up. In truth, she quite enjoyed the uncertainty it created, providing her with immediate impact. It was especially useful when working in a male dominated environment, although up to now no one had fallen off their chair. This morning had been a first.

'I'd like to start this again,' said Lucas exhaling noisily. His calm had returned, and he was conscious he still hadn't replied to her question. 'We're all a little on edge over this, please accept my apologies.' He got to his feet and extended his right hand.

'Accepted.' Jo Sells shook his hand with a firm handshake. She smiled broadly. 'I'm Dr Jo Sells from the Behavioral Science Unit at FBI Quantico. I'm pleased to meet you. Oh, and by the way, in case you're wondering the Jo is short for Josephine.'

Lucas smiled. 'Welcome to Tallahassee, Dr Sells. I'm Ed Lucas, the station Lieutenant here. Oh, and by the way, in case you were wondering, the Ed is short for Edmund.'

Chapter 12

Lucas and Sells sat facing each other across the conference table, hot black coffee steamed out of chipped white mugs in front of them. Jo took a sip and, wary of the heat, pulled a face.

Both were still making small talk and Jo was sharing a little more detail on her impressive CV. As she talked, she absent-mindedly lifted six packets of sugar from the bowl, tapped them onto the tabletop to square the edges, then tore the tops off them all in a single movement. Lucas was mesmerized as Jo expertly manipulated the sachets. She held them between her thumb and first finger and emptied the entire contents into her cup. She flattened out the packets on the table top and folded the torn tops into the paper over and over again. This made a single folded strip. By now Lucas was no longer listening, he was fascinated by the origami lesson taking place in front of him.

Still talking, she flattened the strip on the desk top, then picked up one end in each hand and twisted in opposite directions. This turned the strip of sugar packets into a compacted spiral. She applied more pressure and then released the sachets onto the tabletop. It formed a perfect double helix which rolled along the desk.

Lucas picked it up. Jo stopped talking.

'Interesting,' said Lucas.

'Oh sorry,' said Jo, retrieving the spiral out of Lucas's hand. 'When I was younger I was embarrassed by the amount of sugar I took in coffee. I'd fold the sachets up like this so people didn't know how many I'd actually had. Now I make these automatically – most of the time I don't even know I do it.'

'Well, that's a first. I've never come across that before,' said Lucas.

'My friends called them sugar twists,' she said, holding up the white spiral. 'It's silly, I know, but …' It was as if Jo had divulged a little too much in her eagerness to explain away her unusual addiction. It was time to get back to business.

'So what do you have?' she asked, recoiling from the mug which had burned her lip.

'Two days ago we had a burglary at a beachfront property out Keaton Beach way. At first we thought it was a routine robbery, but we started to suspect that something wasn't right and doubted the true motive was theft. We then turned up a fresh print from a serial killer known as Mechanic. A regular nightmare of a guy with twelve kills to his name. He has a peculiar but predictable style. Blows the brains out of the father and kids with a .45, bumps the mother on the head but doesn't kill her, ties her up in her own nightclothes and leaves her on the bedroom floor. He then loads the bodies into the family car and secures them in place with seat belts. And he always places a thumbprint in the centre of the TV screen as a calling card.' Lucas stopped briefly for Jo Sells to nod her comprehension. He then continued.

'For some reason, at the end of his killing spree, he went haywire and operated in an uncontrolled, almost random fashion. He killed a lone FBI guy who was working on the investigation by shooting him through the head on a piece of waste ground a few miles from his hotel. This was completely out of kilter with his normal MO. And if that wasn't strange enough, a month later Mechanic loaded the bodies of his latest victims into a car, drove to the very same spot of waste ground, doused everything in petrol and set it ablaze. With himself inside.' Lucas gestured with his hands, as if to exaggerate his incomprehension. 'Then, after all this, he turns up on my patch three years later still in possession of a recognizable thumbprint.'

'Initial thoughts?' asked Jo.

'Well, apart from how the hell does that happen, the main thing that jumps out is this dramatic deviation from his normal kill pattern. The FBI guy he blew away on a piece of waste ground just doesn't make sense. His name was ...' Lucas got up and fished around in the box file at his side.

'Victor Galbraith.' Jo interrupted his search.

'What?'

'The man's name was Victor Galbraith.'

Lucas eyed Jo with extreme suspicion. 'That's right, it was,' he replied. 'Either you have an uncanny knack of guessing the names of dead people or you are remarkably well briefed, Doctor. Do you want to tell me which one it is before we continue?'

'I'm well briefed, Lieutenant.'

'But that doesn't figure. We haven't had time to compile a summary case file for you.'

'I don't need one.' Jo could feel Lucas's stare burning into her.

'So how the hell do you know details like that?'

'Victor Galbraith was my boss at Quantico when he was killed by Mechanic. Victor headed our division in the Behavioral Science Unit.'

'No shit. Go on.' Lucas felt outmanoeuvered.

'Sure, okay.' Jo took a deep breath. 'Having completed my psychology degree, I did a post-grad in criminology. Victor Galbraith was a visiting fellow at the university. He tutored me and I gained my doctorate quickly. Then he steered me into taking a job with the FBI. With his sponsorship I couldn't fail and was recruited into the Behavioral Science Unit. I'd been there a couple of years when Mechanic first started killing. The FBI were involved, and Victor was the natural choice to develop a psychological profile of the killer on such an important case. Victor thought it would be good experience for me to see how what we did worked in practice, so I went along with him as part of the team.'

Jo continued, not allowing Lucas to interrupt. 'The other reason Victor was selected was that, at the time, the guy running the show here at FPD was a real hard knock called Dick Harper. Harper thought that all shrinks should be strangled at birth and welcomed us to the investigation like a dose of crabs. Victor was very senior and they thought that he could handle Harper. They couldn't have been more wrong, it was a bloodbath between them.' Lucas held his hand up for Jo to stop.

'Why did Harper hate shrinks so much?' Lucas asked.

'He always thought they were there to make excuses for the criminal low life rather than to make sure the real victims got justice. But as much as he hated shrinks, he hated Victor more. They had some previous history between them. Years earlier, Harper had arrested a guy for the malicious wounding of a woman. Victor didn't work for the Bureau then and when the case went to trial he was called by the defence to provide expert testimony. Victor told the court that the guy's upbringing was so bad he didn't know any different, and that's why he behaved the way he did. Instead of going to jail, he was sent to hospital to undergo psychiatric tests. After three days he escaped, tracked down the woman and killed her for grassing him up. Of course, he was arrested again but all through his trial he taunted Harper that he had tricked the system and fabricated the whole home-life story. Harper went ballistic and was very public in his opinion of Victor. He blamed him and all of his profession for the killing. Then, years later, they locked horns again in the Mechanic case, both of them having serious scores to settle, and it all kicked off again.'

'I see,' Lucas replied, motioning her to continue.

'Harper wouldn't let Victor in on the case and kept him in the dark. Victor, on the other hand, fought tooth and nail to work his way in. Their public outbursts were often as much front page news as the case itself. It was a journalist's dream. They wasted no opportunity to blame each other for the slow progress of the investigation.' Jo stopped speaking to give Lucas time to absorb all she'd said.

'What a pantomime,' Lucas said. 'What happened next?'

'There was massive press coverage. The papers never tired of saying the entire state was gripped in "Mechanic panic". Some catchphrase, eh? Harper was under incredible pressure to catch this guy, but drew nothing except blanks at every turn. To add to his troubles, he was receiving notes in the mail from Mechanic, taunting him that he wasn't smart enough to catch a cold, let alone a serial killer. This was kept well under wraps, no one outside of a few people about it, but the notes gradually tore him apart. Mechanic even sent Harper his suicide note the day before he torched himself and his final three victims in that car. This proved the last straw and Harper retired shortly after the case was wound up.'

'But why was Galbraith shot?' Lucas asked.

'That was never clear. The problem was that there was so much public euphoria at Mechanic's death that loose ends like that were never resolved. Even the police assumed that Mechanic killed Galbraith, and now Mechanic was dead. Case closed.'

'How did they positively identify Mechanic from the bodies in the car?' Lucas was on the edge of his seat.

Jo looked uncomfortable. 'I suppose they didn't, or more to the point couldn't. We only had burned remains to work with. The thumbprint was the only thing we had to identify Mechanic and without it there was nothing to make a positive ID. The ballistic tests proved that the gun found under the driver's seat was the weapon that he'd used to commit the murders. That's all we had.'

'Let me see if I understand this correctly. A man dies in a burned-out car along with three of Mechanic's latest victims. Based purely on circumstantial evidence, the conclusion is that he must be the killer.' Lucas looked at Jo for confirmation. 'Oh, and of course not forgetting the suicide note which was leading you by the hand to reach that conclusion.'

'That's about the strength of it,' Jo replied, then went on the offensive. 'I don't think you get it, Lieutenant. You're grossly underplaying the public's need to have Mechanic off the streets, any way they could. The entire state of Florida was in a complete frenzy. You have to realize this happened at the same time they arrested Ted Bundy. He'd been wreaking his own havoc, killing two women and attacking two more at Florida State University, then killing a fourteen-year-old girl in Lake City. Following his arrest, he had a massive show trial in the June of 1979, in Miami, which was televised to the nation. Two hundred and fifty reporters camped out around the court room. It climaxed when he was sentenced to death twice. He had a second trial in Orlando six months later and was sentenced to death again.' Lucas stared at her, unimpressed. He knew all about Ted Bundy and it was no excuse for sloppy police work in the Mechanic case.

She pressed on. 'Bundy had the whole state terrorized, even though he was in captivity. This guy decapitated at least twelve of his victims and kept severed heads in his apartment as mementos. All this took place over the same six-month period that Mechanic was on the rampage in Florida. It was a manic time. No wonder there was a tidal wave of relief when the news broke that Mechanic had died in that car. To question the validity of that would have been catastrophic, not only for the authorities but for the politicians as well.'

Lucas held his head in his hands while his elbows rested on the desk. He raised his eyes to meet Jo's gaze.

'So it was buried. No difficult questions, no embarrassing forensics, no further action.'

'Yep,' Jo replied.

'Great. Just fucking great.' Lucas made no apology for his first swear word of the day.

They drained the last of the coffee from the flask. The silence between them was long and painful. Lucas glanced at her, wondering what revelation she was going to come out with next.

Lucas was resentful. He kept telling himself that it should be an advantage that Jo had previous involvement with Mechanic. It would give them the inside track on so many things, but he felt left behind. That annoyed him. He needed to formulate his own theories and draw his own conclusions, not have them handed to him on a plate. He broke the silence.

'I want you to brief my people. They need to know everything that we've talked about. Later you and I will drive over to the Mason place to take a look at the crime scene and see if it triggers anything.' Lucas rose from the table and pulled on his jacket.

'Will you be at the briefing?' Jo asked.

'No, I'm going to pay Dick Harper a visit, see if the man and the legend match up. I'll pick you up from the station later and we'll go to the Mason house together.' Lucas was on his way out of the door.

'I have a rental car. I can drive myself and meet you there.'

'No, you and I need a period of quality uninterrupted time together for a long chat. We can do that in the car.'

'If we need to talk, why not now? Anyway, shouldn't I be with you when you talk to Harper?' Jo was irritated at being sidelined.

'To answer your points in order, Dr Sells: one, I'm not ready to talk and two, I don't need a doctorate in psychology to work out that Harper won't be very forthcoming in the presence of the late Dr Galbraith's protégée. I'll see you around lunchtime.' Lucas got up to leave. 'And, by the way, it's thirteen,' he said on his way out.

'What is?'

'It wasn't Mechanic in the burned-out car. So when you brief my guys, it's thirteen kills, not twelve.' He banged the door shut behind him.

Jo Sells sighed. The impact of her arrival had already faded.

Chapter 13

Lucas had done his homework on Harper. He was five feet ten inches tall with a barrel chest and broad shoulders. To describe him as thickset was a ludicrous understatement. He'd never married. 'Always married to the job' was the excuse he always gave, but the truth was that he was a lost cause where women were concerned. At nearly fifty-six years of age, he was invisible to women and had developed into a resentful individual with a prickly and uncompromising nature. He was predisposed to push people away and hence had no close friends, only drinking buddies. Therein lay the origins of his long-running drink problem. He used to be a functioning alcoholic, able to operate at a reasonable level in work, but not anymore. He was now barely functioning at all. He was a full-blown testament to the effects of excess alcohol and personal neglect.

His behaviour had become increasingly erratic and aggressive and the force had retired him early as an alternative to firing his ass out the door. His pension was adequate for a reasonably comfortable lifestyle, but Harper chose to forego that option and drank his way through the lion's share, which only left him enough money to live in squalor. Even the thirty dollars it would cost to replace his glasses, he preferred to spend behind the bar, which left him with a semi-permanent squint to compensate for his short-sightedness.

Of course, he hadn't drunk away all of his cash by himself. If he had, he'd almost certainly be dead by now. He'd used it to engage a loose association of ex-police buddies he substituted for friends. In this way, Harper had no need to invest anything in the acquaintances he drank with, no regular contact, no shared interests or interesting conversation. No, all it required to remain transient bosom buddies was an investment in Bourbon and beer.

He occasionally used a hooker, usually an older streetwalker who needed the cash to feed her kids rather than to feed a drug habit. He considered prostitution an important part of the social fabric of life and a necessary service. It was the pimps he loathed, and when he'd been in charge of the force, he'd used every asset at his disposal to eradicate them.

As a younger man, he'd been drafted into the Korean War. In the middle of the terror, carnage and loss of young life he felt completely at home. He loved it. He could be himself. The physical hardship and the constant threat of death – mixed with a heady cocktail of endless opportunities for extreme violence – enthralled Harper. There were no friendships, no attachments, just a random stream of people who supported the same cause, but seldom matching Harper's skill and enthusiasm.

The one black spot on this cherished time was the death of his brother. Matthew was two years older, but was called up around the same time. One day in Osan he foolishly ventured into an underground tunnel, following a guy suspected of stealing fuel from the base. The fourteen-year-old girl sitting near the entrance and watching the proceedings with childish innocence, counted to thirty and then detonated the charges. They only buried bits and pieces of Matthew Harper. It was all they could find. The military put bricks into the coffin to give the illusion of weight as they carried him into Arlington National Cemetery.

Initially Dick Harper grieved for his brother with dignity and restraint, but the process lasted just long enough to bury Matthew's pitiful remains. Then Harper went to war like no man ever should. He realized that the more Korean insurgents he killed, the less his grief hurt. His kill rate was phenomenal. He had a charmed existence, walking out of fire fights without a scratch, while a procession of casualties were medevaced out. He'd been decorated more times than he cared to recall, but the shiny metal trinkets weren't important to him. His only priorities were to minimize the pain from his grief and to even up the score.

Once the war was over, the prospect of army life without the excesses of war wasn't for him. He found life as a soldier dull, dull, dull. He got into fights with other men on his base and soon became a liability. So he bought himself out and returned to civilian life. Four months later he joined the police and, after a shaky start, he performed beyond expectation.

His style and approach suited the times and, just as his kill rate had got him decorated, so his arrest rate got him noticed. He rapidly rose through the ranks and became Lieutenant at a relatively early age. That's when it all began to unravel for Harper.

Lucas had some sympathy for the man. He was a product of his environment and unable to adapt to the demands of modern policing. Lucas stood in Harper's neighbourhood and looked around him wondering if his predecessor now regretted his inability to change.

Harper wasn't difficult to find. His apartment was well known to the older guys at work. It was in a run-down part of town where a short walk meant your shoes would be covered in pavement grease. Lucas made his way past the bleak tenement blocks, every doorway he passed stinking of urine, the noise of a passing train thundering off the dilapidated buildings.

Some places, like people, wear the bruises of the past. As with people, these bruises are often starkly visible long after the black and purple has faded. Harper lived in such a place.

Lucas entered an apartment block, making his way up the internal stairwell to number 506. He'd tried to telephone before he left the station, but the number was unavailable. Looking around him, he supposed that Harper had been cut off for not paying the bill. He supposed right. At the fifth-floor landing he thumped his fist on the door marked 5 6, the zero long since departed. The loud knock prompted a lot of scuffling inside the apartment and a gruff voice barked, 'Piss off.'

Lucas raised his eyebrows and clicked his tongue on the roof of his mouth disapprovingly.

'Harper, this is Lieutenant Ed Lucas from the station. I'd like to talk to you.'

'Piss off,' came the reply. The door remained firmly shut. This was proving more difficult than he'd anticipated.

'Harper, I need to talk to you. Max Redford gave me your address and said it would be okay for me to drop by.' Lucas's voice was upbeat, guessing that dropping the name of a police drinking partner into the conversation would gain him some ground.

'Don't know any Max Redford.' Harper was having none of it.

'Harper, open the damn door. I need your help with something.'

'What about?' Since Harper's reply hadn't used a swear word, Lucas felt encouraged. There was a pause as Lucas weighed up his options. Provide a wrong answer now and the door would probably remain closed forever. Or he could grab Harper's attention by taking a risk. Lucas gambled.

'Mechanic.' The word was greeted by complete silence on the other side of the door.

'Fuck off.' This sounded like Harper's final word on the subject. Lucas waited to see what might happen, but after several minutes he gave it up as a bad job, vowing to return with a warrant and a sledge hammer. The warrant to make it legal and the hammer to hit Harper over the head. He was one flight down the stairs when he heard the sound of the sliding dead bolt and the chain rattling against the wooden door as it opened on squeaky hinges.

'You'd better come in.' The gravelly voice sounded resigned and reluctant. Lucas went back up the steps and elbowed open the door, stepping inside the apartment. After the gloom of the stairwell, the flood of light from the window at the far side of the room caused spots to circle in front of his eyes, all he could see were large floating blotches. Harper said nothing.

Gradually, Lucas made out Harper's silhouette against the window. Between them lay an obstacle course of newspapers, food wrappers, dirty dishes and clothes, all strewn across the floor so that it was impossible for Lucas to make out the colour of the carpet. An orange sofa was against one wall with a big box television opposite it. A set of chairs and a table had been crammed into one corner and a stove and sink shoehorned into the other.

Lucas's vision was fully restored by now. To his left he saw a bedroom with a single bed and a chest of drawers. Each drawer was open, clothes hanging out, and the door to the bedroom was missing. The place looked as if it had been burgled.

Harper stood with his back to Lucas, staring out of the window. 'Well, Lieutenant. You wanted to talk to me. I'm all ears.' His voice was hard and challenging. Lucas cleared his throat.

'Yes, I wondered if you would help me to tidy up a few loose ends.'

'About a three-year-old case, Lieutenant?' Harper spun around and stared hard at Lucas. 'Come on. That's a clumsy line and you know it. Which particular loose end did you have in mind?' Harper had lost none of his disrespect for the force.

Lucas didn't answer. Harper was still a big man, though the ravages of neglect and years on the booze had taken their toll. His hair was lank, greasy and badly cut, while dark rings circled his eyes above a stubbled jaw line. He wore a shapeless sweatshirt and jeans and had nothing on his feet. He fitted his surroundings well.

Lucas eventually said, 'I need to understand more about the relationship between you and Victor Galbraith at the time of the Mechanic case.'

'What the hell for, man? The damn case is dead and buried and so is he. What relevance could that have today?' There was a crackle behind Harper and a voice came from the back of the curtain. He reached over to switch something off. Lucas saw it was a police scanner. Harper caught his look. 'I like to stay in touch,' he said, moving away from the window and sitting on one of the dining chairs.

'It would help with an inquiry.' Lucas detected flashes of interest in Harper's eyes.

'Okay, Lieutenant, let's cut the crap. I know the score. I'll play along with your game for now. Let's do some dancing.' Harper got up from the chair, swung it around in front of him and straddled the seat with his arms folded on its back. 'As you can see, the force has been good to me in my retirement, so the least I can do is to cooperate.' His retort was thick with sarcasm but he couldn't hide the intrigue in his eyes.

Lucas began slowly and carefully. 'You and Galbraith worked together on the Mechanic case. All of the standard stuff I can read in the reports. What I want right now is some insight into Galbraith. What was he like?' Lucas threw a packet of cigarettes at Harper who caught it in one hand.

'Oh, you want insights? I don't know if I can provide you with insights, Lieutenant.' The sarcasm was knee deep. Harper struck a match and held it below a cigarette which glowed red. Smoke puffed into the air. 'Galbraith was the ultimate shrink. In his world, every action we take, every thought we have, has its roots in our past experiences. Our fears, our pleasures, our little quirks, can all be explained by analysing what lurks in our past. The problem was that it didn't stop there. The stupid prick also considered that if people committed a crime it wasn't really their fault but a product of their previous experiences.' He withdrew the cigarette and inhaled deeply, closing his eyes as the smoke hit the bottom of his lungs.

'To him, the criminals were helpless to resist their preordained destiny to be dirtbags. He also figured that he could describe the characteristics of a killer by what he saw at the crime scene. He could tell their age, colour, personality type, and even in a number of cases what they did for a living. Psychological profiling, he called it. Psychological horseshit, more like.' He drew hard on the cigarette and watched the glowing red band suck its way up the white tube. He blew out a great cloud of smoke which spiralled up to the nicotine-stained ceiling.

'In Galbraith's head it was their experiences in society that had led them into crime and he thought society had a responsibility to care for them, to shoulder part of the blame.' Harper was raising his voice, his anger still clearly visible. 'In doing so, all he achieved was to get the fuckers reduced sentences.' He hurled the words at Lucas.

'I can understand your frustration when Galbraith provided mitigating circumstances for the defence, but that's different from psychological profiling. Didn't you find that the profiling helped the investigation?' Lucas probed gently, aware that the ice was thin.

'It has its place in narrowing the scope, but that's all. The problem was that Galbraith rammed it down our throats. He insisted that without a profile we would never find Mechanic. The harder he pushed, the harder I resisted. I wouldn't use his damn profile, he could shove it up his ass. I told him we'd catch the bastard without it. The only thing it was good for was to provide the defence lawyer with a head start.'

'But you didn't catch him, did you?' Lucas realized his question was unwise as soon as it left his lips.

'The hell we didn't,' Harper exploded, standing up and thumping his fist into the back of the chair, knocking it to the floor. 'We tracked Mechanic down, but the slippery son of a bitch torched himself in that car before we could nail him. We had the fucker, Lieutenant. We had him, and don't you forget it.' His voice subsided along with his flush of anger. Harper set the chair upright and sat down, rubbing the knuckles of his right hand.

'Yes, you did. You're right,' Lucas placated him. 'Why did Galbraith die?'

'I don't know for sure.' Harper slowly shook his head, looking at the floor. 'The only thing I can think of is that he might have worked out Mechanic's identity. And for that reason, Mechanic shot him. But if he had figured it out, he kept it to himself. It's the only rationale that makes any sense. Galbraith had fingered the killer and arranged to meet with him on that piece of waste ground. What I do know is that he didn't tell me or any of my team about it.'

'But why did he keep it to himself?' asked Lucas.

'Oh, that's easy. To prove he was right all along and that his methods worked and mine didn't. The only problem was his damn profile failed to predict that Mechanic would kill him.'

'Do you have any idea of the identity of the person that Galbraith met that evening?' asked Lucas.

'That's the worst of it. Not a clue. Up to that point the enquiry had uncovered absolutely zilch. So how in God's name Galbraith miraculously hits the jackpot is beyond me.'

'How did you know it was Mechanic who killed him?'

'The slugs dug out of the body were an exact match to those found at the previous crime scenes.' Lucas was gripped. His mind raced with facts from the case notes. He fired another question.

'How do you mean, "dug out of the body"?'

'We removed two bullets, one from his chest and the other out of the ground underneath his body. The round passed straight through his stomach.'

'But the file notes said he died from a bullet fired at point-blank range to the head.'

'Yes, that's right it does. But we also dug out two other bullets which matched those found in other murders.' There was an edge of annoyance in Harper's voice since he had to repeat himself. Lucas backed away – he didn't want to switch Harper off now he was talking freely.

'When did you start receiving the notes from Mechanic?'

'They happened throughout the case. We kept them quiet. The press coverage was so heavy in terms of detail that any sicko could have pretended to be Mechanic and given a good account of themselves. The notes contained specific details only the killer would know, we had to keep them secret to have any chance of using them as evidence.'

'That must have been hard.' Lucas was losing Harper who was drifting away to a safer place.

'They crucified us every step of the way.' Harper's eyes were watery and vacant. Lucas saw that it was time to leave. He thanked him for his time before walking to the door, his mind still racing with unanswered questions.

'Did Galbraith keep records, or notes of any kind? These scientist types often do.'

'Yeah, he sure did.' Harper rose from his chair. 'He used to get through a new pen just about every other day. He wrote everything down, must have recorded every time he took a crap. The man was a fanatic.'

'When did you last speak to him?'

Harper thought for a while, then replied, 'He phoned me when I was in a bar on the night he was killed. The jerk tracked me down to ram that damn profile down my throat again and banged on about how I'd got it wrong. Phoned me in the damn bar. Can you believe that? I was so angry – I couldn't even have a quiet beer without that bastard having a go. This time he wouldn't let it drop, went on and on about how I'd got it wrong. In the end I slammed the phone down and never spoke to him again. We found his body the next day. Whatever he knew, he took it with him. He was an annoying prick.'

Lucas walked out of the apartment and onto the landing, not looking back.

'Give my regards to Max Redford,' Harper called after him.

Chapter 14

Driving back to the station, Lucas replayed the conversation with Harper in his mind. He again had that nagging sensation that something wasn't right.

Why would you blow a hole in a person's head, then pump two bullets into their body while they were lying on the ground, obviously dead? He sucked his teeth and clicked his tongue against the roof of his mouth. *You really are a convoluted son of a bitch, Mechanic. I can't trust anything I hear or anything I see.*

He pulled into the station, shoved the gear shift into park and got out, slamming the door. At the front desk, the officer was talking on the phone. Lucas interrupted, 'Do you know where Dr Sells is?'

The officer covered the mouthpiece and replied, 'Yes, sir, she said something about getting her kit and going to the gym. She may still be there.' He returned to his caller.

Lucas made his way to the basement and peered through the gym window. It certainly wasn't the usual hive of sweaty activity as he opened the door and walked in. Several guys were milling around, playing on pieces of equipment but with no serious effort taking place. Then he spotted the reason, Jo Sells on the bench press.

Unlike the others in the gym, Lucas didn't have the excuse of pretending to operate the weights. He just stood and stared. He couldn't figure out which was the most distracting – her legs splayed either side of the pressing bench, or the enormous weight which was lifted rhythmically and effortlessly from chest to full arm extension and back again. Lucas forced himself to snap out of it and walked over to Jo.

As he reached her, she exhaled strongly and sat up.

'Oh hi! Been there long?'

'Long enough to know why your handshake is so firm.'

Jo laughed and threw her head back at the weights. 'This is nothing. I haven't trained seriously for a long while. This is only a warm-up.'

Lucas's eyes widened. He estimated that she was pressing almost her own body weight. 'Hell of a warm up,' was all he could think of to say. He continued, 'Fancy taking a ride out to the Mason house?'

'Sure, I'll take a shower and meet you in the front office in twenty minutes.' She jumped to her feet and followed Lucas to the door. The men who'd been pretending to train clapped as she left the gym. She flashed them a smile and quipped, 'Keep practising guys, it's all in the wrist action. But then you'd know all about that.'

Nice put-down, Lucas thought, despite the fact he was still annoyed with her.

Lucas pulled out of the station car park and headed south with Jo beside him. They sat in silence for the first few miles, watching the afternoon shoppers buzz around and the local hobos getting their first slugs of cheap alcohol for the day. When they hit the freeway, Lucas spoke.

'I need your help.'

'Sure,' Jo said looking straight ahead. 'That's why I'm here.'

'No, what I mean is I need your help now.'

'Okay. With what?'

'This thing is progressing fast and I need a crash course in serial killers. Why they do what they do, what are the different types, what are their motives? You know, the basics. I don't know what I'm dealing with here and that's not good.' He paused. 'I need you to help me.'

'Okay ... Wow, there's a lot to say. Where to start? Er ...' Lucas wasn't sure if it was the question that had fazed her or the fact that he'd asked for her help.

'Just talk and we'll see how we get on. What did the profile say about Mechanic?' Lucas felt that he had provided enough of an introduction and so stopped talking.

'It said that Mechanic was a white male in his late twenties, early thirties. He probably had a steady job and was a reasonably intelligent and affable individual. He was socially adept, was likely to have had a girlfriend or a family and he probably lived in a steady place, in a stable environment. He was an organized killer who—'

'What does that mean, an organized killer?' Lucas interrupted.

'Serial killers can be divided into two categories: organized and disorganized. A disorganized killing has the characteristics of being unplanned. The murder is a spur of the moment thing. Disorganized killers don't plan their attacks. A victim can be chosen merely by being in the wrong place at the wrong time. In these cases, the killer makes no attempt to hide the body and tends to use items found in the immediate vicinity as murder weapons. More often than not the bodies are disfigured after death or the killer has sex with them post mortem. These guys are loners and don't develop attachments to others. They have a low IQ, move around a lot doing menial casual work and are socially dysfunctional.' Jo was recalling extracts from numerous lectures that she'd given on her favourite topic.

'But that's *not* our guy, right?' asked Lucas.

'No, ours is well organized. He's a predator who meticulously plans every detail. He brings with him all the tools he needs to carry out the killing and will have selected his victim against a set of clearly defined criteria. He'll probably stalk his prey until the time is right to kill. Then he destroys any evidence and hides the victim. For such people the act of killing is a piece of theatre. They run the kill over and over in their heads until it's perfect, then they carry it out in line with the fantasy. After each one, they replay it over and over to find where they can make improvements. Our guy probably has a higher than average IQ and is most likely to have taken tokens from the kill site as a reminder.'

'That exactly fits the bill for our guy, given what I've read.'

'Yep, he fits it well.'

'What about his motive?'

'Now that's tough to call. Serial killers have been known to have such wacky reasons for killing, it's difficult to predict. Take David Berkowitz. He killed because he said his next door neighbour's dog told him to, and Herbert Mullin believed that he had to kill to stabilize the San Andreas fault. The precise nature of the motive we might never know, but we can make educated deductions. Motive is usually divided into five categories. The first is Visionary, where they believe they are compelled to murder by God or the Devil or voices in their head. The second is those who are Mission Orientated. These tend to think they are ridding the world of certain groups of people, like homosexuals and prostitutes. They actually think they're doing good in society. The third is Hedonistic. These kill for the rush of it, for excitement, for lust or sex. Murder is a total turn-on for them, they really get their rocks off on it. The fourth are those who kill for Comfort. These tend to be women who kill for money or lifestyle reasons. The last category is the Power and Control freaks. These will more often than not sexually abuse their victims prior to death and it's being in control that really matters, not necessarily the ultimate killing.' Jo stopped. She felt she was giving a lecture and that Lucas's mind had wandered off. But he was hanging on her every word and soaking it all up. She continued, 'Another example of how screwy this can be is the famous case of two female killers, who killed five people in a nursing home because the first letters of their Christian names combined together to spell the word MURDER. They were caught before they could complete their sick game of Scrabble. Motive is very difficult to predict.'

'Okay, I get that it's difficult, but what is the likely scenario for our guy?' Lucas asked.

'In each case the victims are families with Mechanic murdering the husband and children but leaving the mother alive, though badly beaten. That would suggest a pathological hatred of fathers and siblings. Something must have happened in Mechanic's past to instill such feelings. Maybe abuse, either sexual or violent, or it could have been generated through neglect. It could be due to a whole host of reasons, but one thing is for sure, it's driven by a hatred of fathers, brothers and sisters.'

'Is that what Galbraith deduced?'

'Yes, it was, and it perfectly aligns with the pattern of kills. It was also my view at the time. Now that I'm taking a fresh look at the cases, it still fits.'

'What's behind putting the bodies in the car? That's a weird twist.'

'I'm not actually sure. It's why the case was given the code name Mechanic. One of the people on the team said the killer must have liked garages. I agree it's a freaky thing to do, but it's obviously significant.'

'Why do you say that?'

'Two reasons. The first is that it takes time to do it. Once he'd made the kills, you'd think the murderer would want to get the hell out of there. The second is that the longer Mechanic remained in the house and the more he acted out his elaborate fantasy, the greater the chance that he would leave behind forensic evidence. He must have known this, so the fact that he went through such a protracted ritual with the bodies it must have had real meaning for him.'

'What do you think it is?'

'That's the big question. One theory is that the symbolism denotes them leaving, as if they're in the car ready to go. This could signify abandonment. Maybe Mechanic was deserted by his father or siblings in the past. It was never something we got a firm handle on.'

'Yeah, I can see how that figures. So what makes these people kill? Are they born or are they made?'

'Probably a little of both. We all harbour fantasies of doing serious harm to someone who has hurt us, but we don't carry it out. That's because we have a social and personal framework which prevents the fantasy from being put into practice. In serial killers this framework is missing. There's nothing to prevent thoughts which should stay as fantasies from being played out for real.'

'So we're all serial killers at heart.' Lucas was being flippant.

'That's one view.' Jo was deadly earnest. 'There's a common belief that serial killers follow the same basic model. A trauma occurs in their early life which causes a fracture in their personality. This will normally produce a feeling of disassociation in the individual to help him cope with the event. This inevitably leads to low self-esteem which the killer tries to overcome with elaborate fantasies. These become more and more violent and are fuelled by a facilitator of some description. The most common facilitators tend to be drugs, alcohol and pornography. The pattern escalates and the individual eventually carries out the fantasy, and so the cycle repeats itself.'

'Why did Mechanic stop for three years?'

'I have no idea. There could be many reasons. Maybe he was convicted of another crime and sent to jail. There are well documented cases where the killer learns to overcome the compulsion to commit murder through other means, such as finding a branch of pornography that meets his need so he doesn't have to kill for kicks. It might be that Mechanic was ill and unable to continue. But, given the long time lapse, that's unlikely.'

As they drove, the questions continued and the answers flowed. Lucas often interrupted Jo to seek clarification of previous points, as if his mind was playing catch-up with the deluge of new information. She was patient with his eagerness to find out more and had an answer for everything he asked. Jo Sells' doctorate was well deserved.

They arrived at the Mason house and Lucas reluctantly opened the car door. He could have stayed talking to Jo all day. The seventy minutes they'd had together wasn't nearly long enough. Lucas felt as if they could have driven all the way to San Francisco and he'd still have had more questions. The more questions she answered, the more questions he had. She was easy to talk to and had been patient with his schoolboy curiosity – and his schoolboy misunderstandings.

'Thanks, I appreciated that,' he called to her over the roof of the car as he got out.

She nodded, 'That's okay. We can go over it again if you want.' He smiled another thank you and made his way to the front door with Jo following.

The key fitted snugly in the lock and the mechanism opened with a solid clunk. The door swung open and Lucas went inside. The house was strangely quiet compared to the last time Lucas was there. He ushered Jo into the hallway.

The blinds were closed, but shards of bright light danced across the rooms as the breeze from the open door swayed the strips of material back and forth. The effect made it difficult to focus on the interior. Lucas closed the door to prevent the onset of a migraine.

'Okay. Talk me through what you know,' said Jo.

'Mechanic approached the property from the beach and cut open the pool netting to gain access. He taped the netting back in place, levered the patio door from the runners and placed his thumb in the middle of the TV screen. That much we're certain of, but afterwards it becomes less clear. He made it look as though the property had been burgled, took a number of items and left. So we can only conclude that Mechanic had a change of heart and chose not to kill the Masons after all.'

'That's easy,' said Jo. 'The Masons don't fit the profile.'

'What?'

'I said, the Masons don't fit the profile.'

'Why not?'

'Well, look at the photos.' Jo went to the large decorative table which had an oversized lamp on it. Surrounding the base were eight photos of Celia and her husband, Charles, on various holidays and family events.

She held one up and turned it to face Lucas. 'Look, no kids. Mechanic has always gone for a traditional family unit: mom, dad and two children. These people didn't have kids. It doesn't fit.'

'So why would he go to the trouble of breaking in? From what you told me in the car, Mechanic would have meticulously planned this because he's an organized killer. He would have known they were just a couple.'

Jo sank into one of the sofas, shaking her head. 'This is screwed up. This killer is a real detail merchant. He would have rehearsed everything in his head before he made his move. The only thing I can think of is that something went wrong. He made an error and ended up here at the Masons'. Once he gained access, he saw the pictures and realized he was in the wrong place.' She shook her head again. 'But that doesn't figure.'

Lucas listened intently, the grey matter working at warp speed to make sense of what Jo was telling him.

'Are you saying that he just got the wrong house?' Lucas asked, with more than a hint of challenge in his voice.

'What other explanation can there be? The Masons are so obviously not his target group. He got in here, came to that conclusion and made it look like a burglary to cover his tracks. It's the only logical explanation I can think of, but it's so out of character.'

'It's plausible, I suppose,' Lucas said. 'But it's a major departure from the clinical performance you described to me earlier. Why leave a print for us to find? That's careless.'

'Maybe he panicked and somehow messed up. I know I'm making assumptions here, but I'm just trying to figure out what might have happened.'

They looked at one another in silence, each willing the other to make sense of the situation. A loud knock at the front door snapped them out of their state of mutual confusion.

'I'll get it. It's probably Bassano. I asked him to meet us here,' Lucas said.

He opened the door to a tall, middle-aged man who clearly enjoyed the Florida sunshine just a little more than he should.

Lucas allowed his eyes to adjust to the bright light. 'Yes, can I help you?'

'I was supposed to meet my friend early this morning to go fishing, only he didn't show.' The man spoke in a very clipped and earnest fashion. *Maybe ex-military,* Lucas thought. The stranger continued, 'He isn't answering his phone so I wondered, since you're police, if you could maybe do something. It's not like him at all. He lives for fishing.' He stared at Lucas.

'I'm sorry, sir, but we're in the process of conducting an investigation here, so my advice is to call the station if you're worried about your friend.'

'But can't you do it? I can't raise anyone at his house and that's really odd.' He was not to be put off.

'Sir, I can understand that you're concerned about your friend. If you'd like to call this number …' Lucas groped around in his wallet and handed him a card.

'But that's just plain stupid. Why would I want to call these numbers when you're here already? Why can't you help?'

'Sir, we're in the middle of an ongoing investigation. Please call one of the numbers on the card and explain the situation to them. They'll be able to ...' Lucas let his sentence tail away as he started to close the door.

'But you're a police officer.' The man was shouting. 'What's the point of calling the station when you're here? You could do it right here, right now.'

Lucas was about to exert the last few pounds of pressure to shut the heavy front door when something in the way the guy said the last four words made him stop. He slowly reopened it.

'What do you mean, I could do it right here, right now?' asked Lucas.

'My friend lives in the house next door to this one. His name is Dave McKee.'

Chapter 15

Mechanic's head was feeling slightly fuzzy. It was always the same the morning after, like coming down from a massive high. The surge of endorphins meant that even the background pain from Mechanic's burned and lacerated stomach didn't feel so bad.

The late morning sun poured in through the big picture windows which overlooked the park. The air conditioning in the apartment kicked in, ready to do battle with the July Florida weather: ninety-three degrees, ninety percent humidity with scattered showers. The apartment was well furnished, neat and tidy and the smell of polish hung in the air.

Mechanic got out of the bath, dried, put on a bathrobe and walked to the kitchen looking for coffee and anything sweet.

It was odd the way sugar played such a major part in the recovery process the morning after. But sugar it needed to be and lots of it. Mechanic put four Pop-Tarts in the toaster and set the kettle to boil before sitting at the breakfast table to bask in the gentle glow, smiling broadly.

The fuzzy head didn't matter, it would soon clear. The important thing was that last night was a job well done. The screw up the previous evening wasn't important. The success of last night had erased it. The crucial thing for Mechanic was that the mistake had been corrected with such style.

The Pop-Tarts sprang from their glowing red slots. Mechanic lifted them onto a plate and devoured them hungrily. Sugar rush.

Once they'd been demolished, Mechanic refilled the slots with another four and made coffee while the answering machine blinked an impatient red from across the room. Mechanic tried to ignore it to concentrate on the hot sweet black liquid steaming in the cup, but it just blinked on and on demanding attention. The fuzzy feeling subsided as the sugar coursed around Mechanic's body and the excitement of a new message took over.

Mechanic rushed into the bedroom and returned with a small leather-covered book. Sitting by the phone, Mechanic hit the play button.

The tape rewound in the machine. It whirred and spooled back to the beginning. This was a long message. Eventually it stopped, clicked and started to play.

'Hi, my name is Kaitlin, we've spoken briefly before. If you recall, I saw your advertisement and thought I'd get in touch again.' The voice was high pitched and tentative. There was a long pause. 'I was really interested in what you said on the poster.' Another long pause. Then Kaitlin's words came out in a rush. 'I really got what you were saying. It was as if you were talking directly to me. You understand what's going on and what it's like. I feel as though you've been there too and I'd like to talk with you, I think you could help.' There was a pause before she suddenly said, 'I'll give you a call another time.' And with that, Kaitlin hung up.

Mechanic sat in silence. This one was promising. The choice of location had paid off. It was always beneficial to think these things through and carefully target the next victim. After all, it would not serve Mechanic well to have a blanket campaign. No, careful targeting was the answer.

There were indications that this one could be good. Mechanic replayed the message and ticked off the mental checklist. She only gave her first name, a sign that this was a covert call. Kaitlin probably wasn't even her real name, but that didn't matter. The hesitations and pauses signified someone who lacked confidence, who was confused about what to say. Vulnerability was key. The poster had struck a chord with her and the chances were that she hadn't spoken to anyone about getting in touch. She sounded frustrated at the end of the message, as though she had built herself up to make the call, only to be disappointed when Mechanic wasn't there to take it. Then there was the killer line, 'It was as if you were talking directly to me.' That was a fantastic phrase. Kaitlin was hooked, completely hooked.

Mechanic made notes in the small book and closed it with a satisfied grin. Message left 8.30pm. She'll call back, she'll definitely call back. A knot of thrill and exhilaration built up in Mechanic's stomach.

Just one final check. Mechanic lifted the receiver and dialed *69 to get Kaitlin's number, but it had been withheld. She would call back. Mechanic hit the button on the answer machine to wipe the message tape clean before getting dressed, still nursing the cup of coffee.

No sooner had Mechanic reached the bedroom door than the phone rang.

Chapter 16

Lucas was back at the station, looking deep into a cup of lukewarm black coffee. He felt drained of energy. The morning at the McKee's had rushed by in a blur of hectic activity and had taken it out of him.

When the guy at the Mason house had said that Lucas could do it 'right here, right now', the realization went off like a fire cracker in his head. Ignoring his visitor, Lucas ran to the back of the next-door property. Sure enough, he found the netting had been cut and taped back in place. Across the pool he could see the patio door propped up against the frame.

Inside the house he found Hannah McKee tied up and lying on the floor. A pool of congealed blood stained the bedroom carpet where she'd been beaten into unconsciousness. She was still alive, but in a bad way. Lucas was relieved when the ambulance arrived quickly, her injuries were way outside his abilities to help. The garage contained the sickening theatre of Dave McKee and his two children buckled up in the family car. Dad in the driver's seat with the kids in the back. Each one had been shot through the head.

Lucas stood in the corridor which ran from the bedrooms to the lounge. The walls, floor and ceiling were splattered with brain, blood and bone. He imagined Mechanic squeezing the trigger and the core of carnage erupting from the back of McKee's head. The gun must have been silenced because everyone else was in their rightful place when the fantasy played itself out in cold reality. There's never an adequate professional shield to protect you from the crushing horror of young death. Lucas felt it weighing heavily on him.

He got the wrong house, he thought.

Jo Sells stayed at the property and waited for Bassano to arrive. She wanted to immerse herself in the crime scene, while Lucas went back to the station. He needed time to think.

Lucas was staring out the window in his office when Bassano burst in. 'Sir, I think I know why Mechanic went to the Mason house the previous night.' He spread a large street plan of Ridgeway Crescent and the surrounding area onto the conference table.

'But I thought you were at the house,' Lucas said, puzzled.

'Never mind about that,' said Bassano impatiently. 'Okay, let's retrace Mechanic's steps on the night he broke into the Mason property. We'll make a few assumptions but I don't think I'm far off.' Lucas nodded his head for him to continue.

'The chances are that he got to the general location by car. It's the safest, most controlled method and allows for an immediate getaway. But he'd want to park far enough away from the target house not to be spotted. So ...' Bassano stabbed his finger into the map and described Mechanic's route, '... He drives down Ridgeway Crescent passing the Mason house on the right. It's a long road with a cul-de-sac at the end where there's space to park. He travels five hundred yards and pulls up at the parking lot. Now he gets out of his car and walks back along the water's edge to the target house. No one will pay attention to someone enjoying a walk along the beach. It's perfect. When he gets to the target house, and when no one is looking, bam! He's in.'

'That's great,' said Lucas, 'but he went "bam!" and broke into the wrong house.'

'That's right, and that's where the error was made. The McKee house was the intended target and they live at 1315 Ridgeway Crescent. All the properties are located on the beach side of the street and the house numbers run in numerical order. Mechanic drives to the end and looks at the number on the last house, number 1287. He subtracts 1287 from 1315 and counts twenty-eight houses when he walks back up the beach.'

'Brilliant piece of deduction, Sherlock, but he still gets the wrong damn house. Are you saying that with all his high IQ and meticulous planning, Mechanic can't count to twenty-eight?'

'No, sir, he counts pretty good.' Bassano tried hard to instill calm into his boss. 'He counts twenty-eight houses as he walks past them on the beach side of the properties.' Bassano straightened up from the map on the table. 'Only, the twenty-eighth house is the Mason house,' he said, emphasizing each word as he spoke.

'But how can that be?'

'Because one of the residents of Ridgeway Crescent is superstitious and there is no number 1313. The house numbers go 1311, 1312 ... 1314, 1315. Number 1313 is missing, I checked it out. Mechanic counted twenty-eight houses but without number 1313 he ended up in the next door house to the one he wanted. That put him in the Mason house, not the McKee house.' Bassano looked triumphant.

Lucas slumped into a chair, exhausted by the events of the day.

'That's brilliant,' he said to Bassano who gave him a wide smile. 'But do you know what?'

'What?'

'While it solves a little riddle for us, it doesn't get us any further with the big questions. Like, what's the connection between our victims? How is he selecting them? Why did Mechanic kill Galbraith?' Bassano nodded agreement, his smile fading away.

'It does tell us one thing, sir,' Bassano offered.

'Oh, what's that?'

'It tells us he can make mistakes. It tells us he's not foolproof.' Bassano looked at his boss for any flicker of recognition.

'You're right,' Lucas said. 'Let's hope he makes a few more. How are the rest of the team doing?'

'They're working hard trying to provide answers to all the questions you just raised, but they're drawing blanks at every turn. That's why I got excited about unravelling why Mechanic hit the Mason house. So far it's the only thing we've managed to crack.'

'Keep at it and call me if anything else turns up.' Bassano left and Lucas returned to his desk, tilting right back in his chair. From this angle the mountain of paperwork looked even bigger. Even the arrival of a previously dead psychopath on your patch didn't stop the administration machine churning out endless numbers of forms to fill. He jerked the chair back into its upright position, dragged the pile towards him and removed the top sheet. It was a request from the Governor's office to comment on a performance stat. Lucas picked up his pen and started scribbling.

It was late in the evening when Lucas gave up on his paperwork and made his way to his car. There'd been no further revelations from the investigation teams. Lucas had joined them in the incident room on several occasions during the afternoon, as much to get away from his admin as to get himself briefed.

Walking across the car park, he could see someone standing by his car, hands in pockets. As he got closer he recognized it was Harper. He was dressed in a suit you could trick or treat in and a white shirt sporting a tragically frayed collar. He was shuffling his feet and staring at the ground. Lucas couldn't work out if his hair was gelled flat to his head or he had a new haircut. If it was the haircut option, it looked like he'd done it himself.

As Lucas got closer, he noticed that Harper had shaved and had made an effort to smarten himself up. He didn't stink of fags or booze. Though it was hard to mask the long-term effects of alcohol with an ill-fitting suit, some soap and a bad haircut.

'Hey, this is a surprise.' Lucas tried to sound upbeat.

'I thought it best not to make a show of myself in the station. There are still a lot of guys I know there, but it's not such a happy place for me, you know.'

'That's okay. What can I do for you? Do you want to go for a coffee?'

'No, here will do fine for what I've come to say.'

'Go on.'

'When we spoke the other day, there was something I didn't tell you.' Harper looked as though he was in the confessional box at church. 'In fact, it's something I haven't told anyone. But I think it's time.'

There was a long pause.

'Well,' Harper cleared his throat, 'on the night Galbraith died, I told you that he called me in a bar to chew me out again about his damn profile and how I was wrong.'

'Yes, I remember. What of it?'

'I'm not sure that's really what happened and it's bugged me all these years. It was early evening and I was already drunk. When he called I just went into orbit because I thought he'd tracked me down to ram his ideas down my throat. I was aggressive and I guess I didn't listen to him properly. That final conversation has haunted me for three years. I've played it over and over in my head and I think he said something else. I think what he actually said was, "I've got it wrong." He said something about throwing the investigation off course and I thought he was accusing me. But now I think what he actually said was that the profile itself was wrong.'

'Wrong in what way?'

'He didn't say, or if he did I wasn't listening. I was bawling him out so much that he couldn't get a word in. In retrospect, I'm sure what he actually said was, "I've got it wrong." But, whatever it was, he took it to his grave. I never spoke to him again. The next time I saw Galbraith, he was dead.'

'Why haven't you told anyone this before?'

'Because there was no need to. Galbraith was gone and shortly afterwards Mechanic torched himself. It took weeks for the realization to dawn that I might not have heard him right. I'd dream about taking that call and the conversation we had. Piece by piece it dawned on me but by the time I had it straight in my head the opportunity to say something had passed. Besides, this is hard. It's not easy for me to admit to myself. He might've been reaching out to me and all I did was to drive him away. If I'd have been different on that call, maybe he'd still be alive.' Harper looked down at his shoes. 'It was one of the reasons I quit.'

'Do you have any idea how the profile was wrong?'

'No, none at all. He made notes on everything but there wasn't one scrap of paper with any mention of an alternative profile. There was nothing.'

'Did you ask Jo Sells?'

'Yes, sure, but she was just as much in the dark as me. I didn't tell her about the phone call, I just asked if there were any other profile options we should be considering. She was a junior member of staff and played second fiddle to Galbraith. His death hit her really hard and she went back to Quantico quickly after the case concluded. She took time off to come to terms with it. No, she didn't know anything.'

Harper ground to a halt once he'd said all he'd come to say. Lucas sensed that the message had been delivered and the conversation was over.

'Well, I'd better be going. I just had to get that off my chest. Make of it what you will. You know where I am if you need to talk again.' With that, Harper turned and walked away.

Lucas chanced one last question. 'What were the other reasons?' he called after Harper.

Harper turned. 'What?'

'You said it was one of the reasons you quit. What were the others?'

Harper strolled back toward him with his hands deep in his pockets, his head tilted down. He stopped in front of Lucas.

'They are wide and varied, Lieutenant, wide and varied. But, without question, the straw that broke this camel's back happened when I went to see Julie Tate after we'd confirmed Mechanic's death to the press. She was the wife and mother of victims four, five and six. I went to see her to give her the news myself. We were really pumped up that Mechanic was dead. It felt like a good thing to do. I suppose I was expecting a positive reaction from her but she was just numb. We talked a while and at the end she thanked me for coming and said, "Lieutenant, you know, the agony continues for those that remain. I wish I were dead." The words still keep me awake at night after all this time.' Harper paused, drifting away. 'That was it. I was all hyped up because Mechanic was gone and this poor woman was still living through her own private hell. Being dead was a better option for her. It was the final straw for me. My responsibility was to protect people like her. It was my responsibility and I failed.'

'You can't shoulder that degree of guilt.' Lucas felt duty-bound to defend Harper's position. 'It happened years ago and you can't keep beating yourself up over it.'

'Oh, but I do, Lieutenant. When I look in the mirror I tell myself that every day.' Harper turned and again walked away. Lucas didn't call him back a second time.

Back at home, Lucas found himself in the unusual position of having a poor night's sleep. His wife was away on a conference, which generally meant a relaxing evening watching wall-to-wall sport on TV, eating chili dogs and drinking beer. These were banned activities during the week but when the enforcer wasn't there Lucas enjoyed his contraband evenings.

Under normal circumstances such an evening would have guaranteed a restful night, but not on this occasion. Lucas tossed and turned, replaying the conversations of the day in his head. Round and round the events span into increasingly bizarre dreams. A faceless woman swaying back and forth in a rocking chair crying, 'I wish I were dead. It's those that remain. I wish I were dead.' Over and over. In another room, the carpet was stained dark with blood and Hannah McKee was on her knees trying to scrub clean the thick pile. The more she scrubbed, the more the blood smeared across the floor. And there was Harper trying to get to the bottom of a whisky bottle as fast as he could, staggering around and slurring, 'It's the profile, it's the profile.'

Try as he might, he couldn't shift the images which kept sleep at bay. He looked at the green digits on the bedside clock: 3.15am, cursed and turned over, trying to find a comfortable position. He closed his eyes and the faceless woman appeared again, wringing her hands. 'Those that remain, I wish I were dead.' Her voice swirled around Lucas's head. 'I wish I were ...'

He woke up. His mind was completely alert. Leaping from the bed, Lucas raced down the hallway to his study, opening drawers for pens and paper. He took a piece of paper and covered it with what looked like the doodles of a crazy man. There were circles and squares with writing in them and a rat's nest of connecting arrows. He scribbled furiously, reaching for more paper and covering it with the same graphic scrawl. Putting his pen down, he picked up the phone and barked instructions to the startled desk sergeant back at the station.

Replacing the receiver in its cradle, he leaned back and surveyed the papers side by side on the desk. His breathing was slowly returning to normal.

'We've been looking in the wrong place,' he said to himself.

The clock by the bed read 4.47am.

Chapter 17

Lucas marched into his office at 6.50am. Bassano and Jo Sells were already seated at the conference table, coffees in hand. Another large mug full of hot black liquid was placed on a coaster at the head of the table. Lucas claimed it, as he joined them.

He looked across to see a perfectly formed sugar twist by the side of Jo's mug. He estimated it contained more than her usual six packets. She looked immaculate in a grey trouser suit and white blouse with a button-down collar. Her hair was drawn into the same long plait as yesterday and she wore just a hint of make-up.

Bassano looked as if he'd dressed himself straight from the dryer and had made no attempt to tame his bed hair. The previous day he'd suffered the same reaction as Lucas when Jo Sells walked into the briefing room, he'd nearly fallen off his chair. She'd proceeded to give a very polished, competent performance, showcasing her expert knowledge and experience. However, for Bassano, all he could remember from the briefing was, 'Man, she's hot.'

Lucas pulled a buff coloured file from his case and removed a sheet of paper covered with manic scrawl. 'Thanks for coming in early,' he said, pleased that his barked instructions had worked. 'I need to share with you a few ideas and I wanted to do it before the rest of day kicked off.' Bassano and Sells nodded.

'This case bothers me. There is so much of it that doesn't add up. Why is it with thirteen previous kills and three new murders we can't find what connects any of the victims? I've never known a case where we have so much information and yet so little idea of the common thread. I was with the team yesterday, they're hitting this really hard. But what have we got so far, Bassano?'

'Absolutely nothing, boss. Not a single thing which connects the men or the kids.'

Lucas shook his head. 'I shadowed a couple of them and they're doing everything possible to get a result, but we don't have a damn thing. Our profile tells us Mechanic is a father and sibling-hater, right? Something happened in his past to cause him intense trauma, which fractured his personality and drives him to kill. Right, Jo?'

'That's right,' she said. 'The initial murders pointed to that conclusion and the most recent killings at the McKee house support it.'

'But, what if that's not right?' Lucas stood to pace around the office. 'What if that theory is wrong? What if that part of the profile was incorrect?'

Jo Sells stiffened in her chair.

'But it's not. The evidence is clear,' she said flatly.

'Okay, but let's suppose for one moment it's wrong. Let's park the evidence and look at it from a different point of view. Ask yourselves the question, who are the victims here?'

'Mechanic killed the men and the kids. They are the victims,' Jo said, folding her arms tight across her chest.

'Yes, that's what the evidence says, but what if the true victims here were the women? Think about it. Mechanic takes away everything they love and leaves them to cope with the agony of losing their family. What could be worse than knowing that your family was executed, and for some bizarre reason you were spared. How could you live with that? Just think about it.' Lucas stopped to let what he'd said sink in.

He continued, 'What if Mechanic actually hated the women and the most vengeful thing he could do was to kill their families, while he left them alive.'

'That's an interesting hypothesis,' Jo leaned forward placing both hands on the table, 'and one that is completely ridiculous.' She emphasized every syllable of the last word. 'The profile is clear, very clear. Mechanic is a father and sibling hater. He leaves the women alive. To suggest that they're the focus of his attention and the true victims here is complete nonsense.'

'Yes, I know what the profile says, but do you know what Julie Tate said? She told Harper that the agony continues for those that remain and that she wished she were dead. Think about it. For her, being dead was a better alternative to what she was going through. Just think about that.'

'This is absurd.' Jo flung herself back in her chair. She was beginning to lose it a little.

'Go with it, Jo. What if the profile was wrong, what if—'

'So, now you're the expert? Only yesterday you needed a crash course in serial killers and today you're the damned authority on it. No, the profile is correct. It's you who's wrong.' She raised her voice with every phrase and with every phrase Bassano lifted his eyebrows higher.

Lucas stood his ground. 'We need to cover all the options and this is merely a different viewpoint. Let's face it, we've got absolutely nothing from concentrating on the murder victims so let's shift our focus to the women instead.'

Jo leapt out of her chair, banging the table with the flat of her hand. 'This is getting us nowhere. The evidence is clear. Mechanic kills the men and the kids, they are the victims and we need to focus all our efforts on them before he kills again.'

'You're not running this investigation, doctor. I am,' Lucas said, leaning over the table to meet her gaze. Jo kicked her seat back before storming out of the office. 'If anyone wants me, I'll be at the McKee house,' she shouted over her shoulder, slamming the door behind her.

The room fell silent. 'What the fuck was that about?' asked Bassano.

'Damned if I know. Maybe these academics don't like it when you challenge them. Redirect the team to focus on the women and see what comes up. It might be nothing and if so I'll have to eat a shit load of humble pie. But until then, get cracking on the women.' Bassano left, eager to get to work.

Alone in his office, Lucas lifted the piece of paper from the table and placed it back into the folder. In doing so, he pulled out the other sheet covered with the same array of arrows and scribbles. He looked at it, took a deep breath and exhaled slowly. 'I don't know how I'm going to deal with this one,' he said to his empty office. He replaced it and gazed into the distance. 'One step at a time, one step at a time.'

Lucas spent the rest of the morning in routine tasks while Dr Jo Sells was nowhere to be seen. He'd tried to find her and the desk sergeant said that she'd passed him on her way out saying something about 'needing to get some fucking air'.

The phone rang, it was Bassano. 'Sir, can you come down to the incident room. We've got something.'

Lucas was out of his office door and down the stairs as if the building was on fire. He burst into the room. 'What is it?'

'Looks like we were looking in the wrong place. The answer is country clubs.' Bassano waved several sheets of computer printout.

'What?' said Lucas.

'All the Mechanic women were members of country clubs. Not the same one but a country club nevertheless.'

'I knew it!' Lucas punched the table. 'Let's get the details and start making some visits.'

'On it, sir.' Bassano was buzzing.

Lucas walked slowly back to his office. 'One step at a time,' he told himself, thinking of the buff folder in his desk drawer. 'One step at a time.'

With the connection between the women now established, the next logical conclusion, which was scribbled on the second sheet of paper, would blow the investigation wide open. As he reached his office, Lucas was still unsure how to use it.

Chapter 18

Mechanic was on the late shift taking care of business, the usual routine, things to do, people to see. The second morning call had indeed been from Kaitlin and the prospects were looking good. She had continued with her lack of confidence and hesitant speech which Mechanic relished. The call had gone well.

It was best not to rush things. The first conversation was the ideal opportunity to subtly escalate the caller's anxieties while appearing to empathize. This was a fun part which Mechanic enjoyed. The sheer thrill of manipulation, it was a real rush.

Kaitlin had been guarded when it came to providing specific details, which was normal in the early days, and Mechanic was used to playing a waiting game. In fact, for Mechanic, the longer this part lasted the more satisfying the end result.

From their conversation Mechanic discovered that Kaitlin was married with children and she was a troubled woman. Her husband was relatively successful and she was well provided for, but that wasn't enough for Kaitlin. She didn't work and was in a rut. The kids took her for granted. She was constantly ferrying them around to clubs and friends' houses for which she received no thanks. They expected her to be there whenever they wanted and she was nothing more than a glorified home help. She felt completely unappreciated and a spare part in her own home.

Her husband constantly worked late and on the occasions he was home was holed up in his study making phone calls. He was totally blind to the way she was feeling. He didn't even recognize there was a problem and glided through the week without a care. He was frequently away, calling from restaurants or bars in the evening to catch up on the day. Kaitlin never went to restaurants or bars, and she resented it with a passion.

During the call, Mechanic heard the familiar beep beep as the mechanism prompted Kaitlin to put more money in. She was using a pay phone, calling from a place where she was unlikely to be disturbed or to bump into anyone she knew. Kaitlin couldn't make the call from her home phone as the number would appear on the bill and might prompt questions she didn't want to answer. No, a payphone was the right option.

For a first call it had gone well. Mechanic explained that it was a service which was free of charge. Mechanic too had been in the same position as Kaitlin many years ago and had felt isolated. Someone helped by providing sound advice and support, and Mechanic was repaying the debt.

Mechanic described how the counselling worked. The initial consultations would be done by phone to guarantee anonymity for the client. In most cases this would be sufficient to bring about the necessary improvements. Once completed, that would be the end of the arrangement. But in certain circumstances, face-to-face conversations would be required, though these were rare and would carry with them a small fee. For the majority of cases, the telephone was fine.

During the twenty-minute call, Mechanic poured petrol on the fire, fuelling Kaitlin's anxieties. Kaitlin asked for another consultation the following day. Mechanic skilfully talked her out of it, saying that Kaitlin needed time to collect her thoughts in preparation for their next conversation. In truth, Mechanic wanted the carefully placed suggestions to grow in Kaitlin's mind to increase her anxiety further.

At the end of the call, Mechanic hit *69 and once again the number had been withheld. Mechanic knew that would change as the trust and dependency grew.

But, Mechanic couldn't invest all the available time thinking about Kaitlin, because there was already a victim in the bag, waiting to go.

Chapter 19

It was the end of the day and Lucas was heading for his favourite after work drinking hole. It was a stone's throw from the station but you would never know it was there. The bar was in the basement of a large building, reached by walking down a set of narrow stone steps. Lucas shouldered his way through a heavy unpainted door with a bright neon drinks sign above it. Inside, the owner's affection for bright neon signs was obvious, they were everywhere. An ex-policeman, he accumulated the signs partly because he liked them and partly because when they were all switched on the richness of the glow meant he could turn off the normal lighting which he said cost a frigging fortune. With no windows, the array of fluorescent colours gave the place an automatic party feel, no matter what time of day it was. Lucas liked it a lot.

Lucas wandered over to Bassano who was sitting in one of the half-moon booths at the back of the bar. In front of him were two beers with the ice frosting still shimmering an iridescent white on the outside of the glass. When they said they served ice-cold beer, they meant it.

'Why the change of venue, boss?' Bassano asked Lucas, savouring the prospect of the beer.

'I need to talk with you about the case and it's best we're not in the station.'

'Okay, I'm all ears,' Bassano said, taking a long pull at his beer.

'There are too many aspects to this case which simply don't add up and the further into the investigation we go the worse it gets. Yesterday was a prime example. I couldn't for the life of me figure why we were drowning in information about the murder victims but were unable to identify a single common thread linking them. Not one. We needed to look at the evidence differently. It was not how it appeared. That's why I challenged the profile, it was driving us in the wrong direction.'

'Yeah, that was a great call, though I'm not sure our doctor was too impressed. And she'll be even less impressed when she finds out we've found a connection. She's still at the McKee house, you know.' Bassano slurped at his beer.

'Yes I know. We'll let her cool down.'

'What's the other revelation? You didn't bring me here to congratulate ourselves on the progress of the day. Is it to do with the other piece of paper you had in that file this morning? I am a cop you know, and I do notice things.' Bassano sat back against the push-button leather of the curved seat and folded his arms. 'So what is it?'

'Okay. If we accept that the profile is wrong, and the evidence from today would strongly suggest that it is, then there are a number of potential follow-on deductions. The other big piece which doesn't fit in this case is the killing of Victor Galbraith. When we were in the Mason house, I asked Jo Sells why Mechanic didn't kill them, and she said that was easy, they didn't fit the target grouping. And, she was absolutely right, they didn't. All Mechanic's victims have been families with kids, right?' Lucas paused. 'Wrong, because Galbraith doesn't fit the target grouping either, he was a major deviation from the norm. So why kill Galbraith?' Lucas paused again and took a long slug from his beer. 'I think Galbraith was killed because he'd worked out the profile he'd drawn up was wrong, and he was about to alter the course of the investigation.'

'Wow,' Bassano nearly spat his beer onto the table, 'that's a long shot.'

'Yes, I know but it gets worse. Harper told me that the night Galbraith was killed he called him in a bar. Harper was drunk, angry and under immense stress. At the time he thought that Galbraith was telling him that his investigation was going in the wrong direction, but, in the weeks following Mechanic's death, Harper revised his recollection of this conversation. He told me that he realized that what Galbraith was actually trying to say was that he, Galbraith, was wrong. In other words, the profile was wrong. Of course, Harper was in such a rage he only heard what he wanted to hear, and the next time he saw Galbraith he was dead.'

Bassano stopped drinking, his head working overtime. 'But that would mean Mechanic *knew* that Galbraith was about to change his profile and change the direction of the investigation. And that would suggest he had a direct line into the case. Are you saying there was a leak?' Bassano couldn't believe what he had just said.

'I'm not sure how, but in the same way I had an uncomfortable feeling about our inability to find a link connecting the victims, I have the same feeling about the murder of Galbraith. To compound matters, there's another significant deviation around his killing.'

'What's that?' asked Bassano.

'All the victims were shot through the head at point-blank range. Even Galbraith took a head shot and must have been dead when he hit the floor.'

'Yes, agreed.'

'So why shoot him in the stomach afterwards?'

'Maybe he was shot in the stomach first.'

'No, he was shot in the stomach when he was lying on the floor. The bullet passed right through the soft tissue and they dug it out of the ground. He was shot post mortem. Why would Mechanic do that?'

Bassano shook his head, unsure where this was leading.

'I think he shot him again to ensure we found a bullet which could be matched to the previous shells found at the kill scenes. A bullet in the head could mash up on impact, making identification impossible. Mechanic wanted to make sure we knew it was him, so he shot into a fleshy part of Galbraith's body so we'd find a good match.'

'Why would he want to do that?'

'I think Mechanic wanted to forge a positive link between the kill site and himself. Why was that important? Because that was where he staged the burn-out in the car and faked his suicide. He did it in the same damn place.'

'You said it got worse and you weren't kidding,' said Bassano. 'It all fits but it's one hell of a piece of elaborate deduction. So now we have a leak in the initial investigation. Galbraith's murder was to prevent a new profile from ever seeing the light of day while the location of his death was used to secure the impression that Mechanic was in the burnt out car. That's a shit load of deduction.'

'I know, but at least it begins to put a few of the pieces together. It begins to explain some of the loose ends. It's a long shot, I agree, but then this morning we thought the same of viewing the women as the real victims.'

'What do we do now? What about Jo Sells – do we tell her?' Bassano asked.

'I think we keep this between ourselves for now. We need to tread carefully with our dear doctor. Her reaction was completely over the top this morning. I'm not sure how she'll respond to further bombshells. This is a huge leap of faith, for which we have little supporting evidence. We need to get a list of all of the people who worked on the initial Mechanic case and do a little quiet digging. As far as anyone else is concerned, you're focusing on the country club lead. I'll have another chat with Harper to see if he has anything which might help.'

'Okay.' Bassano finished his beer. Both men stood up and moved across the curved bench seat to get out of the booth. Bassano stopped and looked at his boss. 'The theory about the Galbraith killing stacks up, but for one thing.'

'Oh what's that?'

'The matching bullet merely puts the gun at that location, not necessarily Mechanic.'

Lucas sat back down as Bassano left the bar.

Chapter 20

Mechanic's shift was coming to an end. One more job and that was it for the day. But this was no ordinary job at no ordinary club. This was the club where Sophie Barrock was a member.

She was a small Barbie doll of a woman who, despite approaching forty, could still pass for a cheerleader half her age. Her dyed blonde hair and elegantly applied make-up were always immaculate and she strutted around the club, doling out disapproving glances to anyone outside her circle of loyal followers. Sophie had a level of self confidence which was stratospheric and her overall demeanour could best be described as club owner rather than club member.

For Mechanic, the most annoying feature of Sophie Barrock was that she was one hell of a sportswoman. While she was always dressed in the latest and most expensive designer sports gear, it wasn't merely for show. She was an excellent tennis player, consistently top of the ladies' ladder competition, and would regularly play against men as they gave her a better game. In the winter months, she pounded the gym and every aerobics class on offer. Yes, it was annoying for Mechanic to admit, but Sophie Barrock was the real deal when it came to competitive sport.

It was an unfortunate personality trait for Sophie that she couldn't let her sporting talent speak for itself. She felt it necessary to brag her latest successes at every opportunity. She had a significant following of female friends who were mesmerized when Sophie held court in one of the coffee shops or when relaxing by the pool. She would talk about who was in and who was out of the latest social crowd, passing sweeping judgments on people she barely knew and telling her admiring followers who they could interact with and who they should not. Mechanic suspected that these women kept close to Sophie as a defence mechanism, to avoid being in the firing line for her cutting comments and bitchy asides which she used so liberally with others. It was a case of either being in the Sophie Barrock crowd and relatively safe, or outside the group where it was open season.

While the outside world saw a woman brimming over with her own self-importance, Mechanic knew different. Behind the façade, Sophie Barrock was a morass of insecurities and anxiety. Despite her portrayal of herself as a woman who had her act together, her home life was a mess. The whole country club routine was purely a means of escape for her. At the club she could be the person she wanted to be. Behind her front door she was forced to be somebody different. Her list of grievances was endless. Even for Mechanic, this was an impressive set of neuroses, anxieties and hang-ups.

Sophie was in a total rut, tied down by her kids' constant demands: 'Mom, can you do this?' 'Mom, can you take me there?' 'Mom, have you ironed my shirt?' She resented her lack of control. Home definitely controlled her. Her husband was unsupportive, excluding Sophie from what she saw as his blast of a social life. His life revolved around work and baseball. When he was at home, he'd be in his den watching games on the television or down at the sports bar with his friends from work. Didn't he see enough of them in the week? Did he have to see them at weekends as well?

In the bedroom any supposed action was a joke. Of course, to her ardent admirers at the club she had an active sex life and her husband found it hard to keep up with her demands. He also found it hard to keep up with her constant requests to try something different. Yes, as far as the outside world was concerned, it was fair to say that Sophie Barrock had a better sex life than her entire circle of female followers put together.

Other than the so-called friends at the club, Sophie didn't have a close friend she could talk to. In fact, when she thought about it, she had never had a close friend to share her secrets or discuss her problems. That's why the offer of someone completely neutral to talk to felt so compelling for Sophie. It was a chance to offload and air her resentment. That's where Mechanic came into the picture.

Sophie had undergone around fifteen telephone counselling sessions and the situation was beginning to improve. Mechanic had convinced her that she was entirely right in her assertion that she deserved to be fulfilled in her own life. If her family stood in the way of that, then she should do it without them. In truth, Mechanic had done very little convincing in any of their conversations. Sophie was a steamroller of obsession, more than capable of convincing herself of anything, even if she hadn't made up her mind what any of this actually meant.

Did it mean divorce? Did it mean leaving her family or taking a lover? She was constantly wrestling with what action to take. One thing was for sure, she was determined that her life was going to change. Of all the plans, ideas and thoughts Sophie had, this was the statement which Mechanic agreed with most.

Mechanic had been grooming Sophie for around six weeks, fostering a sense of dependency while at the same time manoeuvring her into more and more desperate positions. The calls fuelled Sophie's complex anxieties, she was a perfect target.

There were a couple of items which Mechanic had to finish off, and the scene was set. The preparations for Sophie Barrock and her ungrateful family were nearing completion.

During that afternoon Mechanic had been running through the details of the McKee killings, ticking off the various aspects which had featured so strongly in the fantasy. Once the initial euphoria had faded, Mechanic was feeling increasingly unhappy. After having basked in the delights of a job well done, as the day went on there was an overwhelming sense that it hadn't gone well. It was the whole Dave McKee thing which ruined it. The fact that he'd got out of bed and Mechanic had had to dispatch him as he emerged through the archway into the lounge was not in the script. Mechanic was pleased with the clinical way McKee had been dealt with, but overall this deviation had spoiled it.

Mechanic knew this would lead to a problem. When the kill was perfect, Daddy would go away satisfied and not compel Mechanic to kill again for months. But this one was far from perfect. Mechanic feared it would only serve to bring on another command to 'Go please Daddy' much earlier than expected. Keeping the urge at bay only worked in the early stages of a new attack and, under the circumstances, would probably only buy an additional couple of days.

Mechanic knew another kill was only weeks away. The preparations for Sophie Barrock needed to be stepped up.

Mechanic observed Sophie from a distance of about fifty yards across the club car park. She was going through the ritual of saying her theatrical goodbyes to those people who were in the 'in crowd'. Mechanic pressed the button in the arm rest of the truck and the window glided down to half open. Even at this distance you could hear Sophie's voice trilling on the wind. It was difficult to make out exactly what was being said, but one thing was for sure, whatever it was, it was being said a little too loudly. Mechanic strained to listen and not for the first time thought that Sophie Barrock had all the vocal qualities of a Sea World dolphin trainer.

Eventually, she got in her car and drove away, down the tree-lined boulevard to the interstate. Mechanic eased the big truck across the car park and followed. Sophie made the busy junction well before Mechanic.

It didn't matter. Mechanic already knew where she lived.

As Mechanic sat patiently waiting for a gap in the traffic, Lucas was climbing the stairs to the fifth floor landing and the flat marked 5 6. He hadn't called ahead as he correctly figured that Harper's phone was still disconnected. In any case, Lucas didn't want to give him an excuse to be out when he arrived. He rapped on the door.

'Who is it?' asked Harper from deep within the flat.

'It's Lucas. I want to talk to you, if that's okay.'

'Can't we do it in the morning? I'm busy.'

Lucas paused for a few seconds. 'No, tomorrow's no good. Can we talk now? It won't take long.' *And tomorrow you'll be conveniently out when I call round*, Lucas thought.

'For fuck's sake.' Lucas could hear shuffling from inside. The door clunked open and Harper swung it wide open.

Across the room was a single bright orange armchair with a low table directly in front of it. On the table was a microwave lasagne, still in its plastic tray, with a grubby fork sticking out of the top. In front of the table was the television. All three pieces of furniture were in a dead straight line, Harper's very own version of feng shui. Around the base of the armchair, Lucas counted six empty cans of cheap beer, and in a bucket on the floor another four cans bobbed gently in cold water. Harper watched Lucas survey the scene. It was obvious why Harper hadn't wanted an unexpected visitor. As he made it back to his seat, Harper was swaying, his eyes bloodshot drunk. He left a cloud of alcohol vapour trailing behind him.

'The damn fridge broke and I'm waiting for the landlord to replace it,' Harper slurred, explaining the presence of the bucket.

'Oh,' was all Lucas could think to reply. 'Please, eat your food. Don't let it go cold.'

Harper swung his leg over the low table and flopped into the chair. He picked up the fork and shovelled a slab of food into his mouth. His hand shook as he waved for Lucas to continue.

'It's about what you said when we last met. You said Galbraith was trying to tell you that his profile of Mechanic was wrong.' Lucas watched Harper swallow down the food in one gulp.

'What of it?'

'Turns out you were right.' Lucas allowed this to sink in, waiting for a response. Harper was about to cram another wedge of congealed pasta into his mouth but stopped in mid-air. He replaced the fork on the plastic tray and picked up a beer.

'Go on,' he said, taking a long drink from the can.

'The original profile said that Mechanic was both a father and a sibling hater. But the problem with that was that neither you nor I could find one shred of evidence to connect the victims. It didn't add up. We've uncovered evidence that suggests that the real targets were the women. He figured the worse thing he could do was to murder their families and leave them alive. The profile should have read, 'Mechanic was a mother hater'. I believe Galbraith had come to that conclusion and that was what he was trying to tell you.'

'Have you found a connection between the women?' Harper took another long draw on his can.

'Yes we have.'

'What is it?'

'Can't say at this stage, it needs validating.'

'So whats do yous want to talk to me about?' Harper slurred, draining the can in his hand and crushing it before letting it drop to the floor. He reached into the bucket and retrieved another, the water dripping from the outside of the can into his rapidly cooling dinner.

'I came here for two reasons. The first is that I wanted to tell you that it looks like you were right.' It was clear to Lucas that his attempts to build a conversational rapport with a half-cut Harper were failing badly. 'Secondly, I wanted to ask you if you had any suspicions about the investigation. Was there anything which didn't feel right?'

'Yeah, plenty, but we had no time to tie up all the loose ends. The heat from the media was too strong. They'd have lynched us if it came out that Mechanic might not be dead after all.' Harper took a huge slug from the newly opened beer and burped loudly. He waved the can at Lucas in a curious circular motion. 'We had a shit load of suspicions, Lucas, but absolutely no motiv … motiva … motivation to turn over any more stones than we had to.'

Lucas was thoughtful, not about the answer Harper gave him but about how to phrase his next question without giving too much away. Even a drunk Harper had keen instincts and could put two and two together and get somewhere close to four.

'Did you have any suspicions about any of the people working on the investigation?'

Harper looked at Lucas and screwed his face up. 'Shushpicions … about our people? No nothing. What do you mean?' The words merged together as the heavy alcohol session closed Harper's brain down.

Lucas was regretting his question as soon as it left his lips. He was ill prepared to have an obtuse conversation with Harper in this state. He tried again. 'What I mean is, did you ever question any of the decisions or motives of the people in your team?'

'Shome of them barked up the wrong tree from time to time, but then we all did. Mechanic was a devus … a devinus … a devious bastard. We often spent time on dead ends.'

'Sorry to bother you, I'll leave you to your dinner.' Lucas was keen to hit the eject button on this visit. He wasn't going to get what he wanted without giving too much away, and Harper was fading fast. The best tack now was to bow out and come back another time. 'I wanted to call by and say you were right and to thank you for taking the time to see me the other night.' Lucas was trying to cover his tracks after his clumsy question.

'But, I don't get it. What do you mean sushpinions? Like what?' Harper was grappling with his inability to string a short sentence together. 'What do yous mean?'

Lucas ignored him and made his way to the door. Harper made a weak effort to get up to see his guest out but slumped back into the chair. 'Shee yous again Lieuten .... Lieutenen …' he called as Lucas closed the door behind him.

Lucas made his way back home to another evening of chili dogs and beer. After seeing Harper, he'd probably make that chili dogs and Coke.

Harper slumped in the chair, his eyes closing in a drunken stupor. His dinner lay half eaten in front of him while his right arm was draped across the side of the chair, still clutching his can. A pool of spilled beer soaked into the pile, soon to be invisible amongst the other stains on the carpet. The gravity of what Lucas had told him seemed to have been lost on Harper. However, as he slept, his brain would gradually unravel his words. His dreams would put the facts in order and churn them over and over in endless possibilities. Possibilities which, deep inside, Harper had always known were there.

When he woke in the morning, the full impact of his conversation with Lucas would hit him like a freight train.

Chapter 21

L ucas attended the morning briefing. There was a different feel to the investigation and the room buzzed with energy. Bassano gave the team their orders for the day. One group would visit the country clubs while Bassano and another team would interview the women who'd survived Mechanic's attacks. The enquiries needed to be low key because no one outside the investigation knew of Mechanic's reappearance. Lucas was clear that was how it had to stay, although an annoying voice inside his head kept reminding him – *No one else knows, that is, except Harper*.

Lucas was annoyed about his conversation with Harper the previous evening. He should have trusted his instincts and left well alone. Instead he'd persevered and ended up giving away far more information than originally intended. Frustratingly he'd got nothing in return. While his questions had been vanilla enough at first glance, a seasoned cop like Harper would now be putting the pieces together, albeit with a thumping hangover. Lucas was mad with himself but was trying not to let his frustration show.

He left the briefing and made his way back to his office. He opened the door and there was Jo Sells sitting in the same seat which she'd abruptly vacated twenty-four hours earlier. In front of her was the obligatory cup of steaming coffee along with an expertly crafted, bright white sugar twist.

'Good morning, Lucas,' she said in a quiet voice.

'Well good morning doctor, how are you today?' Lucas was well aware that his tone was patronizing. Jo allowed it to go unchallenged, conceding that she probably deserved it.

'Much better, thanks,' she replied. 'Look. About yesterday— '.

'What about it?' Lucas spoke abruptly. He wasn't going to let her off lightly.

She held her hands up. 'I apologize for my behaviour. It was out of order and unacceptable.'

'Yes it was, and hiding out at the McKee house didn't help matters.'

'I got angry and I shouldn't have. When you challenged the validity of the profile, all I could hear was you challenging the validity of Victor and that hit a nerve. When he was killed I not only lost a talented mentor but also a dear friend and it still hurts. He was with me all through my research and was inspirational for me at Quantico. I'm sorry. I saw red and had to get out.'

Lucas joined her at the table. 'Losing people goes with the territory in this job. Sometimes we have to separate our personal feelings from our professional responsibilities. Yesterday you let them get the better of you.'

She nodded. 'You can put in a request to have me removed from the case and I won't challenge it.'

'Is that what you want?'

'No. Far from it. I want to catch this bastard for real this time and stop him once and for all. I can help, I know I can. It won't happen again, I promise.'

'Have you spoken to Bassano or any of the team this morning?' Lucas asked.

'No, I came to see you first. If you wanted me off the case, I figured there was no point in making any further grovelling apologies. So, no, I've seen no one.'

'Then I suggest you get down to the briefing room, take Bassano to one side and start building bridges. He'll brief you on the tasks for the day.'

'Okay. Thanks.' She got up to leave the office.

'Oh, and by the way. We found something which connects the women – country clubs. Bassano will fill you in.'

Jo Sells looked stunned.

On the other side of the city it was a tale of two sofas.

Kaitlin was at home sitting by the telephone, her mind in turmoil. She wasn't due to have another counselling call until 8.00pm the next day but her anxiety levels were through the roof. She needed to offload. The strain was driving her crazy.

She had tossed and turned all night only managing a couple of hours of fitful sleep which only served to cloud her judgement further. She was dog tired and irritable. Should she call or not? She was so desperate that she was thinking of breaking her own golden rule of always phoning from a call box. This morning she was stranded. Her car was at the garage for a service while the location of the pay phone was several miles away in a rundown roadside café. Her rationale for choosing this place was sound. She wouldn't meet anyone she knew there since it was off the beaten track and anyway who would go for a coffee in such a dump? If she did meet someone, she could say there was something wrong with the car and she was calling home. She'd spent a long time choosing a safe location but was now prepared to blow it with one reckless act.

Her hand hovered over the receiver for a second then picked it up. She quickly banged it back onto its cradle and put her hand to her mouth. Mechanic had done a good job on Kaitlin. She was a wreck.

A mile and half away, Sophie Barrock sat on her sofa staring into space. *What the hell should I do?* she asked herself over and over again. With the kids dropped off at school and her husband working God knows where, this was her quality time to think. Only it wasn't filled with quality thinking.

Should I leave? She churned it around in her head. She could pack a bag and go to her friend Jane's place. But who was she kidding? She didn't know Jane well enough to turn up on her doorstep with an overnight bag. *I've left my husband and two kids and thought I could stay here for a while.* That would be absurd. She was getting desperate.

Alternatively she could confront her husband with a list of ultimatums and force the issue that way. But that course of action was fraught with uncertainty. What if he just said, 'Okay, I think we should separate.' That would be awful. Not because of the separation, but this needed to be on her terms or not at all. This had to be done in the way they'd discussed it in the counselling sessions. She had to be seen to be in control and she had no intention of jeopardising what she had at the club. For Sophie, it was crucial that she should be seen to be driving whatever changes were going to take place. *What to do?*

Back on Kaitlin's sofa, the situation was getting worse. Mechanic had told her focus on her issues in preparation for their next chat and doing so had made her even more agitated. She was now thinking all sorts of outlandish thoughts which had never entered her head before. She was falling apart.

She picked up the phone again, took a crumpled piece of paper from her bag and punched in the numbers. It rang five times then the answer phone kicked in. Kaitlin cursed and banged the handset down. The counsellor was out. She couldn't wait until tomorrow, she was going out of her mind. She picked up the phone again and called the garage to see when her car was coming back.

Sophie sat staring into space. The ultimatum option sounded good, she could make it work if she stayed strong. This thought was interrupted by a loud knock at the front door. Sophie dragged herself back to reality, unlocked it and opened it wide. The Florida morning sunshine flooded the hall and Mechanic stood in the doorway smiling.

Chapter 22

For most of the day, the police station was deserted and strangely quiet as Lucas sat in his office alone. Everyone was out working on the tasks they'd been given at the morning briefing. Despite the peaceful atmosphere, Lucas had experienced a troubled day. He couldn't shake off his misgivings about the previous night's conversation with Harper. He had overreached himself, divulging sensitive information through his clumsy line of questioning. Anyone with an ounce of common sense would have been able to join the dots. Lucas hoped that Harper's drunken state would stop him making the connections.

He also spent time agonizing over the two pieces of paper which contained his thoughts and doodles from the sleepless night. Placing the sheets side by side on his desk, he racked his brains, trying to make sense of the convoluted deductions set out in front of him. But whichever way he twisted the chain of events leading up to Galbraith's death he reached the same conclusion – there was a leak. Mechanic had known the direction of the investigation was about to shift and killed Galbraith to prevent it. The more times he went through it, the more times he reached the same uncomfortable conclusion.

He was about to embark on another painful game of 'What ifs?' when Bassano and Jo Sells walked in, casually chatting about the events of the day. Jo must have made her grovelling apologies.

'What have you got?' Lucas was pleased to have company at last and a break from the turmoil inside his head.

'We uncovered something interesting,' Bassano said as he flashed one of his winning smiles Jo's way, which she ignored. 'We're having difficulties with a number of the country clubs. They aren't being cooperative in granting us access to their member information, even though some of it is twelve years old—'

'You said you had something interesting,' Lucas interrupted

'We do,' Bassano continued. 'We interviewed Julie Tate. She's the wife and mother of victims four and five. She was wary at first, but opened up when we told her we were pursuing an alternative line of enquiry about the killings. It appears that, following the murders, she's had a dreadful time making any kind of adjustment. She's had several stumbling attempts to pick herself up which have spectacularly failed. She lives on her own and swings between being a virtual recluse and other times when she's a social junkie.'

'What do you mean "social junkie"?' Lucas asked.

Jo stepped in, 'She shuts herself away for long periods and sinks into a morbid depression. Then she breaks out with episodes of completely the opposite behaviour. She goes to clubs, parties, rekindles old friendships and drinks heavily. She flips between one and the other.'

'Is this a coping mechanism? Does it help manage the grief?' Lucas asked.

'Well, that's the strange part,' said Bassano. 'It's not driven by grief, more by guilt.'

'But that's understandable, right? I mean the woman was left alive when her family were murdered. That's bound to trigger a massive guilt complex.'

'Yes, that's true, but it's not that. At the time of the killings all was not well in the domestic world of Julie Tate. Her guilt is driven by the fact that she was planning to leave her husband and kids. Her marriage was on the rocks and she hated her family life. She was about to walk out. The way she behaves now is a reaction to the guilt, it's like she's in self-destruct mode.'

'That sounds very sad, but I still don't understand why you think it's interesting?' Lucas left the question hanging.

'Bear with me on this, boss.' Bassano was determined to prove his day had been fruitful. 'None of this came out in the previous investigation, this is new. On the surface she was playing happy families with her husband and kids but underneath there were major problems. Tate was one unhappy woman.'

'Okay, I get it. But most people have skeletons in cupboards. We of all people know that,' said Lucas.

'I agree. But what is unusual is that Lillian Lang, the woman from the first set of killings, was hiding exactly the same skeleton.'

'What?' Now Lucas was interested.

'I had a hunch that this could be important. So while Jo continued to question Julie Tate, I contacted the officers who were interviewing Lang. I asked them to probe along the same line of questioning. Sure enough, she was in a similar predicament with her marriage and family life as Julie Tate. And, just like Tate, her situation was never identified during the initial investigation.'

'You're quiet, Jo. What do you think?' Lucas was keen to bring her back into the fold.

She looked up and shook her head. 'It's too much of a coincidence for both women to be going through the same private meltdown in their relationships. And in both cases it was a meltdown that was so well hidden it wasn't apparent to anyone at the time.'

'But the investigation didn't focus on the women, so it wouldn't have come out,' Lucas countered.

'No, I don't mean apparent to us, I mean to others who knew them. Harper and his team did a thorough job interviewing close friends who knew the murdered families well. They got a consistent picture of a stable family life with no sign of any such difficulties. In both cases, it was wall-to-wall happy families. There was nothing to indicate that the women were about to leave.'

'Why would they talk about it now but not at the time?' asked Lucas.

'Two reasons, I guess,' Jo continued. 'They have no reason to keep it quiet now. Their families are gone so there is nothing to be gained by hiding the fact that all was not rosy in the garden.'

'And the second?'

'I think it's as simple as no one asked them. At the time, these women were trying to come to terms with the ritual killing of their families. It probably didn't feel appropriate to ask if their marriage and home life had been a happy one.'

Lucas nodded in agreement. 'So in a way, this is another brutal twist of the knife, well after the actual murders took place.'

'Yes, I suppose so. In the case of Julie Tate, it took a long time for the crushing guilt to kick in. It may have only come to the forefront once she came to terms with the original grief. The fact that she was considering leaving them, and now they're gone, has destroyed her.'

Lucas scratched his head. 'What was it Julie Tate said to Harper? "The agony continues for those that remain. I wish I were dead."'

'Mechanic is a mother hater, right?' Bassano fixed the other two with a piercing stare. 'Could it be that Mechanic manipulated the situation in the Tate and Lang households to make the tragic loss of their families even worse for these women? It would add a whole new level of suffering and pain for the women left behind.'

'That's operating at a highly complex level,' Jo suggested. 'It would mean Mechanic was somehow involved with each of the women, intending to destabilize their marriages and family life.' She let out a long sigh. 'That's a massive stretch of the imagination.'

'It is,' Bassano agreed. 'But that doesn't negate the fact that we have two women whose families were murdered by Mechanic, and both of them shared a secret. They were both about to walk out. It's a long shot for sure but that's what we have.'

'It's worth following up. As far-fetched as it sounds, it could lead us to further connections between the women. Who are the others we need to talk to?' Lucas's mind was racing ahead.

'Coleen Stewart,' Jo replied. 'Her family were torched in the car along with the unknown victim who we thought was Mechanic.'

'What are her circumstances?' asked Lucas.

'As yet we don't know. We're having trouble tracing her, she may have emigrated. The team are working on it,' Bassano said.

'And Janet Andrews, the woman who died in hospital, do we have any similar leads on her?' asked Lucas.

'Not as yet. We're tracking down her close family. But if she was in the same boat as Lang and Tate we won't find anything because no one had any idea, the problems were well hidden. Now she's dead the chances are we'll never know,' said Bassano.

'Ask anyway. It's unusual for a woman to reach such a crunch point in her relationship and for no one to know about it. Surely she would confide in someone? Go back and interview Lillian Lang and Julie Tate again. I agree with Jo that this is too much of a coincidence. Find out if there is anything that connects this aspect of their lives. Dig around with the other two, find out if they were in the same situation. And when Hannah McKee recovers enough to be questioned, make sure we follow this line with her.'

They disbanded their impromptu meeting. Jo Sells and Bassano made their way back to the incident room to prepare for further late afternoon interviews and Lucas was once again alone with his disturbing thoughts.

Mechanic, on the other hand, was ecstatic. The last piece of preparation was now in place.

Chapter 23

Mechanic sprawled on the sofa listening to the soft strings of Pachelbel's Canon in D. This was always part of the ritual. The music signified the end of the preparation phase and the beginning of the contact planning phase. For Mechanic, this was mental spring cleaning, when all the junk and clutter were swept away to make room for fresh and exciting thoughts. Thoughts which involved the method of entry, the spit of the gun as the first bullet tore into the head of the sleeping husband, and the dull thud as the rubber baton beat Sophie Barrock into unconsciousness.

The visit to Sophie's house had gone well. The counselling sessions were having a profound effect. She was preoccupied, taking no notice of the person who'd come to check out her pool netting. Mechanic's job was the perfect cover to get a closer look at the house.

Country clubs have outdoor pools with extensive sundeck areas. The guests love the relaxed setting and the waiter service as they lounge by the pool in the Florida sun. But they hate bugs, especially the flying kind. Hence they all have large framed netting to cover the pool and decking areas, and these need regular maintenance. There were country clubs scattered all over Florida, which afforded Mechanic a legitimate reason to travel widely – and to seek out vulnerable women. Even better if they also had a husband, two kids and a car parked in the garage.

Yes, it was fair to say that, apart from ritual murder, the one thing Mechanic knew about was pools, decking and netting.

The maintenance visit to the home of Sophie Barrock was free of charge, part of the product guarantee. The manufacturers of the netting got local specialists to do the work, and Mechanic was nothing if not a specialist. The form Mechanic asked Sophie to sign after the check had been completed was a clever fake, but added to the authenticity of the charade.

For Mechanic, this visit was a vital component of the preparation. The back of the house was checked out to establish which section of netting could be cut away to make the initial entry. It also afforded Mechanic an alternative view of the escape route. It was one thing to observe the property from afar but completely different to view it at close quarters. Mechanic could also take a close look at the patio doors to ensure the right tools were brought on the night. This was all essential for a well executed entry.

It also allowed for the first viewing of the interior of the house. Mechanic had completed a rough plan by guesswork, but seeing it first hand was always an exciting prospect. It wasn't difficult to work out where the kids' bedrooms were, along with the master suite.

Of course, during the visit there was some fictitious net fixing to be done. Along with plenty of walking back and forth to the truck for tools, but this was another way of gaining different perspectives on the house and its contents. Each trip gave Mechanic another opportunity to glance through the windows at the side of the house to confirm the position of bedrooms, bathroom and study. Everything was completed in about fifteen to twenty minutes.

For the most part, Sophie carried on as though Mechanic was not there, which was usual when visiting target houses. After all, the service was free and, as far as the owner of the property knew, there were no problems with the netting or the framework so there was no reason to watch over Mechanic's shoulder to see if the work was up to standard. Mechanic was always left to get on with it without interruption. Also, because the visit was routine, it didn't merit being shared with other family members. Let's face it, a wife telling her husband, 'Honey, someone came to look at the pool today,' was hardly a heavyweight news item. It was a brilliant cover.

The other important feature of the visit was that it enabled Mechanic to imagine how the final proceedings were going to play out. Mechanic could visualize standing in the large open-plan lounge, having just lifted the door from its runners, and getting in synch with the sounds of the sleeping household. Tuning in was such a rush.

Now the contact planning phase of Mechanic's work could begin, where every last detail was meticulously run and rerun until the fantasy was perfect. It was true that Mechanic knew about pools, decking and netting. But it was also true to say this was not what Mechanic loved the most.

As Mechanic listened to the seventh consecutive rendition of Canon in D, rehearsing the colourful fantasy of killing the Barrock family, across the city a clean-shaven man was flattening his unruly hair with a generous handful of gel. He was dressed in an ill-fitting suit which you could go trick or treating in.

He was sober now, very sober.

Chapter 24

Lucas swung his car into the driveway. It was getting late and the house was in darkness, a clear sign that his wife was still at the conference. Usually this would mean an evening of rolling out the contraband, but tonight he was too preoccupied for chili dogs, beer and sport. He entered the hallway, throwing his keys onto the side table, and headed straight for the whisky.

He flopped into his thinking chair and kicked his shoes off into the middle of the floor. He'd started the day with two major problems and ended it with three. He slurped at the fiery liquid and grimaced as it rasped at the back of his throat. He didn't even like the damn stuff.

Lucas had only started drinking whisky after the infamous wok incident of '78. He'd never been able to understand why the purchase of a perfectly good kitchen utensil could have triggered such an onslaught of abuse from his otherwise loving wife. He'd latterly had to concede that it probably had something to do with it being a Valentine's gift. Women could be funny about that kind of thing.

His birthday had been a week later. His wife had bought him a bottle of expensive whisky, knowing full well that he hated it. Not to be outdone, Lucas pretended to develop a taste for the liquor, sitting next to her on the sofa while watching TV in the evening with a generous glassful in his hand. But he was clearly bluffing, which made every sip he took another small victory for her.

His relationship with his wife was good, if sometimes a little confused. Lucas always considered himself an up front sort of guy. A set of circumstances occurring on one day would elicit much the same reaction should they occur on any other day. His wife, on the other hand, was different. Whereas one day a bunch of flowers to say sorry would be welcomed with a smile and displayed prominently in a cut-glass vase, another day they'd be dismissed with a 'so you think that's it do you?' and left in the cellophane wrapping on the kitchen table. To Lucas there seemed to be only two things in the world which produced a consistent reaction in his wife, one was chocolate and the other Paul Newman. He loved his wife but running a police station was far more straightforward.

As the whisky warmed him on its way down, Lucas smiled for the first time that day.

He assessed his position. First, he'd made a complete hash of his conversation with Harper and given far too much away. Second, there was a strong likelihood that in the first investigation Mechanic had had a window in on the case. And third, Mechanic didn't only murder the families, he somehow manipulated the women's emotions prior to the crime, pushing them to the brink of walking out on their husbands and children. Then to cap it all he had an FBI special agent who didn't react well to challenge.

Fuck, that's four problems, he thought taking another sip.

Lucas looked across the room at his citation for bravery which hung on the wall. It served as a constant reminder that career progression was seldom a function of competence, it was more a result of being in the right place at the right time and blind luck. He was no more able a police officer after the blast than before it. He couldn't write reports any better, he hadn't gained an encyclopedic knowledge of policing practices and guidelines. He couldn't debate more effectively or detect crime any faster. He stayed the same, it was the way the world looked at him that had shifted.

Every time he saw a busted tail light he wondered what life would have been like without that chance encounter. Lucas thought it was ironic that he'd always had the ability to progress up the corporate ladder but it wasn't until his bravery award that his career got going. If he'd admitted that he'd had no idea the car was full of explosives and that he hadn't been brave at all, it wouldn't have gone down well in the press. But then he often asked himself what he would have done if he had known the reality of the situation. The answer always came back the same, he'd still have stopped it.

There was a knock on the door.

Lucas looked through the peephole still clutching his glass. Harper was on the other side. If Harper's appearance was strange the last time Lucas saw him, the distortion from the peephole lens meant he now looked grotesque.

Lucas opened the door. 'Hi, this is unexpected.'

'You keep turning up at my place so I thought I'd return the favour. Do you have time to talk?' While Harper could still be mistaken for a tramp, there was something in the delivery of his speech which demanded attention. This was a very different Harper, sober and serious.

'Please come in.' Lucas stepped aside and welcomed him across the threshold with a sweep of his arm. 'Can I offer you a drink?'

'No, thanks, I had enough yesterday to last me through today.'

'Coffee then?' Lucas was determined to show Harper how a normal host might treat visitors.

'No, I'm fine thanks. I need to talk to you.'

'Yeah, that's okay. Take a seat.'

'It's about last night.' Lucas was dreading this, his heart sank. 'I apologize for my behaviour. I'm not well balanced and I tend to self-medicate with alcohol. You could say I'm a coping alcoholic and some days I cope better than others. I could tell you it's because it dulls the pain, or that it helps me forget what happened in the whole sorry affair that was the Mechanic case. But both those would be a lie. The truth is I get drunk because I like it. And, before you ask, no I don't want help.'

Lucas was hugely relieved. Harper had obviously come to make amends for the previous evening. Of all the scenarios Lucas had in his head, this was by far the best.

'That's okay,' he said. 'We all get a little crazy from time to time. Forget it. I appreciated your help and I thought I'd drop by to let you know. I'm sorry I disturbed your dinner. Let's just forget it.' Lucas rose to his feet as if to show Harper out.

Harper remained seated, staring at the carpet. 'The other thing is …' Lucas's heart missed a beat, '… I think I had a leak in the investigation.'

Harper dropped the sentence like a grenade. Lucas sat back down, his worst fears materializing.

Harper continued, 'You asked me if there was anything about the investigation which didn't feel right. You also asked if I had any suspicions about anyone who was working on the case. The answer to both those questions is yes.'

Lucas couldn't believe that a man who'd been one can of beer away from a coma could remember what he'd said almost word for word.

'Go on.'

'The Galbraith killing was completely out of step. Out of step that is if you compare it to the pattern of the other murders. It makes no sense. I've always thought that Galbraith was killed because he was about to change the profile and that would have exposed Mechanic. The big question is, how did Mechanic know that was about to happen? The only place that could possibly have come from is someone within the team.'

'That's the way I figured it. That's why I came round last night with a lame-ass excuse to get more info and substantiate the theory. I made a complete mess of it.'

Harper raised his hand to stop Lucas.

'Save it, that's not important. The other big question is, who on the team would know that Galbraith had redefined the profile. It sure as hell wasn't me and I was running the damn show.'

'Any ideas?'

'The answer I get to both questions is Dr Jo Sells.'

Lucas sat motionless, the intensity of what Harper was telling him kept him nailed to the chair.

'She was the only one with access to Galbraith's most current work and his most current thinking. They were pretty close so it was unlikely that something that significant wouldn't be shared between them. I have no proof but I'm damn sure she'd have known about the change of profile. She fits the criteria on all counts. No one else had a clue what was going on. The new profile never saw the light of day. It died with Galbraith when Mechanic put a bullet in his head.'

'It kind of fits,' Lucas said, recalling his previous conversation with Bassano in the bar. 'But it might not have been Mechanic who killed Galbraith. All we know for sure is that it was the same gun.'

'I know. And that could explain why Galbraith was there in the first place.'

Lucas finished off Harper's train of thought. 'Jo Sells could have told Galbraith to go to that location. Then either Mechanic killed him or Sells shot him herself with Mechanic's gun.' Both men looked at each other, stunned at what they were suggesting.

'We're running away with ourselves, but whichever way you cut it,' Harper paused to maximize the impact of what he was about to say, 'I reckon Jo Sells had a direct link to Mechanic and my spies tell me she's back on the investigation working with you.'

'Fuck,' Lucas said for the second time that night.

Both men sat in silence, each struggling to absorb what the other had divulged.

'I've a proposition for you,' said Harper. 'If you make known our suspicions over Jo, she'll disappear and, if we're correct, she's the only link you have to Mechanic. You need to keep her close, at least until we have something concrete.'

'What do you mean *we*?'

'Let me work on the outside. I can dig around for evidence that implicates Jo Sells. After all, you can't do it. She's super bright and will smell a rat straight away. I still have contacts and if there's something positive connecting Jo Sells to Mechanic I'll find it. It'll be between you and me. What do you think?'

'It's risky. You're suggesting we run the two in parallel? I can't be seen to condone you operating outside the main investigation.'

'You don't have to condone it. If for any reason I get exposed, then it'd be seen as Harper being bitter and twisted and trying to rake over unfinished business. We write nothing down and only communicate face to face at predetermined locations. You would have ultimate deniability.'

'It might work.'

'And anyway,' continued Harper, 'you got a better suggestion?'

Lucas had to acknowledge he hadn't. He had to keep Jo Sells on the team but also had to keep her at arm's length from their developing suspicions. If she got even the smallest inkling, she'd make a run for it and they would lose any potential link to Mechanic.

Lucas considered his options for the second time that evening.

'No,' he said bluntly. 'It would have to include Bassano. He could watch Jo from the inside. He can ensure she's not getting spooked and he's a damn good detective.'

Harper thought about it. 'That would work. He'd have the same deniability as you and, from what I know of him from my buddies at the station, he's a good guy. Do we have an agreement, Lieutenant?' said Harper cracking a smile. He extended his hand.

'We do Ex-Lieutenant.'

Harper headed back to the front door and then stopped. 'I want you to know this is important to me. This is personal. And, before you ask, as of now I'm on the wagon. So if you see me shaking at any time, it's not because I'm dancing.'

They said goodnight and parted company. Both men had a whole lot more to think about than forty minutes ago.

Chapter 25

While Lucas was negotiating a way forward with Harper, Bassano and Jo Sells had been trying to coax answers out of Lillian Lang. They'd decided that there was little point revisiting Julie Tate. It was early evening and Julie would have at least half a bottle of gin inside her.

Bassano had spent much of the afternoon in the car with Jo, trying hard to impress her. He talked about his home life, his messy divorce and his job. She said very little even though he asked her about her doctorate, her training and what she did for kicks. Despite the one-way conversation, Bassano was sure she was interested, it was just a matter of time.

Bassano wasn't phased by her unresponsiveness, and instead was engrossed by the unruly button on her blouse which kept popping open. Even if she had been talkative, he probably wouldn't have heard a word she said. His assessment of the afternoon was, 'Not as chatty as she could be but great buttons.' Her assessment was, 'He's a dick.'

While Jo battled to keep her blouse under control, Lillian Lang posed a challenge of a different kind. It was clear that she didn't like Bassano and couldn't understand why she had to talk to him. After all, she had spoken to the other, much nicer, police officers only hours earlier. Bassano tried to take the lead in the discussion but it was obvious he was going to get nowhere.

Jo took over and was very skilful. She ensured that any animosity Lang felt remained focused on Bassano, while she gently probed for the information they wanted. After a period of introductory chit chat Jo cultivated an effective rapport with Lillian, despite Bassano sitting there like a sulky schoolboy.

Lillian Lang confirmed that her marriage had been in trouble at the time of the murders and she was considering leaving, but this was information they already knew. Jo persisted with her line of questioning about whether Lillian had told any of her close friends about the difficulties. She was adamant that no one close to her knew how she felt. The more Jo persevered, the more Lang was resolute with her answers. But there was something nagging at Jo and Bassano. Lillian's answers were far too precise, she was being very careful with what she said.

Both sensed she was holding back.

'I find it difficult to understand that a woman in your position wouldn't share her problems with any of her close friends,' Jo said.

'Well perhaps you can't, but that's the way it was. Not one of them knew,' Lang replied.

'You shared it with no one? I'm struggling to believe that, Mrs Lang.'

Lillian hesitated for a moment as if she was fighting with her conscience. 'I didn't say that,' she said in a whisper.

'What?' replied Jo.

'I didn't share it with any of my close friends, but I did share it with a counsellor.'

Now the words came flooding out.

Lillian explained how she'd been ashamed of using a counsellor and had been reluctant to talk about it. She considered it a social stigma and chose to shut it away and forget it. Jo's questioning had forced it back into the open, making her very uncomfortable.

Lillian went on to describe how she used a service provided by the club where she was a member. She liked it because it was anonymous. The sessions were done over the phone. She'd never met the counsellor in person but had had regular discussions in the weeks leading up to the killings. Looking back, she was not convinced of the benefits. At the time it had given her an outlet for her grievances but in hindsight the sessions had magnified her problems and made matters worse.

Bassano's mind was in warp drive, running through the implications of what Lillian was telling them. She was drying up fast after divulging her secret and, despite Jo pushing further, she was drawing back into her shell.

No, she couldn't remember who the counsellor was and, no, she couldn't remember the telephone number she used. Bassano wasn't listening, he already knew where they needed to be and looking at his watch he saw that they needed to be there fast. He drew the conversation with Lillian Lang to a close, thanked her for her cooperation, grabbed Jo Sells by the arm and promptly left.

Bassano gunned the engine and sped along the tree-lined driveway of Brightwood Country Club, the club frequented by Hannah McKee. In her current state it was doubtful that she would be requiring their services any time soon.

Cars passed them on the other side of the gravelled track, flashing their lights to warn him to kill his speed. 'That's what you get for lowering the membership fees,' was the overwhelming conclusion of the drivers.

He slewed the car into the golf captain's parking slot at such an angle that the vice captain's space was also blocked. He and Jo ran from the car and up the steps to the reception. A tall man in an expensive tailored suit met them at the doorway. His face was as shiny as his shoes.

'This is highly irregular. As I said to you on the phone, we are closed. If you would like to return in the morning we would be only too happy to meet any requests for information you may have.'

Bassano stood in front of him. 'We must talk with you urgently about the services you provide at your club, Mr Wainwright.' Bassano was not in the mood to be dismissed by this stuffed shirt of a man.

'And as I told you not twenty minutes ago, we have a presentation evening tonight and we are not open for business.'

He peered past Bassano's shoulder and his face flushed red. His anger was compounded by the fact that Jo and Bassano had committed at least three club parking violations.

'Mr Wainwright, you have two choices. Me and my colleague can talk to you now in a closed office of your choice, or I will call this into the station and have half a dozen cop cars here in full party mode. Then I'll get a warrant, but not until your honoured guests have their faces pressed against the windows wondering what the blue flashing lights are all about. So what will it be?'

'It's I.' Wainwright said.

'What?' Bassano was confused.

'It's my colleague and I, not ...' Wainwright was a stickler for correct grammar.

'So I'll take that as a yes then,' and with that Bassano and Jo brushed past the immaculately dressed Mr Wainwright and walked up the steps.

'Where do you want us?' asked Jo.

'In my office. Follow me.' Wainwright crossed the reception area and entered a wood-panelled office which smelled of furniture polish and aftershave. They all decided to stand.

Bassano spoke first. 'We have an ongoing investigation, Mr Wainwright, and your club could be implicated. I need to know if you offer counselling sessions as part of your portfolio of services.'

'Officer, we are a premium sports facility not a welfare club. We provide top quality activities for those who want to improve their physical wellbeing and social contacts. We are also active in the local business community and host events like the one we have this evening. We do not offer counselling services to our members.'

'Do you offer anything that could be construed as counselling? Maybe life coaching or self-improvement classes?' Jo asked.

'We do not.' Wainwright was exhibiting all the signs of acute boredom for the benefit of his unwanted guests.

'Do you offer meditation or—' Jo continued.

'I cannot stress this enough, officers,' he interrupted. 'We do not offer services of that sort. I don't know what line of investigation you are pursuing but I can assure you that if it entails Brightwood providing counselling, you are barking up the wrong tree. Now, if you don't mind, I have a room of three hundred distinguished guests I need to return to. Melody will see you off the premises. Goodnight.' He walked out of his office and was gone.

Bassano and Jo looked at each other, feeling as if they had just been dismissed by the headmaster. Melody walked in.

'I guess I should show you both out,' she said politely. Bassano and Sells followed her out of the office and into the grand reception area.

Melody was in her early forties, she wore a well cut navy suit, her only jewellery a pair of pearl earrings. She seemed bright and fiercely capable. 'I hope you don't mind but I couldn't help but overhear your conversation with Mr Wainwright.' She spoke confidently and removed her glasses. 'He is of course correct to say that we don't officially have anything like counselling taking place here, but last month I found these.' Melody opened a desk drawer and retrieved several pieces of printed paper.

'Mr Wainwright likes everything to be done by the book and gets a little irritable when that doesn't happen. So when I found these I just removed them. I didn't mention it at the time because he doesn't respond well to anything out of the ordinary.' She handed the sheets of paper to Jo. 'I'm not sure if they'll help but you are welcome to take them with you. I'm sure Mr Wainwright wouldn't mind.'

Bassano and Jo stood with their mouths open. Jo was the first to talk.

'That's very kind of you, Melody. Maybe, don't mention this to Mr Wainwright for now. I agree with you, he strikes me as a man who likes to play by the rules.'

'You got it.' Melody was pleased her new visitors could also see that her boss was a total asshole.

'Can I use your phone?' asked Bassano.

'Of course.'

Bassano punched in a series of numbers.

'Sir, I know it's late but we need to talk back at the station.' He paused to listen to Lucas's predictable reply. 'No, it can't wait till the morning, boss. We need to move fast. Depending on what you think, we might be looking at an all-nighter.' There were further protestations from the other end of the line.

Bassano decided it was time to curtail the conversation. He turned away from the other two, cupped his hand over the mouthpiece and whispered, 'Sir, we might have located Mechanic.'

Chapter 26

The clock on the wall in the station told Lucas it was a quarter past nine when he marched past the desk sergeant. He nodded a 'Good evening' and took the stairs to his office two at a time. He was late. He'd realized after Bassano's call that he couldn't drive, due to the deliciously expensive, damn awful whisky he'd consumed, and was forced to call the traffic boys to pick him up.

He got to his office to find Jo Sells already sitting at the conference table. It must have been a tough day because there were sugar twists everywhere. Bassano was on the phone.

'I don't give a fuck what time it is, I need that address and I need it now,' he yelled.

'Problem?' Lucas asked.

'It will be in the next ten minutes if he doesn't get his ass in gear.' Bassano came from behind the desk and joined the other two at the table.

'Okay, where's Mechanic?' Lucas asked.

'Listen to what we have first. We've spoken to Lillian Lang,' said Bassano.

Jo took over, 'We thought it best not to go back to Julie Tate because we'd already been with her this afternoon and she is way too unstable at the moment. Lillian confirmed that she was having marital difficulties and having a miserable time just before the murders. She talked for most of the interview about how she felt and how the killings had robbed her of any way to put matters right between her and her family. My thoughts are that she is suffering from the same guilt complex as Tate.'

'Good, so now we have a consistent picture. What about Mechanic?' Lucas asked again.

'I'll get to that,' Jo continued. 'I questioned Lillian on why she hadn't shared any of this with close friends. She said she was too embarrassed about the way she felt and was reluctant to talk with anyone in case it became public. She was so screwed up and didn't want to involve any of her friends or family—'

Lucas interrupted. 'What about Mechanic?'

'However,' Jo emphasized the word, putting her hands up to stop Lucas, 'it turns out she did share it with someone, she spoke to a counsellor.'

'A counsellor?'

'Yes,' Jo continued. 'Some sort of anonymous counselling service conducted over the phone. I've never heard of this technique before, but she said she got the number from the country club where she was a member. She couldn't remember the details but she could recall it was a service provided by the club.'

Bassano finished the story. 'We went to the club where Hannah McKee was a member. At first they denied they provided those kinds of services and were indignant at our suggestion that they would. A lady who worked at the reception desk overheard our conversation and gave us these.' He spread out the pieces of paper on the table. They read:

Taken for granted?
Unappreciated?
Feel there's got to be more to life than this?
We can help.
We run a confidential counselling service.
Talk it through with someone who's been there.
We understand.
It's completely free, you have nothing to lose.
You can make things better.
Call 407-863-7124

'She found them at the club and removed them. She didn't report it to the management,' said Bassano.

'It looks like Mechanic doesn't go hunting for victims, they come to him. He put the flier out as bait and waited to hook someone in,' Jo said.

'He uses the term "we". Why would he do that?' Lucas asked.

'To give the impression the counselling is being delivered by an organization. Remember that anyone responding to this is going to be in a vulnerable state. If he said "I can help" or "I understand" it could sound threatening.'

'Have you rung the number?' Lucas asked.

'No. If we call him he could get spooked. I've asked our tech guys to trace his address from the number. I thought it would be better to pay him a visit instead.'

'Get everything in place. We'll move tonight.'

Chapter 27

Mechanic's head rested on the arm of the long leather sofa. Clouds of warm, hazy dreams swept by as Pachelbel's Canon in D played for the eighteenth time that evening. There was something about it that facilitated fantasies. It was definitely Mechanic's music of choice when visualizing the step-by-step slaughter of the Barrock family.

Then the voices began.

The distinct and terrifying whisper started deep within the tangle of Mechanic's mind. Inside Mechanic's head was a labyrinth of rooms, corridors and hallways which had been constructed piece by piece during years of sexual abuse. Mechanic used to hide away in this maze to detach from reality until the pain receded. Sometimes for minutes, sometimes for hours, Mechanic would walk along the hallways deciding which room to enter, escaping from the sickening acts being committed in the real world.

One room housed the summer holiday they'd had in Sarasota. Long sandy beaches and snorkelling in the crystal waters, chasing schools of tiny fish. Another contained the Christmas when it had snowed and Santa brought Mechanic a twelve-speed bike. It was all wrapped up in coloured paper and propped up on its stand by the tree.

There were many rooms, each one providing a defence mechanism which allowed Mechanic to function with at least the outward signs of a normal life – a home, a job and some friends. But the labyrinth of rooms gave the darker, sadistic side of Mechanic's personality freedom to roam, waiting to seize control.

And that darker side came in the form of Daddy.

The abuse had gone on for years. It would strike at any time without warning. It happened when Daddy had a bad day, it happened when he had a good day. It happened when Daddy was happy, it happened when he was sad. The external stimulus which brought on the attacks was hard to identify. One thing was for sure. It generated a rage that could only be brought back to earth in one way, and that was where the young Mechanic came into the equation.

It was clear that, since Mom had left, Daddy was angry a lot. There was no one to talk to, no one to tell. Daddy had made it clear that if Mechanic breathed a word of this to anyone then the next step would be to be taken into foster care. Daddy also made it clear this was all Mom's fault. The only reason he was like this was because of what she'd done. He had never acted like this before the split. It was all because of her and the way she'd abandoned them for that pot-smoking, beach bum fuckwit. Every attack reminded Mechanic of Mom's betrayal. Every slap, every punch, every time Daddy ejaculated, only to break down afterwards and cry like a baby. This was all Mom's doing. The bitch was to blame.

One room held a special place for Mechanic. Inside was the holiday of '66 when they took the VIA train from Quebec City to Montreal. They crossed the St Lawrence River, enthralled by the moving cinema on the other side of the window. Factories and farms sprawled as far as the eye could see. Trailer parks flashed into view and then were gone. The young Mechanic liked it when the train slowed down to little more than walking pace, passing along back gardens in the small towns. This house had kids, probably a girl and a boy. This one was owned by older people who loved gardening. This one had the remnants of an outdoor barbeque party which hadn't been cleared away. It was a kaleidoscope of images for Mechanic's fertile imagination.

All was going well until they pulled into Drummondville. A smartly dressed middle-aged man got off the train holding a briefcase and an overnight bag. He was wrestling with the strap on the bag which was twisted, crouching down to untangle it, when two youths burst out of the jostling crowd and knocked him to the floor, shouting at him to hand over his bags. He went down hard, disorientated due to the speed of the attack but still had hold of his luggage. Mechanic stared out of the window as the assault continued not eight feet away.

'The fucking case, man,' shouted the louder of the two. 'Give us the fucking case.'

Mechanic was transfixed.

Briefcase man was flat on his back with his feet slightly raised. The second youth kicked him just below his ribs. Mechanic saw his face contort with pain as he doubled over to protect himself.

'Give us the bags, motherfucker,' yelled the loud guy. 'The case, man. Give us the fucking case.' The guy who'd kicked him took another swing. Briefcase man blocked the kick, and grabbed his attacker's leg above the ankle.

Everything went into slow motion.

Briefcase man kept a firm hold of kicking guy's leg and swept his own right foot in an arc, taking the legs clean from under the other attacker. As his legs went one way and his body the other, the assailant spun in the air like a no-handed cartwheel and his head crashed onto the platform.

Briefcase man twisted kicking guy's foot clockwise sending him spinning sideways to the ground, and in a single motion got to his feet, still holding the ankle. He snapped the leg sideways and stomped his right foot into kicking guy's groin. He then calmly walked three strides across the concourse to where the other youth was on his knees, looking on in disbelief as his buddy held his busted balls. This was unfortunate because he didn't see the left-foot kick which almost detached his head from his shoulders. The force of the strike lifted him into the air and laid him flat on his back. He was unconscious before he hit the ground.

Briefcase man stood up straight and dusted himself down. He checked his pockets – keys, wallet, all was in order. He picked up his bags and walked off. As the train pulled out of the station there was a piercing high-pitched squeal. Mechanic thought it came from the carriage wheels, but then realized the sound was coming from kicking guy, still laid out on the concrete, both hands clutched between his legs.

That chance encounter changed Mechanic for ever. The tsunami of abuse which would occur in the years ahead made Mechanic a sociopath but it was the chance encounter with an ex-marine on a station platform in Drummondville which drove Mechanic to acquire the tools to inflict extreme violence.

There was one enduring problem with the labyrinth inside Mechanic's head. Since the abuse had stopped, it was where Daddy now lived, wandering along the corridors from room to room.

Mechanic often caught the distant sound of footsteps on wood block flooring as Daddy stalked around waiting for the opportunity to take control. He would talk to himself as he moved about, the soft whispering of a conversation far away.

Mechanic's eyes opened in shock, torn from the drifting clouds of Pachelbel's dreams. The sound of faraway whispering drifted through the labyrinth. Was it really there or was it just a false alarm? Mechanic stopped breathing, beads of sweat quickly formed then broke and ran in rivulets. The sound of footsteps came closer. The voice was becoming clearer.

Mechanic leapt from the sofa and ran to the small room down the hallway where the gym equipment was kept. Grasping a dumbbell in each hand, Mechanic started pumping the weights. First the right then the left, each movement swelling arms and shoulder muscles as they strained against the heavy weights. The footsteps were close now.

Mechanic had learned that intense physical exercise could block Daddy's attempts to gain control. The more painful the exercise, the more chance there was of fighting off the attack. A menacing voice spoke inside Mechanic's head.

'Didn't go to plan again, did it?' Daddy was not happy.

Mechanic was galvanized into increased effort, muscles beginning to feel the intense burn as the lactic acid coursed through swollen veins. The dumbbells were moving slower now as the muscles became tired. Mechanic's face contorted into a grimace, teeth clenched together, snarling against the pain.

'He was in the wrong place at the wrong time. You adjusted well but it wasn't to plan. There needs to be another – soon.'

Mechanic fought against the failing muscles. This was always the most difficult part, the tipping point. If Mechanic allowed the pain and physical exertion to win, then Daddy would be in control. Maintaining the searing pain was the only way to hold him back. It was unbearable. Adrenalin surged through Mechanic's body, making it shake.

Chest burning.

Arms burning.

Mechanic fought against the pain. Daddy was insistent.

'When will we be ready for the next ...' The sentence faded as the voice got farther away. Then, as abruptly as it had started, it was gone.

Silence.

Mechanic collapsed on the floor, arms flopped uselessly against the hessian matting. The pain and exertion had done its job. Mechanic rolled across the floor and stared at the ceiling, gasping for breath. Mechanic had feared that the imperfect way in which the McKee killings had taken place would trigger another attack, but was not expecting it so soon.

On a scale of zero to ten this attack had been a six, a minor assault, which was easily repelled. Mechanic was still in control, but knew only too well the attacks would grow in intensity. Before long it would be impossible to hold Daddy at bay.

The plan for Sophie Barrock had to be accelerated.

Chapter 28

Lucas sat in a black sixteen-seater van in the rain. Fat water droplets hammered on the roof and resonated through the whole vehicle. It was a hot night and the atmosphere in the van was like a sauna.

The windows misted up making it hard to observe the front entrance of the Silverdale Heights block of flats. Holed up in the van with the SWAT team it was difficult to hear, difficult to breath and difficult to see. Despite this, Lucas was struggling to contain his expectation and excitement.

The briefing at the station had been short and sweet. Lucas had decided early on that this raid was not going to be a gentle knock on the door. It was going to be fast and it was going to be hard.

Bassano alerted the SWAT team that overwhelming force was needed to apprehend the occupant of Flat 10. They were fine with that.

The rental agreement said the sole tenant was Mr Ellis Baker, a twenty-eight-year-old white male whose occupation was listed as IT consultant. The team dug around in the files but found nothing on him, not even a parking violation. He was clean. A short telephone conversation with the block manager also told Lucas that Baker lived alone and was often away on business. It also told him that Baker had moved in about twelve months ago.

That was all they needed to know.

The men and women surrounding Lucas in the steamy van were the service's finest, the toughest and the best trained. They were dressed in black paramilitary style uniforms with enough firepower to start a small war.

During the briefing, Jo and Bassano gave them the minimum amount of information necessary to carry out the raid. You could see the knowing glances passing between the SWAT team as Bassano relayed the statistics to them: white male, twenty-eight years old, wanted for questioning, suspected of killing fifteen people plus an FBI agent, all by gun shot wounds. That certainly grabbed their attention.

Bassano and Sells sat about twenty yards away in an air-conditioned car. The conversation was patchy – she talked about the case and the details surrounding Ellis Baker, he talked about himself.

She was determined to ignore Bassano's line of chat and kept bringing it back to the job in hand. This was an irritating first for Bassano. He was used to being the one on the receiving end of the chase and this was putting him off his game.

He knew Lucas would disapprove but Bassano had a gift for ignoring the obvious when it was inconvenient. Okay, so she was a colleague working on the case, his boss didn't trust her and she was implicated in the leak in the previous investigation. But hey, she was hot. However, she was proving to be a struggle and the more she ignored him, the bolder his advances became.

It bothered him that she continued to feign disinterest. From Jo's point of view, he was simply beginning to bother her.

Jo was nervous and kept drawing and then shouldering her hand gun. Bassano had stopped talking and was thumbing a grainy photograph of Ellis Baker taken from the lease agreement documentation. He looked pale and geeky with unruly hair – he looked like an IT Consultant.

The radio in Lucas's hand crackled into life with three short buzzes. This was the signal from the plain clothes SWAT guy to confirm that noises were coming from Flat 10 and Baker was at home. Could they really have uncovered Mechanic's identity at last?

Lucas looked at the digital clock on the dashboard and gave the signal. It was 11.15pm. The side of the van slid back and the black figures jumped down into the cool night air. The apartment block was on four floors with car parking in the basement. It was newly built and well decorated both inside and out. A large glass door led to a reception area with a security guard sitting behind a half moon desk watching TV. As it was after eleven the glass doors were secured shut.

Two of the SWAT team ran to the back of the building where the fire escape ladders were secured to the wall. Another two ran to the underground car park and the rest took up their positions on either side of the reception doors, their backs pressed against the wall. Lucas walked forward and flashed his badge at the bored security guard, hitting the button for the front doors to swing open. The guard's jaw dropped as Lucas entered, closely followed by eight storm troopers who were seriously tooled up.

Lucas held his hand up for the guard to be silent and motioned for him to step away from his desk.

'We have a potentially serious situation here and we need your co-operation.' Lucas was calm and measured.

'Anything, man. Just name it.' The guard was excited by the prospect of an evening's entertainment.

'I want you to sit here until we need you.' Lucas pulled the office chair from behind the desk and put it against the opposite wall. 'When we need something we'll ask.' The guard took up his position as if he had a ringside seat for a big fight.

One of the team hit the button to call the lift. The other went to the electrical cabinet behind the desk and when the lift arrived at reception pulled the circuit breakers. The lift buttons went dead with the doors remaining open. To the left of reception there was a main staircase leading to all the floors with a much smaller set of service stairs in the opposite corner. Two of the team went to the service entrance and the rest took the main stairs, leaving one in the reception area to keep the guard company. Bassano and Sells followed at a safe distance.

On the first floor a young couple came out of their apartment, laughing and obviously drunk. They sobered up fast when a black figure ushered them back into their flat with a 'shush' and closed the door behind them. Ellis Baker had the corner flat on the second floor with what looked like a new front door. *That's unfortunate*, Lucas thought.

One of the team put his ear to the door, gave the thumbs up and stepped aside. This allowed Big Tom to move into position. Big Tom was the name given to the fifty pound steel bar, about two and a half feet long. It was also the name of the six-foot-four-inch, two-hundred-and-forty pound officer who swung it. It impacted with a deafening thud just below the Yale lock and the door frame splintered.

The SWAT team piled into the apartment with their guns levelled, shouting at Ellis to get down on the floor.

Lucas could see that this wouldn't be easy. Ellis was sitting in an armchair with his head back and his eyes shut. His trousers were around his ankles and between his splayed legs sat Lucky Miranda, a thirty-dollar hooker doing what thirty-dollar hookers do best.

'What the f—' Ellis said as he struggled to detach himself from Lucky Miranda, get up from the chair and pull his trousers up – an all-in-one movement he was never going to make.

'On the floor!' The officer shouted, his gun about three feet from Ellis's head.

'Hey man, what is this?' Lucky Miranda was able to join in the protest now she was disengaged from Ellis. She rolled away to the side and sat on the floor drawing her knees up to her chin.

'On the floor, with your hands behind your head!'

'What the fuck is this about?' Ellis said eating the pile of the carpet.

'Clear!' Came a shout from the bedroom and then again from the kitchen.

The guy banged his knee into Ellis's back and pulled his hands behind his back, locking them into metal cuffs. Once secured, he patted Ellis down for concealed weapons.

'Who's the woman?'

'She's a hooker, man, just a hooker. Look, why are you doing this?' Ellis was finding it hard to talk, lying on his front with a policeman kneeling on his back.

'What do you mean I'm just a hooker?' Lucky Miranda had taken offence at the word *just*.

'Shut it lady.'

'You guys are going way overboard with this cleaning up the city shit,' Miranda said as she looked at Ellis face down on the floor, his front door swinging on a single hinge.

The whole thing lasted no more than twenty seconds.

Lucas stepped forward. 'Ellis Baker, I need you to accompany me to the station. We have some questions for you.'

'This is crazy, man,' yelled Ellis. 'She's just a piece of Friday night fun. Come on man this is fucking stupid.'

'Let's talk about it at the station.' Ellis was lifted to his feet, taken down to the waiting van and driven away.

Bassano stood shaking his head in the empty flat, Ellis Baker's picture still in his hand. Not that he had ever met one, but Ellis Baker did not look like a serial killer. He looked like an IT consultant.

Chapter 29

Bassano and Jo Sells sat opposite Ellis Baker in the interview room. Bassano pressed the button on the tape machine and it emitted a long beep. Lucas was the other side of the two-way mirror in the next room, watching Baker intently.

'Right Mr Baker, you are not under arrest and you have not been charged, we just want you to answer a few questions.'

'I can't believe this. I've done nothing wrong.' Baker was very agitated. He had kept asking the same questions over and over again in the van driving back to the station, only to be met with stony silence.

'It was nothing man, people do it all the time.' He continued to protest in the interview room.

'You do have the right to have a lawyer present—'

'A lawyer?' Baker was out of his chair. The officer at the back of the room moved forward but Bassano stopped him by raising his hand. 'Why the hell do I need a lawyer? This is stupid, man. She was just a bit of entertainment that's all. She sure as hell wasn't underage or anything.' Bassano had to agree with Ellis on that point. No one could ever mistake Lucky Miranda as underage.

Baker sat back down and Jo continued. 'Mr Baker, we need you to help us by answering some questions.'

This set Ellis off again. 'Help you? Help you? That's rich. You put me on the floor in handcuffs, destroy my front door and haul me down here all because I had a blow job from a Friday night hooker. And you want me to help you.'

'Mr Baker, you need to calm down.' Bassano was getting irritated.

Jo interrupted him. 'Mr Baker, this is not about the hooker.'

'It's not?'

'No it isn't.'

'Then what the hell is it about?'

Bassano jumped in. 'Do you know a woman by the name of Hannah McKee?'

'Er no. I don't know anyone by that name.' Baker screwed his face up.

'Are you sure? Her name is Hannah McKee and we believe she knows you.'

Ellis shook his head. 'She can't do, man. I've never heard of any woman called Hannah McKee.'

'What do you do for a living, Mr Baker?' asked Jo.

'Look what the hell is this about?' Baker was becoming rattled.

'Just answer the question,' Bassano said.

'I'm in IT. I install business systems. That's what I do. Who the hell is Hannah McKee?'

Bassano ignored his question. 'Have you ever been involved in counselling?'

'Counselling? No I've always been in IT ever since I graduated from college. I took a promotion and moved here about a year ago. I travel around installing business systems.'

'Have you ever offered any type of counselling services, maybe when you were in college?' asked Jo.

'No never. I don't know the first thing about counselling.'

'So how do you explain this?' Bassano pulled out a polythene envelope containing the poster found at the club and laid it on the table.

Baker stared at it as if he was having trouble reading the words.

'This is your telephone number, right?' asked Bassano.

'Yes it is but I've never seen this before in my life.'

'Then why would it have your number on it?'

'I don't know, I can't explain it.' There was more than a trace of desperation creeping into Ellis's voice.

'Well you'd better explain it because that's why we're here,' Bassano replied jabbing his finger into the numbers on the sheet.

'But I can't. I've never seen this before. Honest.'

'Why would this advertise a counselling service with your number on it if you don't do counselling?' asked Jo.

'I don't know. Honest, I've never seen this before in my life. There must be some mistake, you have to believe me.'

'Well, unfortunately, Mr Baker we don't have to believe you. So why don't you tell us how this has your number on it?'

'I can't. Yes, it's my number but I have no idea how it got there. It must be a mistake.'

'Let's try something else.' Bassano changed tack. 'We are investigating a serious incident that took place on Wednesday evening. Where were you on Wednesday night Mr Baker?'

'Wednesday … umm. Oh, I was in Davenport. I was there for eight days and came back late yesterday.'

'What were you doing there?' asked Bassano.

'We had a project going live. I was part of the team commissioning the system cutover from the old installation to the new.'

'You were in Davenport all that time?' asked Jo.

'Yes, we worked crazy hours and stayed in a hotel.'

'Can anyone verify you were there?'

'Yes, I was part of a team. There's got to be six people that can vouch for me.' Ellis was sounding a little more sure of himself.

'Unfortunately, Mr Baker, we need to be much more specific. Davenport is four hours' drive. You could make the round trip without anyone noticing. That's not good enough, Mr Baker. We need names and times. We need details, Mr Baker. Details.' Bassano was beginning to push hard.

'No, no, you've got it wrong. It wasn't Davenport,' said Ellis.

'So now you didn't stay in Davenport?' Bassano was sensing blood.

'Yeah, we stayed in Davenport alright, Davenport England.' Baker sounded triumphant. Bassano fell silent.

'You've been in England for the past eight days?' asked Jo.

'Well no. We were in England for six days – eight days if you take the travel into account. I got back yesterday around 8.30pm. We flew out of Jackson International to Manchester and stayed at the Davenport Stables hotel. You can check all this out, man. Check it out.'

Lucas was swearing behind the glass.

Jo continued. 'Who else knew you were in England?'

'A load of people. I have a lot of friends, and they all know when I'm around and when I'm away with work. I tend to be away a lot and I make sure the guys at the club know my schedule in case they need to cover me for league games.'

'League games?' Before she asked the question, Jo knew where this was going.

'Yes, I belong to a club and play tennis in a league. Sometimes my buddies have to rearrange games if I'm not there, otherwise I forfeit the match.'

Jo paused, 'It wouldn't happen to be Brightwood Country Club would it?'

'Hey, she's good,' Baker said to Bassano. 'How did you know that?'

Jo looked at Bassano who was still lost for words. 'I think we'll take a short break if that's okay,' she said. Bassano announced the adjournment for the benefit of the tape and turned the machine off. They left the room and closed the door behind them.

Back behind the glass, Jo took the lead. 'He's not our guy. He's not Mechanic. His phone number is on the sheet but he knows nothing about how it got there. Can we run basic checks on the flight manifesto and the Davenport Stables hotel? I'm sure he will check out fine. I'm afraid to say gentlemen, Ellis Baker is not who we thought he was.'

'He's a fucking IT consultant. That's what he is.' Bassano was pissed off.

Lucas was stroking his chin. 'He's not our guy but we have moved forward here haven't we? We know that Mechanic frequents the country clubs in some capacity or another and puts up the posters to attract his victims. The number on the flyer doesn't belong to Mechanic but somehow he uses it to undertake weeks of counselling.'

'I'm not sure that moves us forward, boss,' said Bassano, deflated.

'I think I know what's going on here,' Jo said out of the blue. 'Mechanic puts up the counselling poster and waits. The telephone number he uses is for someone he knows is going to be out of town. He taps into their phone while they're away and gets hold of any calls for the counselling service. When the initial contact has been made, Mechanic gives them a different number, and this is the one he uses for the rest of the counselling.'

'Shit, that's elaborate. Why go to so much trouble?' asked Bassano.

'Because it provides Mechanic with a control break in the process. He goes fishing with the first number for a short period, and when he hooks a victim he reverts to the second number. Once he has someone he doesn't need the advert anymore and has no further need for the first number. Anyone using the first one afterwards will just contact someone who thinks they have a wrong number. That way there is no sustained link through to Mechanic.'

'But how does he get to use their number in the first place?' asked Bassano.

'I don't know. He must have a way of tapping into the line while the person is away. I don't know if that's technically possible but he has to be able to access their phone somehow,' said Jo.

'Maybe he just lives in their apartment while they're away,' said Bassano sarcastically.

Lucas and Jo both looked at Bassano, then at each other.

Lucas shook his head. 'There's so much weird shit going on in this case, nothing Mechanic does surprises me. Check out if Ellis Baker has any suspicions his flat might have been tampered with while he was out of the country. It could be that Mechanic just moves in and waits for people to call. This guy has balls.'

'So we need to look for another number?' Bassano continued.

'Well, it's the only way I can read this situation and make sense of it.' Jo looked exhausted.

There was a knock on the door, it was one of the custody suite staff. 'Sir, I have a message for you from the hospital. Hannah McKee has regained consciousness.'

Lucas turned to Jo. 'Well that's a hell of a theory, doctor, and I think we just got the opportunity to test it out. Why don't you ask Hannah McKee in the morning?'

'Hold on, sir,' Bassano said. 'I've had enough of being wrong today. It would be good to end it on a positive note. Just give me twenty minutes, get yourselves a coffee and I'll meet you in your office.' He followed the custody officer out of the room.

Jo looked at Lucas. 'Coffee?'

'It looks like it. You did well in there,' Lucas said pointing through the glass at the interview room, 'and you did well to give us a possible route through with Hannah McKee.'

'Thanks. I could see the whole set of twisted circumstances coming together. Sometimes the most straightforward answer is the best one, however unlikely it might sound.' Jo was pleased that Lucas had recognized her contribution.

'Well, you might just have nailed several parts of the jigsaw to the table. Let's get that coffee,' he said.

Lucas looked on as Jo tipped the sugar from five sachets into her cup, flattened out the paper strips on the desk and wound them together to form a sugar twist. She didn't once look at her hands and spoke nonstop, going over the details of the interview while her fingers worked. Lucas picked up the white paper double helix and rolled it in his fingers thoughtfully. He looked at his watch it was 1.25am.

Both were seated in Lucas's office finishing off their coffee when Bassano returned.

'Where have you been?' asked Lucas.

'I know it's out of protocol but I spoke with Hannah McKee on the phone. She was still groggy but lucid enough to talk. I didn't feel we could wait until the morning.'

'Go on,' urged Jo.

Bassano referred to his notes. 'Yes, she was receiving telephone counselling at the time leading up to the attack. Yes, she saw the poster at the Brightwood Country Club and yes, she was given an alternative phone number to use after the first session. She has the number written down at home. I've already sent an officer to the house to get it.'

Lucas struggled to contain his excitement.

Bassano closed his notebook.

'There's one final thing. The counsellor was a woman.'

Chapter 30

Lucas reached the office the next morning churning over the consequences of the latest revelations. He'd got home around quarter past two in the morning and managed to sleep like a baby until half past seven. Although his mind had been racing when he got into bed, he fell asleep as soon as his head hit the pillow.

Bassano was waiting for him, his face tinged grey with exhaustion, still dressed in yesterday's clothes. He certainly hadn't had a good night's sleep.

'You look dreadful,' Lucas said as he walked into the incident room.

'Yeah, thanks. Been working on that number from Hannah McKee.'

'Is Jo Sells here?'

'No show as yet.' Bassano drained the last mouthful of coffee and headed to the steaming jug on top of the machine to get another. Jo walked in.

'Morning!' She was just that little too bright and cheery for either of her colleagues. 'How are you both today?'

'Jaded,' was the one word response from Bassano. Lucas said nothing but tilted his head in Bassano's direction and grimaced.

'Thoughts, from yesterday?' Lucas was keen to engage them on their new information

'A woman. I didn't see that one coming.' Bassano was first off the mark. 'When we interviewed Lillian Lang it never crossed my mind to ask the sex of the person doing the damn counselling.'

Lucas assumed this was the reason for Bassano not having a good night's sleep, and he was right. He had spent all night kicking himself.

'It suggests that Mechanic is being helped. It could be a wife or girlfriend, someone who holds the same beliefs as him. Someone with the same need to kill but without the necessary strength or resolve to carry it out. It could be a symbiotic relationship,' Jo said.

'A simming what?' Bassano was not at his sharpest this morning.

'Symbiotic. They feed off each other, a marriage of convenience if you like. She provides him with the targets and he provides her with the dead bodies. The other rationale could be she is doing this under duress. Mechanic may be forcing her.'

'Could that be happening in this case?' asked Lucas.

'I think it's unlikely. From what we understand the sessions take place over a considerable period of time and it would be hard to maintain that if you were being pressurized to do it. And anyway, there are far too many opportunities to warn the victim off. No, I don't think coercion is happening here.'

'So now we are looking for two people. At least that gives us a hundred percent more to aim for.' Lucas tried to sound up beat.

'Yes that's what I figured,' said Bassano.

'Right, let's talk about the plan for today?' Lucas was eager to get going.

Bassano consulted his notebook. 'I have the address for the new phone number Hannah McKee provided. It's a disused warehouse about twenty-five miles east of here on the Brunswick Industrial Park. It belongs to a company called GAI Circles Inc which is a landscape gardening outfit. After yesterday's debacle I figured me and Jo could go and check it out.' Lucas and Jo nodded in agreement.

Bassano continued, 'Boss, can you co-ordinate the interviewing of Hannah McKee now that she's conscious and think through how we are going to alert the country clubs without giving the game away? The other thing is, we need to follow up on Mr-IT-blowjob to see if his flat was disturbed when he was away.'

'Okay, the country club is tricky. It's too soon for people to know that Mechanic is back in operation. Let me think about it. We'll meet back here after lunch.'

Jo Sells sat in silence for most of the journey to the industrial estate while Bassano bombarded her with his witty lines and awkward questions. Despite his fatigue he'd decided to ratchet up his game a couple of notches but she still wasn't falling for his winning routine. This wasn't how it usually went for him and the more he flirted, the frostier she became. For Jo the journey was a long one.

They parked on a piece of derelict land located outside the main gates and walked the short distance to the unit identified on the address. There was no security and no fencing around the estate and it showed.

'Are you sure this is right?' Jo asked looking at the dilapidated buildings, glad to be out of the car at last.

'Yes, that's the address they gave me.' He showed her the page in his notebook.

'No one has worked on this site for years, it's a total mess.'

The industrial estate housed an enormous three-story warehouse and several smaller prefabricated office blocks. Every window in the entire complex had been smashed and the doors either kicked in or missing. Paint and rendering flaked from the walls like a bad skin condition and tufts of grass grew between the cracks in the road. Sheeting from the roofs of the smaller buildings had been removed along with large portions of brickwork, presumably stolen to complete someone's home project.

They approached what looked like the main entrance to the warehouse. It housed a large set of double doors which at one time had been protected by a lockable roller shutter. The shutter was nowhere to be seen, taken and sold for scrap, and the doors were hanging from their hinges, their wooden panels ripped away.

Inside the hallway the acrid stench of smoke and urine hung in the air. Fast food wrappers were strewn over the floor.

Bassano pointed to a scattering of syringes and balls of tinfoil on the ground. 'Tramps and hobos. They light fires to keep warm at night and shoot up when they have the gear. Stay sharp, we might encounter a couple of them.' Bassano was trying his hand at a little early morning humour but Jo drew her gun from her shoulder holster.

'Do you know how to use that?' Bassano looked surprised.

'I had twelve weeks field training and I think it's necessary.'

'I was joking. There's only a slim chance we'll run into any hobos. Put it away, you're making me nervous.'

Jo turned on her heels to face him.

'Look, Bassano, I think it's necessary. Not because there's a *slim* chance we might run into a hobo, it's necessary because there's a *slim* chance we might run into a guy who's killed sixteen people.'

Bassano considered her answer and drew his sidearm. 'Good point.'

'And while we're on the subject,' she continued. 'I've seen your training log and it reads like a piece of shit. "You couldn't hit a barn door" was one of the comments from your range assessment. "Consistently fails to follow protocols and drills" was another. So I need this,' she said holding up her weapon, 'to protect the both of us.'

Bassano said nothing.

'And while we're on the subject and clearing the air,' she continued, though Bassano was unaware they were on a subject or clearing the air. 'No, I don't have a boyfriend and I don't want a date.'

'Well, er … I wasn't asking …' he was completely wrong-footed by her direct approach.

'Yes you were. And that's not because I don't date guys from the job, it's because I don't date, period. Got it? So pack it in with your adolescent Italian stallion "I'll crack her eventually" routine, because it's never gonna happen. Is that clear enough for you? Back off.'

Bassano tried to stumble out a reply. 'Er, well I didn't mean to …'

'Focus on my expertise and competence and less on my ass and we'll get along just fine. And just so you don't misinterpret anything,' she paused to be sure he was keeping up. 'That means you focus on my expertise and competence. Are we clear?'

Bassano looked at her and made a gesture that resembled an apology, but just so he was being clear he said 'Sorry.' She fixed him with a glare and he looked away. Jo felt much better.

They exited the hallway in silence and entered the vast open space of the main building. Any equipment which was installed there had long gone, but there was debris strewn all over the floor and empty cable ties hung along the walls. The building had been stripped bare of anything that was valuable: copper cable, light fittings, even portions of the girder work supporting the structure had been hacked away.

'Careful where you put your feet,' Bassano said trying to be helpful as they picked their way across the centre of the building.

'What was the address given by the phone company?' Jo asked.

Bassano stopped and consulted his notes. 'It was GAI Circles Inc, Main Building, Level 3, Brunswick Industrial Estate.'

Jo scanned the cavernous expanse of the warehouse. 'Look.' She pointed toward the north wall. 'There are offices on that mezzanine and, if I'm not mistaken, they're three floors high. Let's take a look.'

They crossed the expanse of cluttered floor to reach the metal steps which ran up to the offices. The structure was unstable as hell. They both took a firm hold of the handrail and walked up the stairs.

'Keep close to the wall,' Bassano said. The whole structure was swaying and he was sure he could feel the metal staircase coming away from the brickwork.

There were three landing areas. The first two lay empty and were used for storage but at the top there was a walkway which ran along the front of three prefabricated offices. Each one had its door open and its windows smashed. They went into the first office crunching shards of glass under their feet.

Unlike the rest of the property this still had signs of its previous occupants. Broken furniture and papers covered the floor and metal cabinets still containing old ledgers and files were lined up along one wall. Bassano opened a drawer and removed a document. It contained pencil sketches of a garden layout showing the patio area, flower borders and a brick barbecue. In another file there were more drawings of tree-lined walkways along what looked like a shopping mall.

'Why is this lot still here when the rest of the building has been trashed?' Bassano said.

'Perhaps even the hobos won't risk their lives climbing up here.'

She approached Bassano with a piece of paper in her hand.

'Look at this. It's a copy invoice for thirteen hundred bucks.' Bassano took it and read the details on the printed document.

'So?' he said, shaking his head.

'Look at the address.'

Bassano read it out loud, 'Glandford Landscapes, Main Building, Level 3, Brunswick Industrial Estate.'

'Yes, it's the same address but the company name is different. We're in the right place but no one has been here for years. Let's check out the other offices,' Jo said.

They walked out onto the landing and into the other office. This one had much less litter on the floor and was empty of any filing cabinets or furniture. Further along the landing it was the same with the third office.

Bassano leaned against the wall and looked at the printed invoice in his hand. 'The tech guys were adamant this was the place. I asked them to check it twice because I knew this was a derelict site. We know we're in the right place because the address on the invoice confirms it. How can that be?'

'I don't know,' replied Jo. 'But one thing is for sure, no telephone counselling went on here.'

'How's that?' asked Bassano.

'Look around. There are no phone lines.'

Chapter 31

Lucas wasn't arranging interviews, nor was he working his head around the tricky problem of how to alert the country clubs without giving the game away about Mechanic. He was pushing the door open on a seedy run-down café wondering what the hell he was going to find on the other side. This was Harper's favourite place to drink coffee.

Lucas entered from the bright sidewalk and couldn't see a damn thing. Even when his eyes had adjusted to the low light, he found it difficult to navigate his gaze around the place because of the smoke. It hung from the low ceiling like seaside fog and left a bitter taste in his mouth. There was a long bar running down the left side with a curious mixture of tables and chairs dotted around the room. Nothing matched. It was a haphazard style of interior design. The one thing that did match was the guy serving behind the counter with the haphazard sort of face. His oversized nose, buck teeth and thick black mono-brow gave him the look of a kids toy.

Customers were drinking various liquids out of cracked mugs. All the tables had just one occupant – evidently no one had any friends.

A lone woman sat at the bar on a high stool, her lipstick the shade of cherry cola and her skirt the length of cut-off shorts: shorter than her dignity should allow but not short enough for her to care. Her four-inch, leopard-print heels were kicked off and her feet in their black stockings swung free. This was a woman taking a well-earned break from her active profession and from the pain of her friend's borrowed shoes which were one size too small.

Harper was wedged into a corner under a bowl-shaped light which hung low over the table. Lucas negotiated his way through the maze of assorted furniture while five pairs of eyes watched him cross to where Harper was sitting. He scraped a chair from the next-door table along the floor and sat down.

'Great place,' Lucas said, 'coffee rings on the tables and smoke rings on the ceiling. Very classy.'

'You can't see the smoke rings because of the smoke and, anyway, I like it,' said Harper who fitted into the surroundings as well as the guy behind the counter. 'You want coffee?' Lucas nodded.

'How have you managed to turn stuff up so quickly?' Lucas was keen to spend as little time there as possible. It would take days for the stink to go from his clothes.

'Let's just say I'd already done my homework.'

Lucas noticed Harper's hand was shaking as he lifted the chipped mug to his lips. He brought the other hand up to steady it so he could take a gulp. It was early in the morning for Harper and the alcohol withdrawal had very noticeable effects at this time of day. Harper saw Lucas looking at his hand and replaced the cup on the table.

'What do you have?' Lucas asked.

'I'm not sure, but I thought we ought to meet up to get this new relationship of ours off on the right foot. So first the facts: Jo Sells graduated from MIT with a first in psychology and went on to do her doctorate in criminology, specializing in psychological profiling. She was a very bright spark indeed but also had a talent for sport and has a list of accolades as long as your arm. She could have become a professional sportswoman but chose the academic route instead. It was during her doctorate that she first met Galbraith.' He went to take another slurp of coffee but withdrew his hand. The morning was not good for steady coffee drinking.

'Galbraith was a visiting fellow at the university and mentored her for two out of the four years of her post-grad work. He was so impressed that he seconded her into the FBI Behavioral Sciences

Unit at Quantico and employed her when she graduated, which she did with high honours. A year into the job, Mechanic struck for the first time and she and Galbraith were dispatched to support us in the investigation. She was very close to Galbraith and there were rumours that they had something going between them, but there was nothing in it. The people in the know say those rumours were from jealous students trying to do some damage. Nothing more.'

Lucas's coffee arrived and was banged down on the corner of the table, making it slop over the rim. He looked at the steaming hot drink. In the gloomy light it was difficult to see if it was black or white. He lifted the mug and drank.

Harper continued, 'Her home life was stable in the early years. Father was in the forces and they moved around quite a bit. Then he got discharged on medical grounds when he was injured in a training accident. He never worked again. Her mother held a number of lower paid roles, moving from office job to office job as her husband took up different postings. Everything was going fine until shortly after he was posted to San Diego when she left him and ran off with a younger guy. The kids were only twelve at the time and Jo had to become the woman of the house. She has a sister, Jessica, who is proving a bit of a mystery and I only have sketchy details. She was also very bright and excelled academically and, just like Jo, was very sporty. They were like carbon copies of each other in terms of achievement. Jessica left college and went into the army and from what I can work out did some pretty tough shit, she was as near as a woman can get to being front-line. She was in the army for six years then had a huge meltdown which resulted in her being kicked out. She'd been a real high-flyer but something very bad must have happened because I'm struggling to get any details on why she was booted out. What I do know is that after she came out she fell off the radar completely. She just disappeared without trace. I'm expecting more info later today but her time in the military is proving difficult.'

'That's a lot of digging for such a short period of time.' Lucas was impressed.

'Well, like I said, I'd already done my homework. Those are the hard facts, now I'm going to give you the subjective view of Jo Sells. One area where I draw a blank is boyfriends – or girlfriends for that matter. When she was in college she was a complete party animal and put it about. She was the full package and made the most of it, but when she worked at Quantico she supposedly went completely celibate which I for one don't believe.' Harper stopped talking and reached for his coffee. He needed the caffeine and sugar to quell the nausea of going cold turkey.

'Okay, here's the part that sounds like the ravings of a crazy man going through DTs,' he said, steadying the cup. He welcomed the coffee's stabilizing effect.

'I'm ready for it.' Lucas was enjoying this.

'I don't believe Jo suddenly went off men. I reckon she fell for a guy who she needed to keep under wraps, someone she couldn't share with the outside world, someone she needed to keep off the grid. I reckon she got involved with Mechanic.' Harper waited for the peals of derision to come from Lucas, but they didn't come. He was staring down into his cup of sludge.

'You're not laughing,' Harper said eventually.

'No I'm not.'

'It definitely fits. The whole problem with Jo Sells being the leak in the investigation is identifying her motive? If you accept that Galbraith was murdered because he was about to change the profile and expose Mechanic, and if you accept that Jo is the only person close enough to know that was about to happen, then that's her motive. She wanted to shield and protect Mechanic.' Harper paused again.

'That's a whole lot of accepting,' said Lucas.

'Why aren't you laughing me out of court right now?' asked Harper.

'I'm not laughing because we now suspect Mechanic might have a little helper. It looks like that little helper is a woman.' It was Lucas's turn to wait for a reaction. He didn't get one.

'You think that could be Jo?'

'I don't know for sure and it's a hell of an assumption to make, but it ties up so many loose ends.' They both sat in silence looking into their coffee mugs.

'Where do you want me to go next?' Harper asked.

'Keep digging. Find out more about her time at Quantico – friends, clubs, societies and trips abroad. If you're right, she must have met Mechanic around the time she left university and joined the FBI. It gives us more of a defined time window.'

'I'll be in touch. This is heavy shit man,' said Harper.

Much like this coffee, Lucas thought and headed back to the station.

When he arrived, he found Bassano and Jo poring over reams of printouts in the incident room.

'Anything good?' Lucas asked.

'No nothing. We're chasing our tails here.' Bassano had shaken off his lack of sleep but was nursing his wounded pride since Jo had sounded off at him. Okay, so he'd been coming on to her for a while and it had got out of hand, but she didn't have to bring up his poor training record. He was sulking because deep down he knew she was right on both counts.

'How was the warehouse?' asked Lucas.

'Empty. We chased our damn tails in there as well. It was deserted and not a damn phone in sight. We're trying to unravel the complexities of GAI Circles Inc to give us a lead on where to go next,' said Bassano.

'What do you mean there was no phone?' asked Lucas.

'Just that,' said Jo. 'The phone company records show the phone is registered at that address but there's no phone. There aren't even any phone lines.'

'Have you rung the number?' Lucas asked.

'Yes, it rings fine but not on that industrial estate. Needless to say no one picked up,' replied Bassano.

'So what's this?' Lucas waved his hand across the mountains of paperwork.

'Here's the story so far. The original number belonged to a company called Glandford Landscapes based at this address.' Bassano showed Lucas the copy invoice taken from the warehouse. 'It confirms we were in the right place this morning but, believe me, no one has been there in a long time and there's no phone. We got the billing records from the phone company and, sure enough, they confirm it now belongs to a new company, GAI Circles Inc, which supposedly operates from the same address. The records show incoming calls only to that number but they aren't itemized which means we can't identify the callers.'

'What about the bills? Who takes care of them?' asked Lucas.

It was Jo's turn to answer. 'They're sent quarterly to a PO Box in Jacksonville which is also registered under the new company name. We've had the box checked out and all the bills are there unopened.'

'Why doesn't the phone get cut off if the bills aren't paid?' Lucas was full of questions.

'They are paid, by direct debit, from a bank account set up in Jacksonville, and yes you've guessed it, the business account belongs to GAI Circles Inc. The account has around two hundred and fifty bucks in it, which at the current rate of drawdown will keep the line active for the next five and a half years,' replied Bassano.

'Who's putting money into the business account to pay for the bills?'

'No one. The account was set up with four hundred dollars in it and there's no need to top it up.'

'Have you checked the State's Corporate Registry to see if they have details?'

'Yes, they've never heard of it. It's a ghost company which doesn't file any annual accounts and at the moment only owns a phone number and nothing else.'

'So, why can't we just trace the goddamn thing?' Now Lucas was feeling a little of Bassano's frustration.

'We did, through the paperwork, and that led us back to the disused warehouse. The only alternative is to have the line open and active and trace the call that way, but whoever is on the other end isn't picking up so we can't find where it is,' said Bassano.

'We need to get the technicians and the phone company working on it,' said Lucas.

'You won't find anything,' said Jo looking up from the mounds of paperwork. She put both her hands to her temples and let out a long sigh. 'Shit.'

'What?' they both said in unison.

'I said, we won't find anything.' She put her hands back on the desk and looked at both of them. 'Mechanic has set this whole thing up so that if it were to be uncovered nothing would lead back to him.'

'But, how do you know that?' asked Bassano.

'It's been staring us in the face from the time we discovered the second telephone number. It's in the company name, GAI Circles Inc.' She paused and took another deep breath. 'I think it stands for Going Around In Circles.'

Lucas sat down heavily on a chair.

Jo continued, 'Mechanic knows that eventually we would uncover the second number and has set this whole thing up to ensure nothing could lead us to him. He's toying with us, he even gave us a name to play with: GAI Circles.'

'That's just a coincidence.' Bassano was annoyed.

'Is it?' Now it was Jo's turn to flash with frustration. 'Think about it. Why go to the trouble of changing the name of the original company in the first place? He could have set everything up exactly as it is now using the original name, the bank account, the PO Box and the billing address. He could have put it all under the name of Glandford Landscaping. But he didn't, he changed it, and I think he changed it for our benefit. He's playing with us. He knew we would get this far and he's playing with us.'

Bassano retreated under the weight of pure logic.

Jo went back to rubbing both her temples and staring at the desk. Her voice was low and tired. 'So, by all means, get the technical boys to work their magic but I'm telling you now they won't find jack shit.'

Jo jumped up and shoved the mound of paper away from her, the other two had the distinct impression she might be right.

Chapter 32

'So where do we go from here?' asked Bassano. All three of them stared in silence at the wads of paper strewn across the desk, wondering just that.

'We're not getting anywhere,' said Jo. 'Every time we think we have a lead it turns out to be a dead end.'

'We need to go back to the beginning and retrace our steps to see if we have missed anything – something, anything that will move us forward,' Bassano replied and then the silence returned.

Lucas was coming to the boil nicely.

He always maintained three golden rules while at work: never lose your temper, never raise your voice and never swear inappropriately. He was in danger of transgressing all three. Even though it was still early afternoon he felt as though he had already done a full day's work. He had a thumping headache, and a cocktail of frustration and stress was welling up inside him. He balled his hands up into fists and banged them down on the desk making Bassano and Jo Sells jump.

'No we don't. We need to come out fighting. We've got enough to start making life a little more difficult for Mechanic,' he said trying to control the wavering in his voice. 'He's playing with us, he's taking us for a ride and that has to stop.' Bassano and Sells looked at each other unsure if they were meant to respond, so they didn't.

'He's running around playing games, he has us exactly where he wants us, he's laughing at us. Well I think it's time to change tack. We've been on the back foot long enough, it's time to get serious.' Lucas stood up and started pacing the room.

'Bassano get a trace put on that line and wait until someone calls, or if they can't do that, cut it off and disable the number.

Jo, you get over to that damn country club with a team of officers and start finding out who knows what about the poster. Shut the fucking place down if you have to. We need to start disrupting Mechanic's natural flow. We need to let him know we are here.'

They both nodded.

'No more fucking about, no more fumbling around in the dark constantly on the receiving end of this kind of garbage.' He swept his arm across the desk sending the reams of paper thudding the floor. Lucas was on a roll, energized with his new-found grit.

They both nodded again. "No more fucking about," they completely understood.

There was a knock on the door and Metcalf walked in. It was a brave move considering the raised voices.

'Sir, this turned up in the post. It's marked for your attention and urgent. I brought it straight up.' Metcalf handed Lucas a white envelope and left.

Lucas frowned, opened the flap, and took out a single page of lined paper with scribbled writing on it. He held it under the nearest lamp so he could make out the scrawl.

Dear Lieutenant,

Being one out, you may as well be a thousand out, don't you think? Though, it was all worth it. The look on your face was an absolute picture when you eventually worked it out. It took a while, but when it did ... priceless.

Intellectually you are a more worthy opponent but way out of your depth. But then, by now, you know that.

You won't find me but have fun trying.
Mechanic

'Holy shit,' said Bassano, as Lucas read the note out loud. 'What does he mean "absolute picture"? I don't get it.' He was shaking his head.

Lucas reread the note trying to control the emotions flooding to the surface. He was struggling to contain himself in front of the others. He laid the paper and envelope on the table.

'"Being one out you may as well be a thousand out." What the fuck does that mean?' said Bassano, reading over Lucas's shoulder.

'This is what happened last time,' said Jo. 'He sent notes to Harper taunting him. It drove him to distraction.'

Lucas said nothing. He just stared at the letter trying to think straight. Then he got it.

'He was watching.'

'Watching what, Lucas?' asked Jo.

'He saw me at the house.'

Jo just shook her head. 'What house?'

'You and I were at the Mason home and a man came to the front door. He was the older guy who said his friend had not shown up for the fishing trip, remember? He knew we were police and asked if we could check it out as his buddy lived next door. We were next to the McKee house. Remember?' Lucas said.

'Yes,' said Jo. 'I remember, but ...' She still looked quizzical.

'Mechanic was watching. He saw me talk with the guy at the front door and he saw the moment when the realization dawned that Mechanic had killed the family next door. He saw that. He was there.'

Bassano chipped in. 'And that's what he means by "being one out you may as well be a thousand out". He was one number out with the house because there is no number 1313. That's how he ended up in the Mason place by mistake.'

'He must have been there. He must have been watching,' Lucas said for the third time, allowing his brain to process the implications.

'But how?' said Jo. 'How could he have seen what happened?'

'I don't know,' replied Lucas. 'Get this to the lab and let forensics have a go at it.' Lucas pointed to the note as he rose from his chair. 'And then both of you get out to the club and shake them up. I'm taking a drive out to the Mason place.'

Lucas jumped into his car and drove in total silence to 1316 Ridgeway Crescent, not knowing what he was looking for. The other two headed off knowing exactly what they would encounter: the well-tailored delights of Trevor Wainwright.

Chapter 33

Bassano and Jo Sells were travelling much too fast up the ornately bordered, tree-lined driveway of Brightwood Country Club. The large sandstone buildings came into view as they rounded a sharp bend, spitting gravel onto the immaculate lawn.

The car park was full but Bassano had no intention of driving around trying to locate a suitable space. He brought the car to a sliding stop right behind the cars parked in the designated bays. A member of staff scurried to the club house door, but Bassano was already up the steps and into the reception before he could do or say anything.

Bassano spoke to the woman behind the desk. Her name badge said Lucy Prigg.

'I need to speak with Trevor Wainwright, it's urgent.' He flashed his badge at her to stress the point. 'What happened to Melody?' She ignored his question.

'Mr Wainwright is in a board meeting right now and it won't be concluded for another hour or so. If you would like to take a seat,' she waved an elegant hand toward the soft seating area, 'I'm sure he will see you when he's out.'

Jo reached the reception desk just as Bassano was about to get angry. 'I'm not sure you quite get this, lady,' she said in a raised voice.

Bassano continued, 'I need to talk with Wainwright now. You can either tell him to come out and speak with me or I will have you arrested for obstruction and I will find the damn boardroom myself.'

Trying to maintain her poise, Lucy Prigg walked towards a pair of oak doors saying, 'I'll let him know you are here, detective.' She half looked over her shoulder and smiled with a well-practised falseness.

In the changing rooms, Sophie Barrock was sitting on a long wooden bench in front of the lockers with a huge white towel wrapped around her, feeling exceptionally pleased with herself. The last two hours had been fantastic. There was a new guy at the club who'd been coming on to her for weeks, well who could blame him. He was forever saying they needed to play tennis and he'd be gentle with her. He was ten years younger, good looking, had a ton of money and was a total flirt. She enjoyed the attention but, most of all, she enjoyed setting him up.

She played him along like the social pro that she was. The more he challenged her to a gentle game, the more she avoided it. This built up the expectation, and the more she gave the invitation the cold shoulder the more he upped the stakes. By the end, he had turned it into a showboat of a match, telling everyone he was going to teach her a thing or two. It was as if he considered the whole thing as foreplay, and Sophie was more than happy to allow a little club-house foreplay. This of course gave her a rich source of gossip, intrigue and innuendo for her hangers-on. The new guy was very interested in Sophie and consequently her female cronies were very interested in him.

'Are you sure this is just about the tennis, Sophie?' They would ask suggestively over a white wine spritzer by the pool. 'Will you be showering on your own that day, Sophie?' 'You must let us know how big his forehand is, Sophie.' The salacious comments and saucy suggestions spun the whole situation into a Sophie Barrock extravaganza. She was in her element.

When she judged the excitement had reached its peak she said yes. And, of course, the match attracted a large crowd of onlookers, mostly women, who were scrutinizing the new guy and speculating about what Sophie Barrock was going to be enjoying after the game. But that was never her primary goal.

She whooped his ass. She destroyed him on the court and beat him in straight sets. It was a hot day and she always played better in the heat. The hotter it got, the better she played. Under the blazing sun in thirty degrees heat she slaughtered him. He was outplayed in every aspect. She served better than him. She lobbed better than him. She volleyed better than him. She even hit the ball harder than him. She ran him around the court like a child chasing bubbles in the wind.

Sophie smiled as she walked over to the vanity mirrors, took a seat and dried her hair. She had been at her devastating best today, unstoppable.

Wainwright came marching through the large oak doors with Lucy Prigg in hot pursuit.

'This is outrageous,' he protested. 'You threaten to have one of my staff arrested because she is merely doing her job. This is intolerable.' Then he stopped and looked at Bassano and Jo Sells. 'Oh Lord, not you two again. This is harassment.'

It was then that he recalled their last encounter and looked over Bassano's shoulder to where the previous car park infringements had taken place. He almost had a seizure.

'That car is blocking three other vehicles. You will have to move it.' He flapped his arms at the offending car. As he'd run up the steps, Bassano had noticed that the name on one of the blocked parking spaces said 'Chairman'.

'Mr Wainwright, we need to speak with your entire club membership. Can you provide us with a list of names?'

'Certainly not,' came the blunt reply. 'Our members enjoy the strictest confidentiality and we are not in the habit of divulging personal details. It is out of the question.' He was preoccupied with the car parking situation and kept looking outside.

'We are conducting a very serious investigation which involves your club and it is imperative that we contact every one of your members,' Bassano persisted.

'And, as I have said before, we will not provide you with our membership listing because it is private. You will need a warrant or some such paperwork and, until I see that, the answer is no. Now if you don't mind I have a board meeting to conduct.'

'Mr Wainwright, your members may be in grave danger and we need to warn them. I need you to co-operate.'

'What are they at risk from, detective? Dodgy counselling perhaps? This whole thing is a pantomime and now, if you don't mind …' He turned and walked back to the oak doors to rejoin the board meeting.

'It turns out you lied to us sir,' Jo said in an authoritative voice. 'You do provide counselling services here.' She removed the poster from her bag and held it up for him to read.

He snatched the paper from her hand, put on a pair of wire-rimmed spectacles and read the document.

'This means nothing,' he said dismissively. 'This does not concern us.'

'It was found on your premises, so you do offer a counselling service. You lied.'

'I repeat,' Wainwright said as if he was talking to an idiot, 'this means nothing. Where did you get it from?'

'Melody gave it to us when we were last here. She found it here, at the club,' said Jo.

'Well that explains it,' said Wainwright laughing. 'We had to part company with Melody because she was, let's say, getting above herself.' He flashed a knowing look at Lucy Prigg who smiled back compliantly. 'This is nothing more than the workings of a disgruntled ex-employee, someone with a grudge.'

'But that doesn't figure. We turned up unannounced so Melody would not have known we had this as a line of enquiry. No, Mr Wainwright, this was found on your property. You do offer a counselling service and you need to co-operate. You lied.'

Sophie Barrock had finished drying her hair and was applying her make-up. All eyes would be on her when she made her entrance into the restaurant to join her loyal band of followers and she was going to look stunning. She packed her kit away in her bag and dressed in her newest country club attire which she'd bought for the occasion.

By now, Bassano had had enough of this prick giving them the brush off. Jo's reasoning had stopped Wainwright in his tracks and he was staring at the poster, wondering what his next move should be. He decided dismissal was the best course of action.

'I don't have time for this,' he said in his best schoolmaster style. 'Lucy, would you show these ...' he searched for the right word, '... people out.' He put the poster on the desk and once again turned to leave.

'Jo, when the officers arrive can you instruct them to arrest Mr Wainwright for a breach of the peace,' Bassano said.

'Er yes,' Jo looked bemused.

'Breach of the peace?' said Wainwright. 'You really are in fantasy land, Detective. I have a witness here in Miss Prigg who can testify to my good conduct and you are overstepping your authority.'

Bassano picked up the counselling poster and walked back to the front entrance.

'Where are you going?'

'I am going to speak with your membership.' And with that he swung his elbow and smashed the glass out of the square red box on the wall. A chorus of fire alarms screeched into action from every part of the complex. Bassano walked out of reception and down the steps to find the assembly points, behind him the breach of the peace was in full swing.

Sophie Barrock was putting the finishing touches to her victory look when the alarm above her head burst into life. The synthetic two-tone wailing was deafening and she cupped her hands over her ears.

'Damn,' she said, though in the closed environment of the changing rooms she couldn't hear her own voice. That was definitely not in the plan. She cursed, grabbed her bag and headed for the exit. 'Damn it,' she said again.

Her crowning glory for today was always going to be her triumphant walk into the dining hall, soaking up the adoration of her friends. A fire alarm meant that was not going to happen. The last time they had a false alarm people were kept outside at the assembly points for fifty minutes while the fire brigade swept the buildings and reset the system. She was not going to wait all that time. Sophie reluctantly made her way to her car, put her kit in the back and started the engine. Her triumph would have to keep till tomorrow.

As she drove through the car park, she heard a man with a megaphone saying, 'Can I have your attention please,' and holding a piece of paper in front of him. She didn't recognize him as being one of the stewards from the club and he wasn't wearing his regulation fluorescent tabard. Wainwright will be furious, she thought. As she got a little closer, he was also saying something about the police, which seemed a little odd because it was quite obviously the fire alarm that had gone off.

Sophie Barrock drove down the driveway and saw the chaos behind her disappear in the rear-view mirror. She tried to concentrate on her fantastic win rather than her missed lunch opportunity with her girls. She wasn't to know that it would be her last.

Chapter 34

Lucas sat on the hood of his car looking at the Mason property. To the left he could see the McKee house was still cordoned off with bright yellow tape. The front door of number 1316 was clearly visible. He had found what he was looking for.

He was about two hundred yards away, on a broken tarmac road which led to nowhere. He was parked at a higher elevation than the house and had a clear line of sight of the entire plot. Lucas was convinced this was where Mechanic had been when he'd opened the front door that day. He was also convinced that Mechanic had used this as a vantage point to carry out his reconnaissance prior to the killings. With half decent binoculars the spot offered a perfect view.

It felt odd to think that days earlier Mechanic had been in the very same location. Lucas cursed under his breath.

The other reason he needed to get out of the office was that he needed time to think away from the team. When he'd worked out what the note meant, his immediate reaction was that Jo Sells had been with him that day and the note was her work. She knew there was a moment when Lucas realized the real target was next door. Lucas considered this long and hard but then discarded it. Jo Sells was not in a position to know what had happened at the front door, she'd been in the lounge. There must have been another person able to see the front of the house. It must have been Mechanic.

There was another reason the note bothered him. Not in the same way it bothered Harper, he wasn't going to crack up. This was a high stakes game to Mechanic and he kept doing the unexpected with the specific intention of making them look like fools. And that's what bothered him most, it made him look a fool. And then of course there was the GAI Circles name which also made them look like fools. The raid on Ellis Baker's flat made them look like fools. This was a game and Mechanic was winning.

He slid into the driver's seat and reached for the radio mike.

'Get a message to Bassano. Tell him not to cut the phone line, he'll know what I mean.' Lucas stared into the middle distance. *I have a better idea*, he thought.

The rest of the day was a whirlwind of activity. The interviews and briefings at Brightwood Country Club had been productive. The members were falling over themselves to be helpful. They were forthcoming with information in the absence of Trevor Wainwright who was protesting wrongful arrest and police harassment as he was bundled into the back of a squad car. Back at the station he continued protesting but only a drunk and a small time drug dealer could hear him from the adjacent cells.

The picture emerging at the club was polarized along strict lines of gender. The men knew nothing of the existence of the counselling poster while the majority of women confirmed they had seen it. The reason for this split became obvious when they discovered it had been stuck behind the cubicle doors in the ladies' restrooms. Bassano and Jo Sells exchanged knowing glances. This again lent weight to the theory that Mechanic had a female helper.

Lucas had swept the vantage point for anything which could yield a fragment of evidence about Mechanic's presence. He came up with nothing, no tyre marks, no shoe prints, no litter, no nothing. It was surgically clean, Mechanic had made damn sure of it.

They met at the end of the day in the incident room. It was late and everyone was exhausted.

'We got a stack of intel from the club,' said Bassano, still smarting from Jo's comment about his inadequate training scores. 'They were keen to help and wanted to know how the club was involved. Loads of woman had seen the poster but no one we talked to had called the number. We have a list of the remaining people we still have to interview and we need to follow them up. And that phone line tracking you wanted me to check out with the techy guys, they said it should be possible. If it works it will be in place by mid-morning.'

'Good,' said Lucas, gathering up his papers and packing them into his briefcase. 'Well I sure found the place where the bastard watched me at the front door talking to that guy, but there was nothing to connect it to Mechanic.' He was sounding more in control. 'It's late,' he continued, 'let's make a fresh start on those numbers in the morning. But before we go, haven't you left something in the cells?'

'Yeah, I suppose I have,' said Bassano reluctantly. 'I'll drop by and see if Wainwright has been a good boy. I suggest we just drop the charges.'

'Sounds okay to me,' Jo agreed.

Bassano was relieved his boss wasn't going to suggest another all-nighter. He was in need of sleep and some alone-time to mend his dented ego.

'See you both tomorrow,' said Bassano. 'It feels like the balance is shifting in our favour at last. We've been on the front foot today and taking the fight to him.'

Eight hours later, when all three were sound asleep, the balance was about to shift away from them once more.

Chapter 35

Mechanic looked at the illuminated watch dial. It was 3.15am. The air was still but for the faint sea breeze blowing across the beach, while a watery half-moon spilled a silver glow onto the property.

The point of the scalpel cut easily into the mesh, creating a slit in the netting against the frame. Mechanic slid the blade along the edge, watching the black material gape open as it became detached. There was a soft buzzing noise as the sharp knife severed the individual strands. At the corner of the frame Mechanic twisted the scalpel and cut downwards against the metal support.

The flap of netting peeled away and Mechanic eased through the gap. Once on the other side, Mechanic reached into a small pocket, withdrew a roll of black insulation tape and wound off about two feet. Then ran the tape along the top part of the severed netting, sticking it back in place against the framework.

Mechanic crossed the decking and stood at the side of the double sliding doors, out of sight of anyone who might be inside the house, and waited. Listening for anything unusual, anything which could suggest the occupants were not soundly asleep. Nothing. The house was silent.

From another pocket Mechanic slid out two metal bars about an inch and a half round. Each bar had been flattened at one end to form a chiseled edge which curved upwards. The chisels were inserted into the runners at the bottom of the right-hand door until they stood proud like levers. Pushing downwards and pivoting them to the right the patio door lifted from the runners and released the locked catch on the door There was a soft metallic click. Mechanic pushed the levers down further and the whole door eased out. It was suspended in the air on the points of the metal bars.

This was the tricky part.

Mechanic shifted position and brought a well-worn toe cap under the base of the suspended door, supporting it so the levers could be removed. Placing them on the ground, Mechanic grasped the sides of the patio door and lowered the base down, leaning it against the other frame. Mechanic stepped inside and slid the door along the patio decking to an almost closed position. To the outside world nothing was amiss.

Standing in the lounge Mechanic couldn't help but compare it to the previous visit. Someone had been tidying up. The long pile rug near the fire place had the telltale signs of being freshly raked, magazines were stacked neatly under the coffee table and the coasters were all packed away in their ornate box. Even the oversized cushions were puffed up and placed at the ends of the sofas. Maybe today was the day the maid came.

Mechanic fought hard to control the rasping breaths escaping into the cool air of the living room as the adrenaline surged. Absorbing the ambient sounds of the property and tuning into the environment was always a pure rush, no other feeling came close. Now was the time to acclimatize. Mechanic stood and waited, eyes adjusting to the gloom.

Several minutes passed.

Everything was in order, it was time to move.

Sophie Barrock lived in a single-storey house which Mechanic always preferred, no creaking stairs to negotiate. The master bedroom was at the front left-hand corner of the villa adjacent to the hallway. The large TV in the corner beckoned, it was calling-card time.

Now that no one could be in any doubt about the authenticity of what was about to happen, Mechanic moved through the archway toward the bedrooms. The flooring changed from plush carpet to expensive wood block. Mechanic slowed to ensure the wood surface didn't squeak against the rubber-soled shoes. Intensive training had become second nature.

The bedroom door was ajar and the slow rhythmic sounds of deep sleep drifted through the gap. Mechanic went through the steps, the ones carefully rehearsed in the Pachelbel facilitated fantasy. No need to open the door fully, just enough to slip inside. The door glided across the flattened fibres of the carpet as Mechanic edged it open.

The heavy curtain drapes blocked out more light that the rest of the house. Mechanic's night vision needed to adjust. That was easily fixed – just breath easily, keep perfectly still and wait. Absorb the atmosphere and tune in. Soon the defined contours of two figures sleeping beneath white cotton covers came into focus.

One was much bigger than the other. Steve Barrock slept on the right. He stirred and threw his right arm out of the confines of the bedding and rolled over. Mechanic didn't move.

Then, when the breathing of deep sleep had returned, Mechanic unclipped the Browning M1911 from the side holster. It was already silenced which made the barrel look out of proportion to the body of the gun. Mechanic didn't need such a powerful handgun for close quarters work. It was .45 calibre which was way too big but in all the years of trying different sidearms this was always the preferred choice. The weight, the balance when the silencer was attached, the grip and the retort all felt just right. But most of all, it was the suppressed spit it made when Mechanic pulled the trigger which never failed to raise a smile.

Mechanic placed a gloved left hand on the frame at the foot of the bed and rattled it back and forth. Steve Barrock moved a little but didn't wake. Sophie Barrock didn't stir.

Mechanic shook the bed again, this time a little harder. Steve let out a low moan and turned over. Sophie didn't stir.

Mechanic shook the bed again, this time with enough force to cause the frame to make a creaking noise and the headboard to knock against the wall. Steve Barrock woke and sat up staring at the blurred image at the foot of the bed. This part always amused Mechanic. Inevitably the men were the ones to wake, and they would look straight at Mechanic, but it always took a while for the brain to yell 'intruder!' They would just stare and do nothing.

Mechanic kept the gloved left hand on the bed frame, levelled the gun at his forehead and, before he could make a sound, squeezed the trigger.

The gun went spit and the back of his head exploded.

The force catapulted him back and he was once again lying in bed. The back wall was decorated with a star burst of crimson. Sophie Barrock was sitting up in bed rigid with horror.

Mechanic replaced the weapon back in its holster and unclipped the rubber riot baton. Sophie was sat upright when the first back-handed blow struck her. It was aimed at her head but she instinctively put her arm up and deflected it. The baton smashed into her forearm and she yelled in pain. She was quicker than Mechanic had anticipated and, if that was unexpected, what came next was unprecedented.

Sophie leapt from the bed and flew at Mechanic screaming and punching, completely ignoring her broken radius. Mechanic took a step back and swung the baton again. Sophie ducked down and it caught her on the back of her shoulder blade. She screamed with pain but just kept coming low and hard.

Just as Mechanic took aim with what was to be the knockout blow to the back of Sophie Barrock's neck she snapped her head violently upwards, smacking Mechanic under the chin. Mechanic reeled backwards under the force of the blow. This was not supposed to happen. Sophie Barrock was strong and she was fast.

Mechanic tried to take a step back but Sophie bulldozed her way forward, catching Mechanic in the upper chest with her shoulder. Her legs kept pumping after the impact and they both toppled to the floor. The weight of the collision caused Mechanic to lose grip on the weapon and it rolled under the bed. Sophie was now on top with her head buried under Mechanic's chin and her arms swinging wildly.

Mechanic placed two strong arms around the back of Sophie's head and scissored her body with powerful legs, squeezing hard.

Sophie's face was crushed flat against Mechanic's chest and her furiously flailing arms and legs had nothing to grab or hit.

What had started as a fight for life was now a desperate fight for air. Sophie kicked against the bed but Mechanic maintained the crushing hold and squeezed the last drop of breath out of Sophie Barrock's burning lungs. She fought like a wild cat but Mechanic kept increasing the force. Finally, Sophie heard a loud crack in her head as her pretty aquiline nose broke under the pressure. That was the last thing she would recall as she went limp and blacked out.

Mechanic released her from the vice-like grip and rolled her onto her side. 'Bitch,' Mechanic said massaging a bruised jaw and feeling a loose back tooth. There was the unmistakable taste of blood.

Standing up, Mechanic retrieved the baton from under the bed and stood over the unconscious Sophie. Rolling her onto her back, Mechanic brought the baton down full force on Sophie Barrock's left kneecap. There was a loud crack as it splintered under the skin. Mechanic changed position and smashed it down onto the right kneecap. It disintegrated in the same way. Pockets of blood welled up under her skin and her legs began to turn black.

Mechanic rolled Sophie onto her stomach and extended her arms flat to the floor. The baton swished through the air and came down hard on Sophie Barrock's left elbow. Same with the right.

Blood spurted onto the carpet as jagged bones exited the flesh. Around her head a deep red pool of blood formed from her smashed nose.

Mechanic surveyed the damage, the calm and control returning. The kids were next and then the careful arrangement in the garage. The rest was child's play, except that is if you were one of Sophie Barrock's children.

Mechanic tied a gag over Sophie's mouth and stepped over her broken and bloodied body before walking to the other bedrooms.

'Now play tennis, *bitch*.'

Chapter 36

It was 8.30am and the sun was trying its best to penetrate the dust and grime of Lucas's office window. He stood with his second cup of coffee of the day, looking out at the commuters below busying their way to work. The note from Mechanic had rattled him. To think that he'd been so close made Lucas feel very uneasy.

The furious activity that followed had helped. They were finally getting results and that made everyone feel they were moving in the right direction.

Wainwright had behaved himself and Bassano discharged him with a caution and no transport home. The whole experience of being locked up in a cell had served to quiet him down considerably, and he was in complete compliance mode when he left the station. Melody would have loved the transformation.

Lucas took a slurp from his mug and ran through the key tasks for the day. Finishing the interviews with the Brightwood members was top priority – they had gained a ton of new information yesterday. The only problem was that Lucas wanted to keep the team to a minimum, so it was going to be time-consuming. Then there was the forensics team working on the note. Plus another visit to Ellis Baker to see if his flat had been used while he was out of the country. Lucas was feeling good and, to top it all, his wife was due back from her conference that evening. Another reason for it to be a good day.

The phone rang, breaking his chain of thought. He put the coffee on the coaster and lifted the receiver. 'Lucas.'

It was an out-of-breath Bassano.

'Sir, it looks like we've got another one. Westfield Park. The response guys called it in fifteen minutes ago.'

'Fuck,' said Lucas thumping his hand onto the desk. 'I'm on my way, and get Jo Sells over there, I want her to see this first-hand.'

'I tried that, sir, but I can't reach her. She left a message at the desk early this morning saying something about a cracked filling and a dentist.'

'Okay, I'll meet you there, we can talk then.' Lucas slammed down the receiver and stormed out of his office, not feeling quite so good about the day.

Ten miles across town Mechanic was just getting up and experiencing the usual feelings of decompression from the activities of the night. There was a notable difference though. Mechanic had never before had to spit blood into the sink from a loosened back tooth and a badly bitten tongue. Mechanic looked in the mirror with mouth open wide and head tilted back, trying to survey the damage. Couldn't see a damn thing, except the ugly gash along the side of the tongue.

The need for a sugar fix was making Mechanic shake. First job was to fill the toaster with strawberry Pop-Tarts and put the kettle on to boil. To make matters worse Mechanic's jaw hurt like hell, hopefully the painkillers washed down with tap water would help. Mechanic winced as the cold water hit the offending tooth. 'Damn,' Mechanic muttered.

The Pop-Tarts bounced out of the toaster slots with a metallic clatter. Mechanic put four of them onto a small plate and reloaded two more slots. They were difficult to eat – the hot jam burned and chewing was a real problem. But the sugar was good and the first tart was quickly gobbled up. The kettle flicked itself off as the water boiled and Mechanic poured it into an oversized mug, with instant coffee and mounds of sugar. The second Pop-Tart was well on its way to disappearing. The sugar craving subsided and Mechanic walked into the lounge. The red light on the phone said that no one had called. Kaitlin had managed to go through a whole day without ringing to offload her latest set of neuroses. There was an urgent rapping on the front door.

Looking at the clock on the wall Mechanic tutted at the inconvenience of such an early interruption, disposing of the third Pop-Tart. Mechanic opened the door. 'Hey! This is surprise, come in.'

'We need to talk,' said Dr Jo Sells.

Chapter 37

Lucas could see the squad car's blue and red flashing lights long before he reached Sophie Barrock's house. The in-car briefing was a little scant on details, but it appeared that she'd regained consciousness while Mechanic was still at the property but was too terrified to move. The asphyxiation had not been so severe as to cause brain damage but she was physically in a bad way.

Sophie had waited until Mechanic left the house before somehow dragging herself eight feet along the carpet to the bedside table. She pulled the phone onto the floor and dialed 911. She couldn't speak but just left the line open. During her struggle toward the phone, she kept passing out from a mixture of pain and lack of oxygen. The gag prevented her breathing through her mouth and her shattered nose prevented the passage of air. She lost count of the number of times the darkness descended and she went to that woozy place where her body no longer hurt. That simple act of travelling eight feet had taken her almost one and a half hours to complete.

Fifteen minutes later two police officers smashed their way through the side window and entered the scene of carnage.

She had lost a lot of blood and when the response officers arrived they felt unable to move her due to the extent of her injuries. The bedroom carpet looked like the floor of a busy abattoir. With her twisted limbs and blood-soaked nightwear, Sophie Barrock resembled nothing more than a carcass.

Mechanic had dispatched the children while they were both asleep and pulled Steve Barrock out of bed by his feet. His head disintegrated into the carpet pile when it hit the floor. Mechanic dragged his body across the bedroom and over Sophie Barrock. Later she would learn that much of the blood she'd been covered in was in fact her husband's.

The officers concentrated on Sophie until one of them followed the trail of blood leading to the garage. Shining his service-issue flashlight into the window of the Dodge Sebring made the officer think twice before touching anything else. The kids were seat-belted into the back and Steve Barrock was in the driving seat with his hands placed at the ten to two position on the steering wheel.

Lucas parked his car and walked to the house. He was greeted by a uniformed officer and he flashed his badge. The officer nodded and lifted the yellow tape to allow Lucas to step onto the driveway. He made his way to the front door, donned a pair of forensic overshoes and went inside the slaughterhouse.

Chapter 38

Jo sat on the edge of the soft leather sofa, leaning forward with her hands clasped tight in her lap. 'You have got to stop,' she cried, tears of frustration welling in her eyes.

'Don't see why, honey,' Mechanic replied. 'Everything is fine and, anyhow, I have you as my guardian angel. What could go wrong?' The fourth Pop-Tart disappeared off the plate. 'Coffee?'

'I've not come here to drink damned coffee.'

'I appreciate your concern but everything is going well. I mean it won't—'

Jo Sells cut Mechanic off mid-sentence.

'You've killed again haven't you?' Jo said, with complete disbelief, noticing the Pop Tarts and the vacant look on Mechanic's face. 'You've done another family haven't you?' She raised her voice as she stood up.

'You know I can't help it, now sit down and chill out,' said Mechanic. 'It went fine. Bit of bother with the woman but on the whole it went like clockwork. That one should buy us time.' Mechanic minimized the problem Sophie Barrock had caused in an attempt to feel better about the previous night.

'Jesus Christ!' Jo yelled. 'You have to stop. I can't protect you like last time. This Lucas guy is not like Harper, he *will* find you,' she emphasized the word 'will'. 'I'm sure he already has his suspicions about me, this guy is a thinker and he's good. You have to get out while you still have time.'

'Stopping isn't part of the plan, honey. You know when this gets hold of me we just have to go along for the ride. I can keep it a bay for a while but then … bang. Anyway, we are okay, aren't we? I have you to give me top cover. Sooner or later it will stop, and then so will I,' said Mechanic.

'What do you mean *we*? You're not listening, I can't give you the top cover you need. Lucas is different, he will burn me and catch you unless you disappear fast. It's the only way we can get through this unscathed.' Jo sounded desperate.

'You sorted it last time and you'll sort it this time. Anyway it was a great idea to send him a nice little love letter, don't you think?' Mechanic was being playful.

Jo interrupted. 'You don't get it do you? Lucas isn't going to fall apart in the same way Harper did, the notes won't have the same effect. If anything they only served to make him think clearer and act with more conviction. You have to get it into your head he is not Harper.'

'He can be destabilized. I'm sure the next personal message from me will do the trick.'

'Listen to yourself,' Jo shouted. 'Get it through your thick skull, it won't happen like last time. You can't just knock this guy off course with a note.'

'Then we need to fucking find something that will.' The violence of the words filled the room. Jo recoiled, frightened.

'For Christ sake stop saying *we*, this is about you. You're the fucking psycho, not me. You're killing these people, not me.'

Jo balled her hands into fists.

Mechanic broke the uneasy silence. 'Were you followed?'

'Yes, I made a point of getting myself tailed … No, I wasn't.' The tension between them defused and Jo brought herself under control.

'And where are you supposed to be now?'

'At the dentist.' Then the realization dawned. 'Shit, if you've killed another family Lucas will want me there when they find it. I gotta go.'

'Drop by when you have more time and we can get a takeout,' Mechanic said, as if inviting a friend around to play video games.

'A fucking takeout! We need to get you the hell out of here and far away, not eat fucking takeout.'

'Come on, it would be nice to spend more time together, and anyway you work too hard.'

Jo's face was glowing pink. 'The reason why I have to work so damn hard is because you keep killing people and I have to cover it up.' She marched to the door, stopped, took a deep breath and tried to regain her composure. 'You have to stop and you have to stop now. We have to plan an exit strategy and get you out of here.'

'Last time worked like a dream.'

Jo turned to face Mechanic and shook her head, 'We can't do that again it wouldn't work. We need to come up with something else.' She was sounding desperate. 'We need to make it happen quickly. He's closing in and I am not in a position to prevent it. You need to buy a ticket and get on a Greyhound bus to anywhere but here.'

'I can't, it's not done yet, I'm sure a couple more and that will be it.'

'You have to control this better. You have to buy us time. I can sort it out but only if you stop.' Jo was pleading with Mechanic. 'Are you still on the meds?'

'Yes I am, but all the psycho tabs in the world don't help when he gets hold of me. You know what it's like. I'm trying as hard as I can. I'll see what I can do but I can't promise anything. I love you and I love the way you're always there to look after me.'

'But I can't look after you. Not this time. This time is different. Lucas is different. He will catch you if we don't move fast, and you have to play your part and co-operate.'

'Look, I'll work at keeping myself in check, if you promise to visit me again soon. I love seeing you, I miss you. You think through what we need to do next and get in touch when you're ready.'

'I have to get back,' said Jo. 'You've heard what I said, right? You have to stop this, I can't save you this time.'

'Okay, okay, I get it.' Mechanic had the demeanour of a naughty child getting a slapped wrist. 'You'll come and visit, though, right?'

'I will, we need to get you out of here. I gotta go.'

'Love you,' Mechanic called out as Jo let herself out.

Jo drove back to the station frantically rehearsing her trip-to-the-dentist speech. She was acutely aware that Lucas and Bassano were probably, at that very moment, staring at three dead bodies safely seat-belted into their family car.

Chapter 39

Sophie Barrock was down but she was certainly not out. As the lift doors opened onto floor 7A, Bassano could hear her. He had been en route to the latest kill site when the call came in that Sophie Barrock was conscious and wanted to talk. That was an understatement.

He stepped out onto the polished hospital floor which reflected the overhead strip lighting back into his eyes. The smell of hand sanitizer and disinfectant was overpowering. He looked at the scribbled piece of paper in his hand: 7A ward 6. He didn't know where that was but all he had to do was follow the noise. Sophie Barrock was in a side ward and shouting at the top of her voice.

'Get away from me with that fucking stuff. I don't want sedation until I've talked to them. Where the fuck are the police?' she yelled. 'Are you sure you've told them I'm ready to talk? I need to talk with them now.'

Bassano sidestepped the male nurse as he scurried out of the room and peered inside. Sophie was flat on her back in a four-way traction device, with crepe bandages wrapped across her busted face. Her legs were so badly broken she probably wouldn't walk unaided for the rest of her life. And she would be lucky to take the top off a jar of cooking sauce, let alone strike a tennis ball again. A knitted braid of tubes were stuck into her wrists and saline and morphine bags hung from chrome poles by the side of her bed. Both her eye sockets were yellow and black and she stared fiercely out of a swollen face. Mechanic had broken her body for sure, but one thing was clear, her spirit was ferociously intact.

Bassano introduced himself and before he could retrieve the chair from the corner of the room she started.

'I hit the bastard hard and decked the fucker,' she said as Bassano manoeuvred the chair trying to avoid the drips and traction cables. He had the look of a man under siege.

'I nailed him with my head but he was too strong. I nearly had the bastard. I could have taken him.'

'Any distinguishing features?'

'Well officer, apart from the black outfit, the ski mask, the gun and the baseball bat, er ... let me think. No, nothing really to go on. What sort of question is that?'

Bassano wished he could start again.

She continued, 'He was strong but he was relatively short.'

'What do you mean?'

'When I floored him he was standing and I was crouched. My head was under his chin, which would make him around five feet nine. That's short for most of the men I know. And he was kind of narrow about the shoulders.'

'Narrow?' Bassano was unused to someone being described as narrow.

'Yes, narrow. You know, most men have broad shoulders. They tend to taper in at the waist. You know the classic V shape. This one didn't.'

'Not V-shaped,' Bassano repeated the words, wondering if the drip going into her arm was contributing to the strange description of Mechanic – short and narrow, not V-shaped.

'Was there anything else which might be of help to us?' Bassano asked.

'I can't think of anything more. He was fast and strong. It was dark and I did my best. I fought for my family.' Sophie started sobbing uncontrollably. Tears pooled at the fringes of her bandaged face and were absorbed into the soft material.

She turned her face away from Bassano and cried, 'My babies. My fucking babies.' The tears flowed freely.

Hearing the commotion, a stern looking female doctor came into the room followed by the nurse. 'This has to stop, officer. Mrs Barrock cannot exert herself, she's experienced severe trauma.' She went straight up to her patient. 'You have to rest. I'm going to give you something to help you sleep. You won't be any use to anyone if you relapse.' Sophie Barrock was still sobbing and nodded her head in agreement as the nurse adjusted a line going into her arm and she started to relax.

'Just one more minute. No more,' the doctor instructed and left the room.

After a while Bassano said softly 'Do you want to stop? I can come back later.' He got up to leave.

'There was one thing.' Sophie's voice was a bit slurred. 'When the bastard crushed my face to his chest and I blacked out, I remember two things. My nose gave way with a crack like a thunderbolt in my head and ... breasts.'

'Breasts?' Bassano repeated, as if he had not heard the word before in his life.

'Yes breasts. I was crushed into the chest of a man with breasts.'

Bassano was a little lost for words, 'I'm not sure I understand.'

'The bastard crushed my face into his chest with a force you would not believe. It bust my fucking nose it was that strong. But before I blacked out I remember thinking breasts.'

Bassano scribbled in his book. He was losing Sophie to the effects of the drugs.

'I have one more question, Mrs. Barrock.' He said, 'were you receiving telephone counselling?'

'Yes.' She looked at him through the tears.

'And, was it delivered by a woman?'

'Yes it was.'

Bassano thanked her for her help, put the chair back against the wall and left. The sound of gentle sobbing followed him all the way to the lift. He looked at his notebook – short, narrow, not V shaped, with breasts. It was a hell of a message to deliver to his boss.

Chapter 40

Lucas stayed forty minutes at the Barrock house soaking up what he wished he didn't have to. Then a rerouted call broke into his darkness, it was Harper. He needed to meet and it needed to be now.

Lucas was way over his tolerance for blood, gore and tragedy and found an excuse to leave. Driving to the agreed rendezvous he was cursing his poor powers of persuasion. Try as he might he could not convince Harper to meet him anywhere else but the damn stinking coffee bar.

When he'd taken the call over the radio he'd suggested alternatives. 'What about Denny's? It's light and airy and has air-conditioning.'

'No,' was all he got in return, so he thought he'd try something little more earthy.

'What about the truck stop on the corner of the next block? That one serves great coffee in mugs that are big enough for you to drown in. And what's more the woman who runs the place has a cleavage that's also big enough for you to drown in.' *A winner all round,* Lucas thought.

'No,' Harper insisted. It had to be the coffee shop that had nothing going for it, and from what Lucas remembered, didn't even contain breathable air.

Lucas got out of the car, walked down a flight of steps and leaned against the door. He took a deep breath and entered, allowing his eyes and lungs to become accustomed to the toxic interior. The place stank of stale smoke and the fog of a hundred cigarettes hugged him like a stinking blanket. Lucas was wearing his oldest suit. His favourite one was at the dry cleaners, following his previous visit. He picked his way around the randomly placed tables which contained equally random occupants, and made his way to the back where Harper was already seated. Lucas drew a chair up and joined him.

He noticed Harper was sitting with nothing to drink. The customary sludge was missing.

'You want coffee?' Lucas asked.

'Damn thing is being cleaned or serviced or something.' Lucas looked at the bar and saw chrome-plated pieces of coffee machine strewn across the top. The owner was scrubbing, cursing and replacing bits of pipework and filters back into the reluctant machine. Lucas noticed that none of the people at the tables had coffee, except one. Harper followed his gaze to the only guy holding a cup.

'His tasted like iron filings. That's how Jake knows when it needs taking apart, when he gets iron filings.'

'Oh,' said Lucas. 'No coffee then.' He was relieved.

Harper looked okay. His hair still looked like he'd spent forty minutes in a wind tunnel but he was clean shaven, and smelled like he'd had a bath. His hands weren't shaking but he kept them on the table with one on top of the other just in case. He had lost his ashen grey colour and his eyes were a little brighter.

'How have you been?' asked Lucas.

Harper surmised that the question was directed at the state of his health. 'Bit unsteady at times but coping alright considering.'

'You said you had more information.'

'I do, but first I have a question,' Harper said.

'Go on.'

'When you found out the sex of the person providing the counselling, how did you reach the conclusion that Mechanic was being helped by a woman?'

Lucas thought for a moment. 'We didn't really reach a conclusion, I suppose. Jo called it and we just accepted what she said.'

It was Harper's turn to be thoughtful. He said nothing.

'Why do you ask?'

'Let me answer by telling you what I've found.'

'You had luck with the boyfriends then?'

'Not exactly, what I have concerns Jo's sister and it's pretty crazy stuff.'

'Her sister?' Lucas sounded surprised. 'Jessica wasn't it?'

Harper nodded. 'The last time we met, I told you Jessica Sells was a high flyer in the army and she'd been discharged for some really heavy shit.'

'Yes, I remember.'

'Well my guy has turned over a shedload more.' Harper paused to collect himself. 'She worked in a programme which was top secret. You know the type, eyes only and very hush hush. Not sure if it was black ops, but it was way off the mainstream, and definitely covert. That's why my guy struggled to make any headway.'

Lucas put his hand on Harper's arm to stop him. 'If that's true, how did you get hold of it? Is it reliable?'

'To take the last question first, yes this is genuine. And as for the first question, I think you would call it the act of a concerned citizen. However, back in my day,' Harper paused to enhance the theatrical timing, 'we called it blackmail.' Lucas backed off and let him continue.

'She specialized in undercover work, and saw active service in a number of missions all over the world. She was a signals and telecoms genius and was deployed into some high profile hot spots. Jess was heavily trained in special ops and got top marks. She was a weapons and explosives expert, a counterintelligence specialist, and was as tough as any marine. There are documented accounts of her having to fight her way out of tight situations. On more than one occasion she was forced to hit the eject button and be airlifted out, but not before inflicting a shit load of collateral damage. She was a serious piece of work. My guy tells me she was highly regarded and never failed to deliver. She got the hottest and most difficult assignments because she was that good. She was decorated three times: a Purple Heart, an Army Commendation Medal and a Distinguished Service Cross, they don't give those away for fun.'

'So why the dramatic fall from grace?'

'She was sent to a research facility attached to a military base. There was a suspicion one of the guys was passing secrets to the Russians. The target had an extravagant lifestyle which was not in keeping with his salary so they sent in Jessica Sells to investigate. She had recently returned from a particularly hot operation in Belize, which not even my guy could get near, so my reckoning is it got ugly. This research job was meant to be a little R and R for her. It was a playground gig compared to what she usually did, and should have been a soft job.'

'So what happened?'

'It went bad,' Harper said flatly. 'She integrated herself into the team and came to the conclusion that the guy was clean. He was just a lucky gambler and the cars and expensive purchases was him enjoying his winnings. So that was fine. What was not fine was that she was with the target and a few other work colleagues in a bar when a group of soldiers fresh from a tour in Somalia came in for beers. They'd been sent to the base to decompress after a hectic tour of duty. They were still high from their time in theatre and were throwing their weight around. What started out as lively conversation soon turned nasty. They took a dislike to Jessica Sells and her friends and started shooting their mouths off. Jessica tried to defuse the situation but they were just too far gone. She was worried she might be compromised – any trouble involving the police might blow her cover so she was keen to get out of there. But these guys wouldn't let it drop and they wouldn't let them leave the bar.'

'What happened next?'

'Well eventually it got physical and one of the men who Jessica worked with took a real beating. She kept well out of the way and waited for it to stop, while the bar owner called the cops.

The guy was in a bad way so Jessica went to help the injured man and patch him up. One of the soldiers took exception to this and went for her.'

'And?'

'She broke his arm in three places, knocked out two of his teeth and fractured his eye socket. Like I said, she was a real piece of work.'

'Shit. Why did she do that? She should have just backed off to protect her cover.'

'Yeah, I agree. I can only put it down to instinct and training. The soldier lunged at her and that was it, she tore him apart.'

'But how does that constitute being discharged? The army doesn't discharge everyone who has a brawl in a bar, there would be no one left.'

Harper nodded. 'You're right, but it didn't end there. When the cops arrived to break it all up she was still beating the crap out of this guy. Two of the soldiers weren't happy their friend had got a kicking, especially from a woman, so they followed Jessica when she left the bar. It all goes a bit fuzzy after that, but what is clear is at some point they jumped her, knocked her out, and dragged her into an alleyway,' Harper looked up at Lucas, 'and they raped her at knife-point.'

'Hell, this just gets worse.'

Harper took a deep breath. 'They had her on the ground with her hands above her head. The first guy, Private Benjamin Stanek knelt on her arms and held a knife to her throat. The second man, Corporal Winston Westgate stripped her from the waist down and raped her. Stanek held the knife so tight to her throat that she was cut pretty deep. The movement of the other guy banging away caused the knife to slice her up. She regained consciousness during the rape but just let them get on with it. She didn't fight back, didn't struggle. She just lay there and let it happen.'

'She didn't fight at all? That's weird given what you've told me.'

'Yeah it is. She seemed to zone out. She just disengaged. They raped her and she did nothing. That was until the men went to swap places and that's when she struck.'

'Struck?'

'Yeah, while they were concentrating on pulling pants up, pulling pants down and handing over the knife, she killed them both.'

'Shit.' Even in the gloom it was plain to see Lucas had his mouth open.

'Not sure of the exact turn of events, but the result was she snapped Benjamin Stanek's neck and he died at the scene. Westgate later died from massive blood loss and organ failure.'

'She stabbed him?'

'Not exactly. She beat him to a pulp and then sliced off his cock and balls.'

'Fuck.'

'She cut off his bits and pieces, went to a pay phone, called an ambulance and left,' said Harper.

'Why would she do that?'

'The only reason I can think of is that she didn't want him dead. She phoned for the medics so he would have a chance of living, but minus his genitals.'

'Hell, that's calculating,' said Lucas.

'The ambulance got there quickly and he lived for a couple of days. What Jess didn't bargain for was the military police getting hold of what had happened so quickly. They transferred Stanek's body and Westgate to the military base. They froze the police out. You know what the military are like for taking care of their own dirty laundry. Of course, in that environment, Westgate spilled the beans, and after a couple of days the MPs turned up at Jessica Sells' place. By this time Westgate had died too so it was a double homicide and the army weren't keen on one of their brightest and best being the number one suspect. They were eager to make a fast arrest and tidy the mess up quietly.'

'But I don't get it. After a couple of days she would have washed her clothes and scrubbed herself down. They would have struggled to make the DNA fit. All she had to do was deny it. This doesn't figure. There were only the three of them so it was his word against hers and he was dead. She could have covered her tracks and got away with it.' Lucas looked puzzled.

'Wow, slow down there, Lieutenant,' said Harper. 'Don't forget the knife made a mess of her neck and her blood was at the scene. But that didn't matter because when the MPs entered Jessica's flat they found all the DNA they needed.'

'How come?'

'They found Westgate's cock and balls in a glass jar on her dressing table. It was a bit of a giveaway.'

'Holy shit,' Lucas said.

'They took her into custody and during her interrogation she played it cool. After all, the army had spent a million dollars training this woman to cope in these types of situation, she was better equipped than they were. She said that if they pressed charges she would be forced to disclose why she was there, which would blow the lid off the covert op. Also, there were the families of the two dead guys to take into consideration. Did the army really want to make public the true reason for their deaths? It would be a publicity nightmare. She stood up to them and drove through a plea bargain. There was no court-martial and she accepted a discharge in return for sweeping it under the rug. No further action was ever taken.'

'And then?' Lucas asked.

'She came out of the army and it all goes blank.'

'How do you mean blank?' asked Lucas.

'She just fell off the grid. My source is good and well placed. We can only conclude she changed her name, set up a new identity and disappeared. If she is still out there, we can't trace her. No housing records, driving licence, credit card references, social security number, healthcare claims, nothing. The list goes on and comes up with nothing.'

Lucas snapped back to why he was there in the first place. 'That's a fascinating story but what does it have to do with Mechanic?'

'Well, I keep hearing your words about always looking in the wrong place. I think we've been looking in the wrong place again.

It's why I asked the question at the start: how did you reach the conclusion Mechanic had a female helper?'

'Sorry, Harper, I can't see where this is going. I don't get it.'

'We turned over every stone in Jo's past regarding possible boyfriends. Not a thing. After a very lively time with the opposite sex at college, Jo Sells went celibate. We found no one, not even a quick fumble.' Harper took an audible intake of breath, as if to steady himself for what was about to come next. 'I believe Jo isn't protecting a boyfriend. She's protecting her sister.'

Lucas recoiled back in his seat as if he'd been shot. 'That's nuts.'

'Is it? The only reason you think it's nuts is because it's a woman. If you switch the gender, and put a brother or boyfriend into the equation, it becomes a logical conclusion given what we know. Also, you didn't make the supposition about the female helper, Jo did. She put that idea in your head and you went for it. I don't believe there is a helper, it's the same person. It's Jessica Sells. And I believe Jessica Sells is Mechanic.'

Lucas considered it carefully. Someone who was ex-army, special-forces trained, exceptionally bright and psycho would fit the bill completely. There would also need to be the other social triggers to make a monster but it would fit the Mechanic profile perfectly. It would also provide the rationale for why Jo would cover for that person. The fact that the counselling was being delivered by a woman was too close to home for Jo so she misled them with the woman helper argument. Harper was right, they were all eager to buy it because it conveniently fitted the picture. Lucas sat back in his uncomfortable wooden chair and folded his arms. The silence between them was broken by an angry hissing sound from the direction of the bar.

'Gotcha, you little bastard.' The owner said to the machine. 'Coffee's back on,' he said to his customers who waved their hands in the air, a gesture which meant 'Yes, a coffee would be good, thanks.' He lined up a row of ill matching cups and mugs. Lucas wondered if Harper had any further revelations in his box of tricks. He was mulling over the implications of what he'd just heard and the prospect of having to suffer the consequences of a longer stay, coffee of questionable origin and another trip to the dry cleaner.

Harper reached into his jacket pocket and pulled out a dilapidated wallet stuffed to bulging with till receipts. He flicked through and picked out a folded piece of photocopied paper, flattened it out on the table and slid it in front of Lucas. It depicted a small grainy black and white photograph. Lucas lifted it from the table and tilted it against the light. He frowned.

The photo was a head and shoulders shot of Jo Sells dressed in an army parade uniform, her cap under her arm against a backdrop of a large stars and stripes flag. She was smiling broadly into the camera.

Lucas looked at Harper. 'But Jo wasn't in the forces. She went straight to Quantico from college.'

'That's right,' Harper said. 'But that's not her. That's Jessica Sells when she passed out of officer training. Jo and Jessica Sells are identical twins.'

Chapter 41

Lucas sat on the wooden bench in St Clement's gardens and stared into space. He often came here when he needed to push life's reset button and the way life was going lately it was badly in need of pushing.

He was very troubled. It felt as though he was constantly off balance. As if he'd lost his safe pair of hands and kept dropping the ball. He was losing control and drowning.

He thought about Mechanic and how he and his team were being led by the nose. Every time they believed they were making progress, it had been engineered by Mechanic. And more frustratingly, it always turned into a blind alley. And now Jo had once again set them off on a wild goose chase. She'd had them looking for a second person which conveniently explained away the identity of the counsellor as a woman. This was making Lucas angry. He had to be radical, he had to change tack and do something unexpected. He had to take a course of action which Mechanic had not already choreographed for him.

The conversation with Harper was a turning point. He now knew something which Mechanic hadn't gifted to him. He had an edge at last. The big question was how could he use it to jolt the investigation back in his favour?

He looked at his watch. In the distance he saw them coming, right on time. This was a special place for Lucas because he'd discovered them by accident one day sitting in the park fumbling with the reset. It happened at more or less the same time every day in the summer months. Hundreds and hundreds of tiny birds flying in tight formation across the park, swooping down to the ground en masse to devour insects from the meticulously tended grass. They flew through the air morphing into complex shapes as though they were a single organism. Why they did this at the same time every day, Lucas hadn't a clue, but they did. You could almost set your watch by it.

He watched as they plundered their way around the park consuming their prey. In their tight cluster formation they weren't afraid of the human traffic passing by, and soon Lucas was surrounded by the tiny killers. They flooded the ground where he sat and then, without any discernible signal, lifted off and flew to the next spot.

As they got further away, Lucas focused on his course of action. It was clear what he needed to do but there was a problem. It was an all-or-nothing strategy. If it worked he would be a hero, if he was wrong he would be dead meat for sure. For him there was no option. It had to be all in. The reset button had been pushed.

Bassano sat in Lucas's office fidgeting with his watch strap waiting for his boss to return. His notebook sat on the conference table opened to the page which he was sure would be met with ridicule and anger. Short and narrow, not V shaped with breasts. Bassano had a sinking feeling which intensified when he heard Lucas coming up the corridor. Lucas entered the office and cut straight to the chase.

'What did she say?'

'Well, she was agitated and aggressive.'

'So would you be in her position. What did she say?'

'She was full of drugs and the details of what happened were a little strange.' Bassano was determined to put off the inevitable as long as possible.

'She's in shock,' Lucas offered. 'What did she say?'

'She was ranting when I got there but then broke down in tears.' Bassano was dancing around the subject.

Lucas lost patience. 'Well, as you aren't going to tell me what she said I'll tell you my news.' He got up and closed the office door. 'I've just spoken with Harper and there is strong circumstantial evidence that Mechanic could be Jo's twin sister.' Lucas paused and was expecting a howl of derision. But none came. Bassano looked at his open notebook on the table, reached over and closed it.

'Thank fuck for that,' he replied, which was not at all the reaction Lucas was expecting. 'Sophie Barrock gave a description which also suggests she was attacked by a woman.'

'How come?' said Lucas.

'Well amongst other things her attacker had tits.' Bassano was feeling a lot braver now. 'Sophie Barrock's face was crushed into Mechanic's chest so hard it bust her nose and she blacked out. But before everything went dark she recalls thinking breasts. How did Harper come to the same conclusion?'

'He uncovered some heavy shit about Jo's sister which fits Mechanic's profile. She's ex-army and trained in covert ops. She has a clutch of combat medals and, among other things, was a signals and telecoms expert. She was also a total psycho and got herself discharged after killing two soldiers, American ones that is. And when she came out she disappeared and just fell off the grid. It gives Jo a compelling motive to provide cover. It all fits.' Both men sat in silence.

'Where's Jo now?' asked Lucas.

'She's at the Barrock house following her trip to the dentist.'

'Get the tech guys in here. It's about time we did some fishing of our own.'

Chapter 42

It was late afternoon when Jo returned to the station. Her time at the Barrock house had been spent looking at blood splatter patterns, checking their angles of incidence with walls and furniture in an attempt to piece together the chain of events. She'd also assessed every minute detail of the figures in the car and the bloodied pathways to determine the sequence and method of loading. All of which was a charade performed for the benefit of the forensic guys because in reality all she had to do was pick up the phone and ask Mechanic what happened.

She entered the incident room to find Lucas and Bassano deep in conversation.

'Are you sure it'll work? These technical jerks are never very reliable,' said Lucas.

'They said yes. I tested it out and got the message so I think it's a goer.' Bassano was sounding positive.

'Hey,' said Jo. 'Sorry I missed out this morning. I went straight to the house after the dentist. It's trademark Mechanic, a total bloodbath.'

'I know. It's nasty. Did you get anything?' said Lucas.

'I might have new insight into the bodies in the car. I reckon he dragged the husband into the garage and left him on the floor while he went back for the children. The blood is pooled at the offside of the vehicle near the driver's door. This is the same MO as other kill sites.'

'Nothing specific to go on then?' asked Bassano.

'Well, it again represents a consistent and repeating pattern. It must have some meaning for Mechanic, just not sure what. I need to work on it.' Jo went to get a coffee.

'We've decided to go on the offensive,' Lucas said.

'Oh, how?' Jo said looking over her shoulder as she filled a Styrofoam cup, reached for a handful of sugar packets and began the unconscious ritual of making another sugar twist. Bassano lifted the receiver on the desk phone next to him, punched in some numbers and offered it to Jo. She put it to her ear and heard the tinny but unmistakeable tones of Chris Bassano on the line. She looked at him as the message played, transfixed by what she heard. She was silent.

'The technical department have worked out a way of putting a repeating message loop onto the phone line. When someone calls Mechanic's number they will hear the message.' Bassano looked pleased with himself.

'But how does that work? I thought you said we couldn't trace Mechanic's line, so how do they know …' she said, not finishing the sentence, still holding the receiver to the side of her head.

'Still can't,' replied Bassano. 'This just creates an open line so anyone dialling in gets this message.'

It was Lucas's turn to sound upbeat. 'The message tells the caller they are in danger and this is not a hoax. It also tells them to get in touch with us as soon as possible. Maybe Mechanic's next victim will call and we'll get an undamaged person to question. It might also give us more intelligence on his whereabouts.'

Jo replaced the receiver in the cradle having listened to the entire loop.

'How long has it been …?' Jo said, again not completing the sentence.

'We've had it up and running for about two hours now,' said Bassano.

'If it's an open line then presumably Mechanic can hear it as well?'

'Yeah, that's the downside. It wouldn't operate any other way. The boffins have worked hard with the phone company and I agree it would be better if only the caller got the message, but that's the problem with an open line, everyone can hear. It's far from perfect but it's worth a shot,' said Lucas.

'And have you had any luck?' Jo continued, still looking preoccupied.

'No,' replied Bassano. 'If I'm honest, I think it's a long shot but it's worth a try. We know Mechanic goes fishing so we thought we'd give it a go. The other piece of news is Sophie Barrock is conscious. She had some useful information to tell us.'

'Go on,' said Jo sipping her coffee, trying hard to pull her raging thoughts away from the implications of the phone message.

'She was also receiving counselling in the same way as the others, she is pretty lucid and angry as hell. She fought with Mechanic and put up a good show, so we are in the process of getting a physical description from her. Also, there's a good chance that in the fight Mechanic left behind some forensics. I think we're onto something,' said Bassano.

'And there's more,' he continued. 'We checked out Mr IT Blowjob, and he confirmed that when he got back from his business trip he thought someone had been in his flat. Turns out he's got a touch of OCD and is very particular about the positioning of things. You know, coasters, rugs, cushions, that kind of stuff. He reckoned they'd been moved.'

Lucas chipped in. 'And that's good because it ties in the need for the second number. I suppose it also explains why he went crazy about the untidy condition of his front door.' Bassano laughed, Jo didn't.

'He put it down to one of his friends going into the flat to keep an eye on the place while he was gone. We've fingerprinted but turned up nothing. We're checking his phone records to see if it had been used during his time away. The other thing is—' Bassano was interrupted when the phone in the incident room burst into life.

Bassano answered it.

He listened for a while then said, 'Take her to Interview Room One. I'll be right down.' Lucas and Jo looked up.

'There's a woman in reception, says she's called a number and a recorded message told her to report to the police station. I think we might have hooked someone.'

Chapter 43

Gina McKellen could be heard coming up the corridor to Interview Room One. 'What do you mean I have to be interviewed? Why would I need to be interviewed? I just want to know why me and my family could be in danger.' The policewoman escorting her said nothing, just opened the door and motioned for her to take a seat.

'Will you talk to me?' Gina was freaking out.

She removed her jacket and slung it on the back of the chair. Then banged the chair down and sat at the desk staring at the woman officer stood by the door.

Lucas, Bassano and Jo Sells stood in the observation room next door and watched her through the two-way mirror. Gina McKellen was in her early thirties with a shock of red dyed hair that shone like burnished copper, drawn back from her face in a top knot. She was very pretty. Her skilfully applied makeup accentuated her features, while her skinny jeans, tight white T-shirt and high heels accentuated the rest. The muscles in her arms flexed when she assaulted the chair, she looked one seriously fit woman. Bassano was struggling to stay focused.

'I'll take this one, boss, and you two observe,' said Bassano before he could help himself.

'No, I think it's better if I take it. Jo would you observe and Bassano you get back to Sophie Barrock,' said Lucas.

Bassano looked at his boss open-mouthed. 'What? That's not a good split. She's our best bet, I want to be involved,' he said, gesturing at Gina.

Lucas flashed a sideways glance at Bassano. 'That's not how I see it. At the moment Sophie Barrock is our best bet and I want you on that. You've already spoken to her and you need to stick with it. This McKellen woman may not give us anything we don't already have. Barrock on the other hand spent time trading blows with Mechanic, which is the hottest lead we've had.' Lucas paused and Bassano stared at Lucas. 'Jo, I want you in here observing. I need an outside perspective on this woman. Is that clear?' Jo nodded.

Bassano made a lame gesture of protest but before any words came out Lucas pointed a loaded finger and silenced him. Bassano knew when it was discussion over. He slapped his arms to his sides and looked like a sulky schoolboy not picked for the big game.

'If that's what you want,' he said and left, leaving the door behind him open in an act of silent protest.

Jo watched him go. 'Not sure that went down well.'

'I don't give a damn,' replied Lucas. 'This woman could have jack shit for all we know and Sophie Barrock might be our way in. He needs to focus, and not just on Gina McKellen's T-shirt.' Jo nodded, unsure if she was meant to respond. She felt very uneasy.

'Are you sure you don't want me in there with you?' she asked.

'No, I want you out here picking up on the information I miss. I need your perspective to be clear and dispassionate. You need to be at arm's length, okay?'

'Yup,' Jo replied. Lucas walked away and entered the interview room.

No sooner had he opened the door than Gina McKellen was on her feet firing questions.

'Who the hell are you? And will you tell me why I'm in danger?' Lucas pulled up a chair and sat opposite the agitated woman.

'Thanks for coming in, Gina. I am Lieutenant Ed Lucas and I need to ask you a couple of questions.'

'I just asked you a fucking question. So why don't we start with that one.' Her face was red.

'Okay,' said Lucas. 'That fair.'

'Well?' Gina yelled at Lucas again.

'We have reason to believe that when you got the recorded message you were intending to call a counsellor. Is that correct Gina?'

'Er yes, I suppose so.' She was much less on the offensive now.

'I need you to tell me the nature of the calls. What were the calls about?'

Gina hesitated, this was touching a raw nerve.

'I'd rather not say.' She folded her arms across her chest.

'Gina, this is really important. What did you talk about on the calls?'

'I don't like this,' she said. 'It's personal and none of your business. I just want to know why me and my family are in danger.'

Lucas straightened himself in his chair, then leaned right forward with his elbows on the desk. 'Gina, you and your family are in danger because we believe that the counsellor you've been talking to may be working with a serial killer. You could be the next victim.' Gina's eyes widened and her mouth dropped open. 'Now you need to co-operate if we are going to prevent that happening, but we can't if you don't talk to us.' Lucas maintained his close posture and kept his voice low.

She sat staring at Lucas in disbelief. 'But that's ridiculous. I've never met her.'

'Who? What's her name?'

'I don't know her name and she doesn't know mine. It's all part of the anonymity. I call her Josie and she calls me Josie. She is really good and so understanding. She helps me work things out.'

'What kind of things?'

'Family problems, that's all. She helps me put them in perspective. Things are not that great at home and she helps me get myself straight.'

'How long have you been doing this?'

'Oh, I suppose about five weeks.'

'And you call the number and get the counselling, that's the arrangement.'

'Yes. That's how it works.'

'Did you use a different number to start with?'

'Yes, how the hell did you know that? I saw an ad at the club and used that number first. Then Josie told me to use a different number to continue the support. But why am I in such danger and why are my family at risk as well? I don't get it. She doesn't know who I am.'

'We believe she and the killer track you through the club somehow. That part isn't clear to us as yet.'

'But she can't know who I am. She doesn't know where I live or what I do. We've haven't even met yet,' said Gina.

'Look Gina, we are treating this individual as very resourceful and dangerous. We believe this person has been involved in previous murders using the same counselling tactics to engage with the victims. At present we are not sure how ... What do you mean *yet?*'

Gina looked startled by his change of tone. 'She said the counselling was not working, it wasn't bringing the expected results so she suggested we meet up. I said that would ruin the whole anonymity thing, and she said it was usual practice in a small number of cases, and anyway—'

'Meet up?' Lucas interrupted. 'What do you mean *meet up?*'

'She wants me to meet her so she can help me focus on the issues. She said there are times when the problems are so deep rooted it's necessary to—'

Lucas was becoming more and more excited. He interrupted again.

'In a cafe, a park. Where? Where does she want to meet you?' Lucas asked.

'At her place,' Gina replied.

Lucas was on his feet now. 'How are you going to do that?'

'I have her address. During our last call she said it was important for us to explore the deep rooted—' Gina was unable to complete her sentence again.

'You know her address?' It was Lucas's turn to yell.

'No, I have her address. It's written down at home.'

'When are you supposed to meet?'

'She said we would finalize something today. That's why I called, because I hadn't heard from her to make arrangements.'

Lucas reached for the desk phone. 'Get me a squad car out front right now, and get hold of Bassano. Come on Gina, we need you to take us to your home to get that address. And we need to move fast.'

'But, but ...' Lucas pulled Gina by the elbow. She picked up her jacket from the back of the chair and they bustled out of the interview room.

Lucas turned to Gina in the corridor. 'Wait here.'

He went to the observation room and opened the door. 'Come on let's ...' His voice tailed off. Dr Jo Sells was gone.

Chapter 44

Lucas went back into the interview room and picked up the phone. He spoke in hushed tones and replaced it in its cradle. He stood by the table and stroked his chin deep in thought. Gina McKellen, or Officer Gina Spence, as she was better known, came into the room.

'Good job,' said Lucas.

'Thank you, sir,' she replied. 'I hope I didn't overstep the mark when I swore at you.'

'No, that was absolutely fine. You were excellent. There is a car arranged to take you home.'

'Am I allowed to ask, sir, what this was all about? This is pretty irregular.'

'Yeah it is, but I'm afraid not. But if I'm right, you will know soon enough.'

'Well, sir, there is one thing I need to know.'

'Yes, what is it?'

'Can I wash this crap out of my hair?'

Lucas laughed. 'Yes, that's fine. I don't think we'll be needing the services of Gina McKellen again.'

'Thank you, sir.'

Gina Spence left the room and could be heard clip-clopping down the corridor in her non-regulation shoes. Lucas stayed by the phone wondering if the gamble had paid off, or whether he would be the one getting paid off when they fired his ass out of the force. He felt calm and sharp.

Bassano on the other hand was having a dreadful time. Jo had left the station at a hell of a pace and found a taxi right outside the main gates. She figured that a taxi was more difficult to trace than her hire car, so when she saw it she jumped straight in.

Bassano had been waiting across the street in his car. He was in a dilemma: he didn't want to raise suspicion by moving off too soon, but also didn't want to risk losing his target by leaving it too late. He hesitated just a fraction too long and found himself about six cars behind the taxi, getting caught by pedestrian crossings and traffic lights. His car was filled with bad language and inappropriate gestures. The gap between them was widening.

As they left the city limits, the taxi driver put his foot down while Bassano was still struggling to get through the last remaining intersections. He lost them momentarily but then spotted the taxi as it drove up the ramp onto the freeway. In a last-ditch effort before they disappeared, he forced his way through the barrage of angry horns and jumped a red light. Bassano hit the freeway.

In the taxi, Jo's head was spinning. *What the hell was Jess up to? She must have a fucking death wish this time.* The thoughts swirled around in her head and she felt sick. She had to get there and warn her. The phone was not an option and her only hope was that Jess would be at home. She had to tell her they were coming. She had to protect her.

Bassano was now positioned a far more comfortable three cars behind. He reached for the radio.

'Patch me through to Interview Room One.'

The phone rang and Lucas picked it up.

'You with her?'

'Yes, bit of a nightmare but under control now. We are going east on 71st and have just passed intersection nine.'

'I'll get the cars on the road and co-ordinate from there. Stick on her tail and keep me briefed.' Lucas put down the phone and made his way to the control room.

Jo was trying to get a grip of herself as a ball of molten panic welled up in her throat. She had blown her cover but what was she supposed to do? She had no alternative. She had time though.

Lucas wouldn't waste effort looking for her, he would be focused on finding that address and getting to her sister's place fast.

Jo shook her head. Her career was ruined and she would now be as much on the wanted list as Jessica. *Shit, what a mess.* If only her damn sister would behave like any other normal psychopath and not try to be a clever bitch. They had to get away fast, was all she could think of.

She loved her sister and like other identical twins they shared a special bond. It was as though what happened to Jess also happened to Jo. They were exceptionally close, they had to be.

They'd both been Daddy's girls and had idolized their father. He was a marine and they travelled from place to place as his postings sent him around the world. He saw active service many times but refused to talk about what he'd done, even when the girls were old enough to understand.

Their mother was a dutiful service wife, following her husband from town to town, setting up home in whatever accommodation the forces threw at her. She would pick up casual work in bars and restaurants to keep herself occupied while the girls were in school. She did it for the social interaction – they didn't need the money. She was a good mother but always a little distant and she never really connected with her children. As a family they were rubbing along well together right up to the point when Daddy took *that* posting.

San Diego is a beautiful place. They jumped for joy when his latest tour ended and he was posted there. She'd always dreamed of being a San Diego girl. Funny how sometimes you have to be careful what you wish for.

It was fantastic, to begin with.

The school was great and they made friends quickly. The weather was wall-to-wall sunshine and life was very good indeed. Mom took a job working in a bar in the old town which was a pleasant enough place, serving margaritas and Mexican food. There was a large outside seating area with gas fires in the centre of the tables. The girls loved it when they picked Mom up from work and could sit on the high stools, sipping non-alcoholic cocktails next to the burning flames.

Life was good until Mom met *him*.

He was a twenty-something beach-bum-come-hobo, with a ready supply of hash and beer breath. She fell for him, head over heels. Jo remembered it like it was yesterday. Her dutiful mom who only drank on a Saturday, never left ironing in the basket for longer than a day, and had dinner on the table at six thirty every evening became a drunken, pot-smoking, fuck bunny within a period of three months.

The guy was like a Svengali to her weaknesses. Dad was devastated. He tried to reason with her and help her through this little fling. But when that failed, he beat the living daylights out of him and it all went tits up. Mom moved out and disappeared in a cloud of pot smoke, leaving the two girls and a husband who was cracking up.

He desperately tried to contact her but she'd vanished. He stopped going to work and they put him on sick leave. He began drinking and the inevitable mental breakdown ensued. This sent their whole world into free fall and it was then that the abuse started.

Jo remembered that they were about twelve at the time. He'd started shouting and swearing at them, and then occasional slap when they argued back, then came the odd punch. There was no food in the house and the girls were forced into wearing dirty clothes, they were in a bad way.

He would scream that it was their mother that was making him do this. She was the one to blame. As he hit them he would cry and shout, 'Your mother's making me do this. She's the bitch to blame.' It got more frequent and more intense each time.

Then, one night, she remembered him coming home drunk and crashing around downstairs. Jo hid under her bedsheets hoping he'd just collapse on the sofa in front of the TV and fall asleep. But she heard the clumping of boots on the stairs and screwed her eyes tight shut, trying to block it out. He went into

Jess's room and shut the door and all was quiet. That's how it remained all night.

The next morning Daddy was much calmer. He was not spoiling for a fight and the girls went off to school unscathed. Jess never said what had happened, but then she didn't have to. Jo knew it was bad. Jess turned to Jo over the breakfast table, cool as you like, and with not a flicker of emotion said, 'I'm fixing it. I'll look after you.'

Her father visited Jess regularly and it was always the same result. A strange calm descended over him and the slapping, shouting and screaming stopped. After a while he returned to work, gradually got himself together, and the household started functioning again.

All the outward signs said, 'Stewart Sells had a rough time when his wife left him, but he's back on track now.' The truth was that Jess was the one having the rough time. About twice a week Jo would hear the bedroom door click shut and then silence. This happened for the next six years until Jess and Jo went off to college. When Jo asked the question, all her sister would say was, 'Don't worry, I will always look after you.' Jo often wondered what life would have been like if her dad had turned to the left at the top of the stairs instead of right into Jess's room. In her quieter moments she would think, 'There but for the grace of God, go I' but then it was obvious, whichever way you looked at it, the grace of God had given her family a miss.

Jo was so engrossed in her thoughts she was oblivious to the journey and how far they had travelled so when the car came to an abrupt halt she blurted out, 'Why have we stopped?'

'Because this is where you told me to go, lady,' said the driver in a tired I've-been-up-for-eighteen-hours kind of voice.

'Oh yes, sorry,' Jo replied, fishing in her bag for money and throwing notes onto the passenger seat.

'But, lady, your change,' the driver called after her as she got out of the car and ran up the white wooden steps two at a time to the first floor apartment. She could see her sister's truck in the parking lot at the back and banged on the door with thudding urgency. She banged again. Jessica Sells opened the door and was shocked to find her sister barging past her, already talking at a hundred miles an hour.

Bassano swung into the road just in time to see the taxi pull away and head back to the freeway. The driver had a satisfied grin on his face after the twenty dollar tip the previous fare had thrown onto his seat. Bassano clocked Jo racing up the steps. He radioed in the details of the property to Lucas who started running records on the occupants. After several minutes Bassano was joined by another two cars, each with four people. They killed their engines and waited.

Fifteen more minutes passed which felt like a lifetime, then Lucas radioed in.

'There are eight flats in the building and only one of them is let to a single female. Her name is Olivia Dunn and she's in flat 5. I suggest we get the place surrounded. How many men do you have?'

'We have nine including me, sir. That should do it. It's a residential area with plenty of visibility and clean access, there's little room for surprises. I think we should go in, sir.' Bassano was pumped with adrenaline.

The team were impatient and it seemed that Lucas took forever to respond. 'Okay. Move in.'

The car doors swung open and the men spilled onto the road and the sidewalk, fanning out as they approached the building. Bassano gestured and three went around the back as the others filed up the white steps.

They found flat 5 at the top of the second flight of stairs. Two men stood on one side of the door and three on the other. Bassano stood in the middle. He reached for his radio and squirted the transmit button to signal to the guys at the back they were ready. He gave a finger countdown: three, two, one – crash. His right foot ploughed through the mortise lock securing the door to the frame. The door swung back, hitting against the wall in a shower of plaster and paint.

The men either side burst into the flat with their weapons raised. 'Freeze.' They yelled at the crumpled figure crying on the sofa.

'Don't move, Jo,' yelled Bassano as the officers peeled off into the adjoining rooms.

She turned and looked at Bassano, his gun levelled at her head. Makeup streaked down her cheeks and her face was red. Her mouth was open but nothing came out.

One of the officers pulled her off the sofa and forced her to the ground. She yelped in pain as her shoulder hit the wooden floor and the cuffs clicked into place. The other officers swept the remaining rooms shouting, 'Clear!' as it became obvious the flat was empty. Bassano inspected each of the rooms in turn. He shouted to one of the men. 'Get her up.'

He yanked her to her feet and shoved her back onto the sofa. She was still crying with tears streaming down her face and onto her jacket.

'Where the fuck is she, Jo?' Bassano shouted in her face. She flinched at his aggression and turned her head away.

'She's gone,' she said choking back a cough. 'She's not here.'

'Tell me Jo, where is she?' Bassano shook her by the shoulders.

'I don't know,' she said with complete desperation in her voice. 'She's gone, and I don't know where.' She was sobbing uncontrollably. Bassano gestured to the officer and he marched her out of the door to the waiting car outside. Bassano turned to the others. 'Shut this place down and get forensics in here. I'm taking her back to the station.'

Bassano stomped out. This was not the way it was supposed to have happened.

They sat in the car in silence. Bassano drove, with a police officer in the back next to Jo. She was still sobbing. 'What will happen to me?' she asked through the tears.

'That depends on you,' said Bassano looking in the rear-view mirror. 'But I doubt you can do anything to keep your sorry deceitful ass out of jail, and with any real justice you'll take a needle.'

Chapter 45

'Jo, this isn't helping. You're gonna have to talk to us eventually.'

Lucas and Bassano sat opposite her in the interview room. Her head was bowed, she looked a total wreck. She had stopped crying for long enough to confirm her name and date of birth for the benefit of the tape but other than that had said nothing.

They fired a barrage of questions at her but she refused to say a single word. She just stared at the table top, with one hand resting in her lap and the other cuffed to the table leg. As the hours ticked by she said absolutely nothing.

'We can sit here all night if necessary,' Lucas said in his best flat unemotional interview voice. It was now 11.45pm, they had been going at it for three hours.

Lucas continued, 'I've called Quantico and they are sending someone over to join us. They are not happy with you.'

'You will talk to us you know, Jo,' Bassano said. 'We will get to the truth and we will catch your sister. You do know that don't you?'

She looked up and took everyone by surprise. 'I want a lawyer.'

'Wow, now we're getting somewhere,' said Lucas. 'Okay, if that's what it takes to get you talking then let's get one.' Lucas made a call and sat back down. 'So what now, we play the silent game until he arrives?' He knew the answer before he asked the question.

After forty-five minutes of stone cold silence there was a knock on the interview room door. Bassano got up to open it and there stood his favourite attorney, Jefferson Gill, defender of the guilty. Never had Bassano been so pleased to see his nemesis. He shook his hand and said, 'Good to see you Mr Gill.' The warmth of the greeting took Gill by surprise considering Bassano normally looked as if he'd rather shake him by the neck. Bassano ushered him in.

'Can you give us the room, gentlemen?' Gill said. 'My client and I need to talk.'

'Good luck with that,' said Bassano and the two of them left.

They made their way to the small kitchen area located at the back of the interview rooms to make coffee.

'What the hell was going on in there?' asked Bassano when they were out of earshot.

'I have no idea. I don't get it, she could make life a lot easier for herself if she co-operated.'

'Looks like that's the last thing she intends to do.'

The door to the interview room opened. 'My client wishes to make a written statement. I presume that is okay with you?'

'Yeah, of course,' said Lucas, appearing from the kitchen.

'Oh, just three things. She can't do it if she's handcuffed to the desk, she doesn't want you two bearing down on her when she does it, and could you bring us some coffee?'

'I'll send in a supervising officer and the drinks are on their way,' Bassano bellowed as he reached for a tray to assemble the necessary items.

He piled up a stack of plastic cups, spoons and napkins along with milk and sugar. He had an overwhelming sense of relief.

Lucas walked off muttering something about, 'Could have done that three fucking hours ago.'

The clock on the wall in the incident room said 2.05am. Lucas was staring at the boards filled with photographs and sticky notes while Bassano slept with his head resting on his folded arms on the desk. There was nothing to do but wait.

Lucas rose from the hard wooden chair and, deciding not to wake Bassano, made his way back to the interview suite. *What the hell was taking so long?* Even the officers at Jessica Sells' flat had called it a day. They had found very little to suggest where Mechanic had gone, however they had a bucket load of confirmed thumbprints. That much was certain: Mechanic and Jessica Sells were one and the same.

Lucas wandered along the corridors to where she was being held, the place was empty without any of the usual mayhem of late-night policing. Even the interview rooms were quiet and, as far as he knew, Jo was the only one occupying a slot on the board. Lucas passed the small kitchen. He noticed the plastic tray sat on the worktop stacked with discarded Styrofoam cups and an empty flask of coffee. Napkins and spoons littered the tray along with a confetti storm of empty sugar packets.

Lucas stared at the tray in horror.

He ran to the interview room, bursting through the door.

The attending officer was slumped on the floor with his back to the wall and his legs straight out in front of him. There was no obvious sign of injury, just his head lolling sideways against his left shoulder, the snapped vertebrae in his neck unable to support its weight. His eyes were wide open in a dead-fish stare and his mouth gaped open.

Jefferson Gill was sitting upright at the table. His arms hung down by his sides and his head was tilted back looking at the ceiling. Two inches of pen could be seen sticking out of his left eye socket. The spatter of blood and vitreous humour on the wall and table bore witness to the force of its entry. His mouth also gaped open, as if mimicking his dead companion.

Lucas hit the alarm strip which ran around the room and went to the officer first. He put his fingers against his neck to feel a pulse but he was gone. Even with his limited medical knowledge Lucas knew there was little point checking the pulse of Jefferson Gill. Within seconds three officers fought their way through the open door and started attending to the two dead men. Bassano was one of them, having woken and wondered where his boss had gone.

'It was Mechanic,' Lucas yelled. 'We had Jessica Sells, not Jo Sells. We had the wrong one.'

'Fuck,' Bassano said through gritted teeth as he knelt by the officer. 'How did that happen?'

'Damned if I know.' Lucas shook his head and barked orders. 'She can't be far, get a photo circulated, check the outside CCTV, she'll be on foot.'

'Yes sir. I'll set up road blocks at all the major interchanges and alert public transport. We'll get the bitch.' Bassano rushed out of the room.

Lucas noticed three handwritten pages on the desk. He picked one up and read it.

Johann Pachelbel was a Baroque composer. His precise date of birth and death are not known, however he was baptised on 1 September 1653 and was buried 9 March 1706. He was born in Nuremburg into a middle-class family. His father was a wine dealer named Johann Hans and his mother was Anne-Marie Mair. He was an exceptionally gifted musician and received his early tuition from Heinrich Schwemmer. He was enormously popular during his lifetime and composed hundreds of pieces of music. His most famous was his Canon in D which was the only canon he ever wrote.

Lucas read on.

He was forced to quit university after less than a year due to financial difficulties and took up a scholarship ...

He scanned further.

Pachelbel was married twice. His first wife, Barbara, and their only child died in October 1683 during the plague. He married for a second time to Judith Drommer on 24 August 1684 and had five sons and two daughters.

And so the strange biography continued.

The Canon is based on a simple theme of three voices and is a polyphonic device in which several violins play the same music entering in sequence. It was originally scored for three violins and was originally paired with ...

Lucas murmured to himself, 'What the hell is this?' He flicked over to the last page and at the bottom he read.

Music history lesson over, Lucas. By now you will have worked out you had me and let me go. Very, very sloppy. We swapped clothes and you did the rest, so predictable. Jo will be 250 miles away by now and out of harm's way, so it's time for me to go. Sorry about the mess. Must dash
Jess
PS I will kill anyone you send to find me. If you are in any doubt ask my ex-roommates.

The last three sentences were smeared with blood. He looked at the two dead people in the small interview room and a shiver ran down the back of his neck. She had written this Pachelbel essay and then, when the time was right, she went to work. This was her written statement for Gill, after all she had to be seen to be writing something.

Jess was the consummate professional when it came to situations like this. Her training and dozens of successful ops had honed her skills to perfection.

As she wrote her so-called confession, Jess was planning the endgame. This was a three-strike offensive, first the attorney, then the officer. That way Jess could count on a split-second of officer indecision when he thought about helping Gill. A split second of indecision was all she needed.

She had written her fake confession until she was ready, waiting for all the players to be in the right place. Then, she struck with clinical precision. No fuss. No drama.

She had looked up from her paper and waited for Gill to hold her gaze. The police officer stood behind her and with a slight turn of her head, she could see both men. She raised her pen from the paper and chewed the end in an act of supposed concentration. She smiled at Gill.

The officer fumbled for something in his pocket. Her right arm snaked out with a straight jab – strike one. The pen entered Gill's left orbit with a squelch as eye fluid spurted out.

He let out a gargled scream and brought his hands up to his face. The second blow drove the pen deep into his brain killing him instantly. Strike two.

The officer rushed in and the valuable split second of indecision came into play allowing Mechanic to step behind him. Left hand around his face with a tight grip on his jaw, right hand round the back of his head and ... twist. Hard and fast. Listen for the crack. Strike 3.

Job done, she was still smiling.

Chapter 46

Lucas sat in the incident room. The bodies downstairs were being photographed, along with the walls, floor, and anything else which found itself in a camera viewfinder.

He was deep in thought. *How the hell had they got it so wrong? How had they not recognized the switch?* He tried hard to focus on what needed to happen next, rather than raking over the errors of the day. It had been forty-five minutes since his discovery. Bassano was out in his car, racing around the streets trying to find Mechanic, as were the rest of the force.

They had set up roadblocks and were already undertaking random stoppages. They'd found Mechanic's clothes discarded in the gym – she must have found some old clothes to change into. The CCTV footage outside the station showed her wearing a dark hooded top, dark tracksuit bottoms and trainers, like ninety percent of people roaming the streets at this time of night.

Lucas shook his head. It was needle-in-a-haystack time.

Fortunately for Lucas, Bassano was a world-beater at finding needles in haystacks. The streets were empty, not only because of the lateness of the hour, but also because it was pouring with rain. The drains were struggling with the volume of water which caused mini lakes to form at the side of the road. Bassano reckoned the best way for Mechanic to get about was by taxi, but dressed like that it wasn't going to be easy. She looked like a homeless bum. No taxi driver in his right mind would pick her up, and besides, she was going to be soaked through by now.

She must be on foot. There was very little parkland for her to use, so the streets were her only route. He cruised up and down the side roads figuring she wouldn't keep to the main drag.

Then he spotted her in the distance. She was about a hundred and fifty yards ahead. He couldn't see her face and she was walking away from him, but he knew it was her.

Everyone else walking around at this time of night had a slow and shaky gait, born out of excess alcohol or drugs. This hooded figure had neither and walked with a steady purpose, it had to be her. He killed his lights and gained ground on Mechanic.

Bassano thought the hood pulled tight around her head would muffle the sound of the car engine, so he speeded up. It did no such thing, and she turned to see a car cruising towards her with no lights. She changed direction and ran up the main street.

Lucas stroked his chin, 'Where the hell would she go?' he said to no one. 'Think man, think.'

Jo had a six-hour head-start and was by now holed up God-knows-where waiting. Maybe Mechanic was going to lie low and meet up with her sister later? But that was too risky – the longer she remained in the confines of the city, the more chance there was of being caught. If they found Jo, they would find Mechanic. Of that he was certain.

His thoughts came together, at last making sense. Jo and Mechanic had only had a short period of time together to develop a plan to get themselves out of this so it couldn't be very complex. Jess must be going somewhere predetermined. The obvious thing to do was to meet up with Jo, but that was impractical. Or was it?

Suddenly the answer went off in his head like a bomb.

Lucas banged his fist onto the table. 'Damn you,' he said, and reached for the phone. 'Patch me through to Bassano.'

Jo sat waiting, chewing on a breakfast bar in the dark. Despite there being no windows, she wasn't taking any chances and the large strip lights in the ceiling were switched off. Her sugar levels were dropping due to the stress and wrappers littered the floor. She was trying to stay calm and take deep breaths but her panic levels were running close to the surface and kept bubbling up, causing her to reach for more food.

'It will take several hours, so don't worry,' Jess had told her as she hurried Jo from the flat and down the fire escape at the back of her building. 'Just sit there and wait and I will come for you.' Jess had a reassuring way of speaking when under pressure. It made Jo feel safe.

'Okay,' was all she could manage as a reply.

As she sat in the gloom, her head was racing. *What a fucking mess. If only Jess could control it better, if only …*

There were lots of *if only* statements crowding in on Jo. *If only they hadn't gone to San Diego, if only Mom hadn't gone off the rails, if only Daddy hadn't chosen to fuck his own daughter. If only …*

The years of abuse had made Jess ill. Nothing you could see, nothing you could fix with a bandage or a plaster, she was damaged in her head. The only way she could deal with the horror of what was happening was to detach herself from the situation, disassociate herself from the abuse. This was her defence mechanism, which enabled her to live an outwardly normal life.

For the young Jess, she had no option: while Daddy was abusing her, he left Jo alone. This created a deep and violent psychosis in Jess which was always going to boil over one day, it just needed a suitable trigger. It needed the blue touch paper lighting, and that happened with an unexpected visit.

Jess was in the army, stationed in Florida. One Saturday afternoon, there was a knock on the door, and there stood her mom and dad.

'Hi, how are you, honey?' Jess's mouth fell open. It was the first words she'd heard from her mother in over ten years. She delivered them as if she'd seen her last week at the mall. Jess was stunned and unable to speak.

'Me and your mom have something to tell you,' said her dad. Jess was still mute. 'She's back, Jess. Isn't that great? Your mom's come back. We couldn't wait to tell you the good news.'

Tears ran down Jess's face as she tried to get her head around what was going on. She stumbled backwards and sat on the sofa, completely numb.

Her parents followed her into the one-bed, service-issue apartment. 'Honey, there's no need to cry,' said her mom. 'We're so happy, and we wanted to tell you.'

'Isn't it great,' said her dad. Jess said nothing.

He knelt beside Jess and put one hand on her knee while holding her mom's hand with the other. 'Everything is okay now honey, Mom and I are together again.' They both smiled the smile of schoolyard sweethearts.

Jess raised her head to meet his gaze. 'If you don't leave, I'll kill you both.'

'Hey now, just hang on a minute,' said her dad, recoiling back and jumping to his feet. 'I know your mom made a mistake and things were difficult for a while, but there's no need for any of that nonsense.'

With that Jess leapt forward, grabbed him by the throat, and slammed him against the wall. 'Difficult? Difficult? Get out now or I will kill you both.' She hissed every word.

He broke her grip and held his neck coughing. 'Jesus Christ,' he spluttered. Her mom went to help, patting him on the back.

'Get out!' Jess screamed and bundled both of them out of the door. She slammed it shut. *All the years of abuse and he's the one not having any of that fucking nonsense.* Something snapped in her head and Mechanic was born.

From that day forward, it became Jo's turn to look after Jess.

'Triggers,' Jo muttered under her breath as she waited in her underground bunker. 'My whole life is ruled by triggers.'

She recounted the events leading to this latest crisis. Mom going completely yaya with that drug-ridden asshole was the trigger for Dad becoming a sexual sadist. The abuse he heaped onto her sister was the trigger that created Mechanic. And the most inappropriate casual visit ever conceived provided the trigger for twenty-one murders, if you count the two soldiers. Quite an escalation.

When her sister snapped the last time, Jo had been in the right place to rescue her. It was pure chance she worked with Galbraith, and it was pure chance she got included in the investigation. Then there was the total melt down moment when she realized it was her sister who was doing the killing.

Jess's psychotic attacks were uncontrollable. Jo had to get her sister out of the situation, which she did. It cost Galbraith his life, but so be it. The three years which followed were an uphill battle of mind-bending drugs, counselling, and round-the-clock care. She moved Jess into her place in Virginia to support her through the attacks. Jess made steady progress and got better, moving back to Florida as Olivia Dunn, the unremarkable woman who looked after the pools and the netting at the country clubs.

Then there was the final trigger, which brought them all to this.

A simple death in the family.

The illness took her mother quickly, as is often the case with stomach cancer. Her mom and dad had been back together as if nothing had happened, and then she was gone again. Her father was distraught and went off the rails. He went ballistic because only Jo attended the funeral. Jess was determined not to go and had done her disappearing act after leaving the army.

She kept in close contact with Jo and one day Dad showed up at Jo's place when she wasn't in – but Jess was. Jess was paying her sister a rare visit to show how much progress she'd made with her recuperation. Dad was drunk, and when faced with Jess, couldn't tell the difference. She didn't want to raise any alarms, so pretended to be Jo.

He poured his heart out to her. How he missed his wife and how she was the only thing he had to live for.

Jess was devastated. Despite that woman tearing their family apart, despite the years of hurt and anguish, despite the beatings and wilful abuse, Dad still put that fucking woman on a pedestal.

She just sat there and took it. He left, and they hadn't seen him since.

Jess returned to Florida. The trauma of their chance encounter was too much and something inside her head snapped. Unknown to Jo, the final trigger had been pulled. Mechanic was once again in charge.

Bassano gunned the engine and spun his tyres on the wet road. His radio crackled into life. He reached over and turned it off, he had her in his sights now and needed full concentration. Mechanic dodged between the cars as rain bounced off the road. She joined the main street and headed downtown. Bassano mounted the sidewalk and swung into the flow of traffic. He sounded his horn and gesticulated to the other motorists driving in the right direction down the one-way system. Bassano threw the car back and forth across the lanes to avoid the vehicles heading straight for him. His view of Mechanic was constantly being obscured. She was still running hard between the oncoming cars.

Despite the early hour, the congestion was bad and Bassano made slow progress against the tide of angry motorists. Then she was gone. Bassano swung the nose of his Buick at the roadside and stopped. He leapt out of his car, flashing his badge at anyone who was looking and jumped onto the roof scanning the way ahead.

'Shit,' He screamed the word into the air and punched something imaginary. Then he saw her veering off onto a side road again, still running at the same pace as when the chase started. Bassano jumped back into his car, relieved that he hadn't attempted to pursue her on foot. He pulled back into the honking, abusive flow of traffic and tore after her, turning down the same side road, and into a built-up industrial area. In the distance he could see Mechanic on the sidewalk about sixty yards ahead of him, bent over with her hands on her knees sucking air into her burning lungs.

He slowed down and tried to blend into the traffic, but it was no use. Her head flicked up, she spotted him and she was away again.

The Buick heaved forward and sped around the slower cars, accelerating straight for Mechanic. At least he was travelling in the same direction as the other motorists this time. She changed direction and darted down a backstreet about twenty yards to her right. Once in the alleyway she cursed and tried to backtrack but Bassano was already at the top of the road. He slammed the steering wheel to the left and pulled hard on the handbrake. This swung the back end of the car around, blocking Mechanic in.

Mechanic looked around. It was a dead end between two high-rise buildings and a high back wall. The entire alleyway was no more than thirty feet long and featureless, no trash bins she could use, no windows to smash through, no fire escapes she could reach. There was nothing, just an empty, plain, three-walled box with the open side blocked by Bassano in his car.

Mechanic evaluated the situation and cursed again. She collected her thoughts and slowed her breathing. She was facing Bassano, about twenty feet from his car at the entrance to the road. She heard the sound of the passenger window being buzzed down.

'Stay where you are,' he called. 'Back up against the far wall.'

Mechanic stood motionless and said nothing. In the absence of any other options, it was time to play games. Bassano repeated his order through the open window. 'Back against the wall.'

'Make your fucking mind up,' Mechanic replied. 'Either I stay where I am or I back up against the wall. I can't do both.' She was openly mocking him.

Bassano detected the playful tone in her voice and it unnerved him. 'Don't be fucking smart, you're going nowhere. Now, back against the wall. Now!' He slid across the bench seat. The sodium glow from the street lighting struck his face as he moved inside the car.

'It's Detective Bassano isn't it?' Mechanic asked crouching to get a better view.

The words pierced him to the core. *How the fuck did she know that?*

'You know I don't have a shooter, Detective Bassano, or I would have blown your face off, and you know I don't have a knife or I'd have carved my name in you by now. So why don't you stop hiding in that car and face me ... man to woman, so to speak. What are you afraid of?' Mechanic took a couple of exaggerated steps towards the car.

Bassano blinked in disbelief and drew his gun with his right hand. 'Back up against the wall or I'll put a bullet in you.' He made sure the nose of the .38 was visible.

This was rattling him.

'What, shoot an unarmed woman? Detective, that would look so bad.' Her voice cut right through him as she took another swaggering step forward. 'If you won't come out, I'll have to come in and get you,' she said in a childlike sing-song voice, accompanied by her best psycho smile.

Bassano forgot all his training as the rising panic gripped him.

He thrust his gun further out through the window, threatening her. It pointed straight at Mechanic's head – she was now no more than eight feet from the car. She could see his face illuminated by the light from the dashboard and recognized the look of fear in his eyes. She had been here before and she knew this game well.

'I'm coming to get you,' she chanted and took another step closer to the car, waving her hands in the air as if conducting imaginary music. Bassano's right arm shot out of the car window, brandishing the gun at Mechanic.

'I'll fucking kill you,' he shouted.

But it was too late she had already made her move. The game was almost over.

She lunged at his outstretched hand, grabbed the gun and yanked his arm further out of the car. In the same movement she stepped in close, pulling it across her body, and clamped the gun against her right hip. Her left hand slammed through the open window into Bassano's shoulder, sending him careering forward out of his seat. His head smashed into the windshield with such force that the screen deformed into a cobweb of tiny fractures.

245

The reflex of being grabbed meant Bassano let off a round and the shell spun into the empty alleyway. It ricocheted off red brickwork sending fragments of mortar into the night. The muzzle flashed white against the dark and burned a black mark in Mechanic's sweatshirt. The retort from the shot resonated off the walls.

Mechanic brought Bassano back to the upright position in his seat and then shoved him forward again, crashing his face into the windshield with a sickening crunch of bone and cartilage. The screen was now distended outwards from the impact. Bassano's fingers went into spasm once more and another round embedded itself into the far wall.

Blood spattered across the inside of the windshield and bits of tissue tore away from Bassano's face as the shattered glass embedded itself. Mechanic brought him back to a seated position and once again smashed him forward into the dashboard. His fingers failed to spasm this time.

With Bassano forced forward and his head wedged between the screen and the dashboard, Mechanic twisted his arm. Then drove it up in an arc until his elbow struck the upper sill of the door. The sweep continued and Bassano's arm snapped against the joint with the sound of firewood being broken against a wall. The violence and speed of the movement lifted him from his seat as his arm broke in two, only the remnants of connective tissue and tendons holding it loosely together.

His grip on the gun gave way, sending it looping onto the roof of the car.

Blood sprayed into the air as the splintering bone exited the ripped flesh of Bassano's inner arm. The ragged ends of torn arteries pumped plumes of blood into the night. She released her grip on his wrist and shoulder and ducked away to avoid the cascading blood from the almost severed arm.

Bassano slumped back to his seat his eyes closed, a river of crimson streaming down onto his shirt, his face cut to ribbons. His upper right arm was propped on the window ledge with the forearm hanging down the outside of the door. Blood was pooling beneath the car as his heart pumped it from his body and onto the ground. Mechanic put her hood up, reclaimed the gun from the top of the car, and walked away.

Lucas was by now in his own car driving out of the deserted station. He knew where Jo was and he knew where Mechanic was heading. 'No damn transport, everyone on roadblocks and where the hell is Bassano?' He cursed under his breath. 'Do I have to do everything my fucking self?'

Unbeknown to Lucas, as the minutes ticked by, and the rain washed the blood under the car, the answer to his last question was unfortunately yes.

Chapter 47

Lucas sat at a set of traffic lights still cursing, however, this time it was directed at no one but himself. Why had he fallen for it again? After all this time, Mechanic had set a trap and he had plunged headlong into it.

It had hit him like a freight train: the only reason he'd thought Jo Sells was two hundred and fifty miles away was because Mechanic had told him she was. The silent treatment in the interview room and then getting an attorney were delaying tactics to make them think she had got right away.

But the fact was that when they were together in Mechanic's apartment they'd had precious little time to concoct an elaborate plan. The primary objective must have been to get Jo out of there fast and for Mechanic to get arrested in her place. They needed a strategy which was simple but effective and could be achieved with little preparation.

Lucas surmised that Jo must have taken Mechanic's vehicle and escaped from the property just before the police broke into the flat. He also concluded that, if the two hundred and fifty miles was just another of Mechanic's misdirections, Jo was probably hiding out somewhere close waiting for Mechanic to join her. Then the two of them would disappear forever.

The rendezvous would need to be somewhere familiar and capable of keeping Mechanic's vehicle and Jo Sells out of sight. It would also have to be within striking distance of the station. Mechanic was on foot and wouldn't risk public transport. So the question bugging Lucas, even more than his own gullibility, was where could that be? And the answer he came up with was Brightwood Country Club.

Brightwood was around eight miles from the station and could easily hide Jo and the vehicle in its sprawling grounds. Mechanic knew it well and someone with her level of fitness could be there in less than an hour. That was where Lucas had placed his bet and that was where he was heading. He pulled away from the lights still cursing himself.

There was however a significant flaw in Lucas's plan of attack. With everyone out looking for Mechanic there were no patrol vehicles available so he was stuck with his own car which had no radio. He was frustrated at not being able to get hold of Bassano, and left a message with the station controller to give Bassano the instruction to meet him at Brightwood.

It wasn't long before the Club came into view, the exterior lit up in all its glory. Lucas pulled up outside the locked gates and hit the intercom button. It buzzed in irritation. No one answered. He buzzed again. The white box remained silent.

He waited, then a voice crackled into the night air. 'Yeah.'

'This is Lieutenant Ed Lucas. Can you let me in please? It's an emergency.'

'What sort of an emergency?'

'I am not at liberty to share that with you, but can you please open the gates.'

'Well, no actually,' said the white box. 'Any crank could come here and say they are a Lieutenant. So no, you can't come in.' The truth of the matter was the HBO movie was just getting to the good part, so no he couldn't come in.

Lucas was not in the mood for this and objected to being called a crank. 'Open the fucking gates or I will get your ass fired. This is a police matter and you are obstructing a police officer in his duties which is a criminal offence.'

'If this is a police matter, then you'll have a badge. I'll come down to the gates, you can show it to me and then I'll let you in,' the voice said, resigning himself to the fact that he'd now miss the good bits.

'But I need to get in now,' said Lucas. This time there was no response.

Lucas waited, and he waited, and waited. No one came. He buzzed the intercom several times more but nothing happened. He stomped off, left his car at the gate, and walked the perimeter wall looking for an alternative way in. It was dark and the grass verge was soft from the rain. The wall was about ten feet high, much too high for Lucas to scale, and anyway he didn't relish his chances with the drop the other side.

After thirty feet, the wall stopped and was replaced with a wooden fence lined with poplar trees. Lucas crouched down and leaned his shoulder into the wooden panels. They were loose and he worked his way along until he found one which gave way under his weight. He crouched down and shoved hard against the fence. Two of the panels broke away creating a gap big enough for Lucas to squeeze through.

On the other side, he took stock of his surroundings and waited for the late arrival of the security guard. He could just see the headlines in the morning: 'Lieutenant caught in break-in scandal.' He forced it from his mind and tried to focus.

Ahead was the ostentatious grey stone building where the conference facilities, gym and restaurants were housed. To his left was the driveway leading to the grand reception and far off in the distance Lucas could make out the golf clubhouse. The guard still failed to show up so Lucas circled around the back of the main house looking for service buildings and maintenance sheds. As he rounded the corner, a huge pool area stretched out on front of him, with cabanas and loungers awaiting the arrival of the day's more sedate members. Lucas could see three outbuildings about two hundred yards away at the back of the estate. Keeping to the perimeter of the grounds, he tracked towards them.

The security lights turned the place an eerie yellow and the recent rain ensured Lucas was getting a good soaking from the overhanging bushes and branches. He arrived at the larger of the buildings, stood with his back against the side wall and listened. Nothing, all was quiet. He reached under his jacket and drew his gun. He hadn't done that in years but it still felt good.

He made his way around the corner to a large window and peered inside, cupping his left hand to the glass to shield against the light. The building contained pumps, ladders, sit-on mowers and every gardening tool you could imagine. He moved his position to get a better view but saw no more.

Lucas's right leg snapped like a chicken bone as Mechanic stamped on the side of his knee, breaking the joint. As Lucas crumpled, she gripped the gun with her right hand, thrusting her thumb into the back of the trigger guard to prevent a reactive shot. She delivered a fierce back elbow to the side of his head. Lucas didn't even have time to scream before he hit the wet grass, out cold.

Chapter 48

Lucas was coming round. In his woozy state he felt he was swaying back and forth like a long-stemmed flower in the breeze. His consciousness momentarily broke the surface and the agony of a hundred nails being driven into his hands filled his body. He slipped back into the blackness which brought some respite from the pain. Lucas ebbed and flowed, each time coming closer to the surface, only to go back under.

Lucas's eyes flickered open and he was staring at the floor. His head was slumped forward with his chin against his chest and he realized he was standing upright, or more accurately, he was hanging upright. Looking down he could see his legs crumpled below him, his arms taking his full weight. He raised his head and looked up. His hands were stretched above him, his wrists bound together with rope and secured to an overhead pipe.

He tried to focus but his head felt as though it was about to split in two and the pain in his hands was excruciating.

Lucas scanned his surroundings. He was in a dimly lit room and could see pale-coloured block walls and a concrete floor but other than that everything was a blur. He tried to stand to take his weight off the rope but found one of his legs didn't work. Lucas looked down and saw why. The bottom of his right leg stuck out sideways below the knee and a pool of blood had accumulated below his foot. He struggled to shift his other leg under his body and straightened it. The pain in his arms receded but his hands still burned like hell. His broken leg was also coming to life and shards of pain shot up his right side.

He vomited down his front.

The fog was clearing from his head and Lucas realized he was in a maintenance room full of pipes, valves and electrical cable trays. He could see about a twelve-foot radius and nothing more. Work benches lined the walls with mechanical jigs, tools and broken equipment awaiting attention. Beyond that there was darkness, a single naked bulb strung from the ceiling offered no clues as to what lay outside its narrow cone of light. He heard footsteps approaching.

'I heard you puke,' said the figure emerging from the gloom. He stared hard trying to block out the pain. A woman stood before him with all the outward signs of being Jo Sells. The same frame, the same face, even the same hair. But her eyes told a different story. Lucas knew he was looking at Mechanic.

'It will be the concussion, that's what made you vomit. It's your brain swelling due to the little bump you received on the head.' Mechanic was standing right in front of him now about three feet away. 'You don't look so good,' she said conversationally.

Lucas tried to speak but nothing came out. She kept swimming in and out of focus.

'I made it clear I would kill anyone you sent to find me and that includes you. But not just yet, eh? Not yet,' said Mechanic. 'You see, my sister likes you and I have found you a worthy adversary, so killing you very much depends on what you do next. I'm curious about a few things so I thought maybe a little question and answer game first, how about that?' She waited for an answer but got none.

'I'm not unreasonable, Lieutenant, so let's make it a game of even trade. I ask a question, then you ask a question. We'll take it in turns, even trade right?' Lucas was in no position to barter. 'You see I'm intrigued. Apart from making that lawyer's head into my new pen holder, how did you work out the switch at the station? I hadn't been gone long and those guys were all over the place looking for me.'

'Sugar packets on the tray,' Lucas said trying to clear his throat.

'Sugar packets?'

'Your sister has a sugar habit and she twists the sugar packets into a spiral to hide how many she's used. Your sugar packets were flat.'

'Ah yes. Very good, she makes those sugar twists, it's very cute don't you think? That's a great piece of observation and deduction. Now your turn, you ask me a question. Even trade, Lieutenant, even trade.'

'Why did you swap places at the flat?' Lucas asked trying to block out the pain in his leg.

'Good one,' said Jess. 'We swapped because if you had arrested Jo you would have her for good. I love my sister, and she's good at what she does, but in certain situations she's hopeless. Me, on the other hand, now that's a different story. The government spent a huge amount of money to ensure I can get out of tight spots like that. We switched so she could get away before your officers blundered in, and I could just do what I do best. You see we look out for each other. I look after her, she looks after me. In this instance it was me looking after her. Now my turn,' Mechanic paused. 'Whose idea was it to cook up the story about the taped message on the line and the woman coming into the station pretending to be a victim? That was very smart.'

'Mine.'

'Bravo, bravo.' Mechanic clapped her hands in mock applause. 'You see my sister is kind of smart but kind of dumb at the same time. When she told me what happened it was an obvious setup. Good one, though, good one. Even trade, Lieutenant. Your turn.'

'We will catch you and put you away,' Lucas said, coughing blood onto his shirt.

Mechanic came right up to Lucas and put her face in his. 'Strike one, Lieutenant, that's not a question.' She snarled the words, then turned and took a step back. 'I am prepared to let it go on this occasion,' she said, the statement thick with menace. 'You see I'm not sure you will catch me. I'm a great believer in a track record being a good indication of what will happen in the future. And let's face it your track record is shit. You couldn't catch me last time, though admittedly it was that halfwit Harper running the show, but still, even when I gave myself to you, you didn't catch me this time. So I don't think the odds are stacked in your favour. Anyway back to the game that is keeping you alive, it's your turn to ask a question, Lieutenant. Even trade.'

'Why do you load victims into the family car and do the counselling?'

Mechanic shoved her face into Lucas's again. 'That's a double question. Strike two.' She backed away. 'The car loading is a complex ritual. The first point to understand is that our mother abandoned us when we were young and it turned my father into an abusive sadistic bastard. So long as I took the abuse, he left Jo alone. My mother created my father who in turn created me. So this whole thing is about revenge and reparation.'

'I still don't get it ...' Lucas croaked.

'Be patient, Lieutenant. The car ritual signifies abandonment which is what the women are considering doing to their families. So in my head that's a kind of a neat metaphor. The counselling is great fun and is a little like foreplay, I suppose. It makes the main event that much more satisfying. It leaves the women with a crushing sense of guilt. They were going to leave their loved ones and now with the courtesy of my services they are the ones who are left. Nice twist of the knife don't you think?'

Mechanic paced around in front of Lucas. 'To understand my third reason you must first understand the judicial system in this country. Our judiciary is like having your dementia-ridden uncle come to visit – everyone knows something isn't right but you kind of accept it. So, if by some flight of fancy you ever did catch me, I have a better chance of being classed criminally insane. If I simply murdered people, and did nothing else, I would be banged away on death row for murder one. But because I finish off the performance by doing weird shit, I relinquish any responsibility for my actions. A quirky but very useful safety net, so it's a mix of all three I suppose. Again, good question, Lieutenant. My turn, even trade, even trade. Did you ever work out the telephone numbers?'

Lucas shook his head as much to try and clear his blurred vision as to answer the question. 'No, we never got it.'

'That's excellent, you were never meant to. I laughed myself stupid at the GAI Circles name change. I set it up years ago and was afraid I'd never get a chance to use it but I needn't have worried. You see, as well as training me to take care of myself, the government also trained me in all sorts of covert comms, which comes in handy when you don't want to be found. Now your turn, even trade Lieutenant, even trade.'

Lucas was racking his aching head to think of a good question, one which would not only help the investigation when he was rescued, but also one which would keep him alive. He was aware he was on Strike 2, whatever that meant.

The pain from his leg was escalating and the pool of blood on the floor was getting bigger. 'Why did you kill Galbraith?'

'Oh poor selection, a wasted question. Isn't it obvious? He was about to rewrite his profile, which would change the direction of the investigation and put me and my sister in danger. I couldn't allow that, so I posed as Jo, arranged to meet with him, and eliminated the risk. Jo was very upset, but it did give me the opportunity to give Harper and his guys the dumb ass connection they needed when I committed suicide so spectacularly. They were not a smart outfit. Not like you. They needed spoonfeeding when it came to investigating crime. But then you knew that. Wasted question, Lieutenant, wasted question.'

'Now my turn.' Mechanic thought for a while. 'What do you think Bassano's last words were before I killed the sorry bastard …?' She let the words hang in the air. 'I did warn you, anyone you sent to find me.'

'You fucking murdering bitch,' Lucas yelled and struggled against his bound hands.

'Now if you're going to be rude, Lieutenant, then question time is over, and so are you.' She moved in close and Lucas shut his eyes.

'Don't!' Out of the darkness came Jo Sells. She stood behind her sister, carrying an oversized bag. Lucas opened his eyes, it was a surreal picture seeing them together. They were absolute carbon copies.

Mechanic could see Lucas flicking his eyes from one to the other. 'Can you tell us apart?'

'Yes,' he whispered.

'How?'

'Your voice,' he said, tasting the vomit in his mouth.

'Ah, yes, the voice. I agree it is a bit of a giveaway. Mine is deeper than my sister's but then she didn't overdo the steroids. Hers is oestrogen fuelled, whereas mine has more than a little testosterone in it. Nice observation, Lieutenant Lucas. My sister said you were good. It's why when you had me at the station I was crying all the time to mask it, and why when you interviewed me, I said nothing. You were easy to fool.' Mechanic circled Lucas as he tried to balance on one leg taking the strain off his tied wrists.

'There are other ways to tell us apart, but not from where you're standing, or hanging I should say,' Mechanic continued. 'My sister drinks very little whereas I like Wild Turkey bourbon, she is almost celibate whereas I am promiscuous as hell and she is a gentle soul whereas I ...' Mechanic paused, 'Well, let's just say I am not.' She circled Lucas. 'So you see, Lieutenant, unless you buy us a drink, fight us or fuck us, you wouldn't know the difference.'

Lucas spoke over Mechanic's shoulder, 'Jo, think about what you're doing.'

'My sister says I shouldn't kill you, she says you should live. Don't you, baby?' Mechanic draped her arm around Jo's shoulder. She nodded but said nothing. 'I'm kind of convinced otherwise. You know too much and I hate loose ends. And you are a very loose end, Lucas, We've both enjoyed the question and answer game, and with your latest outburst you now have three strikes. There is always a forfeit for that.'

Without warning Mechanic dropped her arm away from Jo, spun on her left leg and sent the instep of her right foot smashing into Lucas's ribs. In the confines of the room, the crack echoed off the walls. The force lifted him off the floor and swung him to the left. Mechanic pirouetted and faced Lucas once more. The blow ripped the air from his body as Lucas screamed in pain, the broken ribs puncturing his lung. Blood erupted into his mouth and splashed onto Mechanic.

Lucas couldn't breathe.

'No!' Jo screamed, pulling her sister away. 'Don't, you said you wouldn't.'

'Jo, you have to stop her. Put an end to this.' Lucas coughed blood and words onto the concrete below. He was beginning to shut down. The room was growing soft and woozy. 'Jo, you have to stop her.'

'I'm being compassionate, Lieutenant. I didn't think you would survive another shot to the head. You talk to me, not my sister.' Mechanic hissed the words through clenched teeth. 'It's me you deal with not her. Do you hear me, Lieutenant Lucas?' Lucas didn't answer, he was fighting for breath as his left lung collapsed. 'Do you hear me?' Mechanic yelled, her voice reverberating in his ears.

'Yesss,' he croaked. 'Yes I hear you.' Lucas could feel the world spinning and the sound of water rushing in his head. He was close to passing out. The blood from his lung filled his mouth and dribbled down his chin.

'Not good enough.' Mechanic slammed the sole of her right foot into Lucas's chest lifting him off his feet. Lucas swung on the rope and screamed in agony. He tried to right himself but his legs gave way under him and a fresh splash of crimson joined the dark pool on the floor. He jerked violently at the end of the rope. It disappeared into the flesh around his wrists and blood ran down his arms.

'No!' Jo screamed, stepping between her sister and Lucas. 'You promised not to kill him.'

'That was before he was disrespectful.' Mechanic moved in again but Jo drove her back. The force of the kick broke Lucas's sternum. He was asphyxiating and bleeding to death.

Tiny light bulbs popped and flashed at the edges of his vision. The lack of oxygen was forcing his brain to shut down, but he was determined not to give Mechanic the pleasure of watching him pass out. His peripheral vision was closing in and he felt very cold all of a sudden. The pain was receding and an overwhelming numbness was creeping through his body. The rushing sound in his head grew louder as Lucas fought for consciousness.

His eyes were open and he could see Mechanic fighting with Jo.

Jo was shouting, 'Just leave him, Jess, please leave him.'

Mechanic was snarling like a wild animal and threw Jo to one side. She took a step forward and Lucas knew this was the end.

Jo stepped in and grabbed her sister. The pair of them swirled round, locked in a savage embrace.

Then a shot rang out. Then another.

One of the women dropped to the floor and Lucas could see the unmistakable unkempt figure of Dick Harper holding a gun. He fired again and everything for Lucas went black.

Chapter 49

It was never clear to Lucas which of his injuries did the most damage. Whether it was the brutal beating at the hands of Mechanic or the ricochet shell from Harper's gun which cut a deep groove in his head. Either way, as Lucas saw it, he had stared death in the face and was still here. Well, in hospital to be more precise, hooked up to more tubes and machines than any one person should be allowed to encounter in a lifetime.

They kept him sedated while he was on life support, his busted rib cage and punctured lungs were unable to cope with the usual function of taking in air and blowing it out. And his shattered knee required major surgery. They told him he would be in hospital for another six weeks before he could even think of going home, but at least the life support in ICU was now being used by someone who needed it more. For Lucas that was a small victory.

Against all the odds, Bassano survived. A patrol vehicle out looking for Mechanic heard the shots and got to the scene just in time to save his life. Unfortunately, they didn't get there in time to save his arm. It was amputated in the same hospital as Lucas and for a brief period they were in ICU together. Neither one knew the other was there due to them both lacking consciousness. Bassano also suffered extensive head trauma which left him unable to walk. The hospital said that would mend with time.

After the operation and his spell in hospital, Bassano moved back to New Jersey to be with his parents. After all, he found it difficult to look after himself properly when he had two arms so learning to cope with one arm was going to be tough. He needed constant care and attention, and that lay at home.

Lucas was pleased his friend had survived but struggled to come to terms with the extent of his injuries. He was gutted it had ruined such a promising career in the force. Bassano was a good officer and a loyal friend. Lucas had let him down badly. Bassano visited Lucas before leaving to join his parents, but Lucas was out of it on a cocktail of morphine and sedatives. He could not remember seeing his friend leave. That made him sad.

Since then Lucas had called Bassano several times but on each occasion his father had declined to put him on the phone. Lucas said how sorry he was but the silence the other end said it all. If it was raw for Lucas it must be unbearable for Bassano's family, so he didn't hold it against them.

Lucas was not strong enough to deal with it anyway so it was just as well. It was difficult to choose which of the two of them had come off worse at the hands of Mechanic. They were discharged from hospital at separate times but neither one under his own steam. Both left in wheelchairs.

Lucas's wife camped out at the hospital during his recovery. This was traumatic for her, because unbeknown to Lucas, his heart stopped several times when first admitted. She maintained a constant vigil at his bedside and stayed strong but when she heard that he had pulled through and was out of danger, she cried for an entire day.

Lucas woke from his drug-induced coma to find his words were slurred. He had difficulty constructing sentences, but as time went by his speech returned to normal. He grilled the steady stream of officers who came to visit him about the case. What's the latest? Have they followed up on the vehicle? Did they get fingerprints?

One of his regulars was Dick Harper. Lucas loved his visits because Harper spoke to him in his usual blunt and to the point manner. It was simple, uncomplicated straightforward conversation.

Harper was oblivious to the fact that Lucas had slurred speech, ignored the fact his lungs didn't work, and never once appeared to notice the knitting basket of pipes and tubes keeping him alive. Harper was also impervious to the usual protocol of bringing the sick person a gift of fruit or flowers. He sat at the side of Lucas's bed, burning with all the intensity of a rooky cop while devouring any grapes, strawberries or oranges which were within arm's reach. Lucas never saw him eat the flowers but he ate everything else.

Between them they had a single topic of conversation, piecing together the events of that evening.

That night, Harper had known about the incident the station from the reports on his police scanner, and when he got to the station the controller told him where Lucas had gone. He found his car abandoned outside the club. Harper was a lot more agile than his bulk would suggest, and he had scaled the gates to get into the grounds. He found the security guard in the bushes near to the grand house with his neck broken, and figured, just like Lucas, that the most likely place to look was the maintenance sheds at the back of the estate. He could hear shouting coming from the basement, saw Lucas hanging by his wrists, and the two women fighting. He shot twice at the women and one of them threw a wrench causing him to fall backwards. His third shot struck the ceiling and then hit Lucas.

When Harper regained his balance, one of the women returned fire and shot him in the shoulder, knocking him backwards into the work benches. As he fell he struck the back of his head, and that was the last Harper knew of anything until the backup units arrived to take charge of the wounded. At least Harper had the presence of mind to tell the desk controller to get a patrol car over to Brightwood club. They were late but at least they got there.

It didn't matter how many times they went over the details of what happened, Harper always maintained one thing. His second shot hit one of the women in the head and he saw her fall. He recounted how her head snapped back and he saw the black hole in her forehead. Harper was adamant he had killed her.

When Harper came round from being knocked unconscious, his first question was about Lucas, and his second was about the women.

Lucas was in a bad way and on his way to hospital.

The women were gone.

Chapter 50

Present day
Wednesday, 23 March 1983
Tallahassee, Florida

Lucas wanted to shoot his visitors. The gun lay in his desk drawer and he was itching to pull it out and blast away. He had to stop them torturing him with kindness, but wasting two FBI agents on his first week back was such bad form. So, in the absence of being able to kill them, he chose instead to only half listen.

The two guys in FBI regulation suits were talking but all he heard was the faint mumbling of soft, understanding voices. They were being ever so gentle and considerate, which would be good, if it wasn't for the fact they had been ever so gentle and considerate for the past three goddam days.

They were well trained to deal with people being rehabilitated back into work after they had suffered significant trauma. But how many times did he have to go over and over the same damn stuff? It was always the same story, always the same chronology, always the same people and always the same outcome.

Monday 21 March was a significant date in the Lucas household calendar. It was the day he finally returned to work. He had been back now for three days. Not that anyone would have known because he had been holed up in his office talking to the FBI suits for the entire duration.

Lucas harboured a dark thought, which he kept securely to himself. *Let them bring a new guy in to run the show and I'll drive a desk in a back office somewhere.* It was once the job he loved, but now the role of Police Lieutenant appeared like a giant nettle which he had no intention of grasping.

After everything that had happened, Lucas couldn't move on. How could he? There was no resolution to what had taken place, just one giant loose end.

One big, fat, ugly loose end.

He was aware that the talking had stopped and the FBI agents were staring at him with a look of expectation that said, 'It's your turn to talk now.'

He looked up and didn't even bother to pretend. 'Sorry, guys, I wasn't listening. You need anything else?'

'It's been a long few days but I think we have all we need,' the taller of the two men replied, nodding his head. Lucas still couldn't remember their names.

You had what you needed two damn months ago, Lucas thought, keeping his mouth shut.

They rose from the circular conference table and shook hands across it. There was a palpable sense of relief that the gentle tones and soft questions had at last come to an end.

'Thanks guys.' Even Lucas had to admit his words sounded hollow and disingenuous. He just wanted them both to piss off.

Lucas ushered them to the door, limping without his stick, and showed them out. He flopped down in his chair and shook his head. There was a knock on the door and his mail arrived.

The plain white document-sized envelope with the handwritten address stood out from the rest. Lucas pulled it from the stack and held it in his hand, turning it first this way then the next, as if examining a piece of evidence. It was addressed to him with a date stamp of Monday 21 March and from the postmark he could just about make out Baton Rouge, Louisiana.

It was written in an ornate copperplate script with flurries of expert swirls around his name: Lieutenant Edmund Lucas. He frowned and edged his finger into the corner of the flap, and then slid it along the top, ripping it open.

The envelope felt empty.

He peered inside.

It certainly didn't contain a letter or a document, but Lucas knew there was something at the bottom. He tipped the envelope sideways to extract whatever was inside.

The first grains of bright white sugar rolled from the confines of the envelope and onto the polished surface of the desk. Lucas was stunned, unable to comprehend what was happening.

He tilted it further. More grains of sugar spilled out and pooled in concentric circles on the table top. The more Lucas tilted the envelope, the more sugar cascaded down, along with what looked like squares of white paper. Lucas upended it and allowed the complete contents to empty onto the desk. He stared at the mess of sugar and paper, holding his breath.

It took a few moments for the cogs to turn and for realization to dawn. Then tears welled up in his eyes and he exploded, slamming his fist into the table.

'No!' he yelled at the top of his voice.

As he punched the desk a second time, the door burst open.

'Are you alright, boss?'

'No, I am not!' Lucas spat the words across the office. 'Get those FBI bastards back here now.'

He was ready to grasp the nettle and spoiling for a fight.

Ten white paper packets, with their tops torn off, lay scattered across his desk among the sugar.

They were perfectly flat.

Mechanic was back.

The End

A Note from Bloodhound Books

Thanks for reading Those That Remain. We hope you enjoyed it as much as we did. Please consider leaving a review on Amazon or Goodreads to help others find and enjoy this book too.

We make every effort to ensure that books are carefully edited and proofread, however occasionally mistakes do slip through. If you spot something, please do send details to info@ bloodhoundbooks.com and we can amend it.

Bloodhound Books specialise in crime and thriller fiction. We regularly have special offers including free and discounted eBooks. To be the first to hear about these special offers, why not join our mailing list here? We won't send you more than two emails per month and we'll never pass your details on to anybody else.

Readers who enjoyed Those That Remain will also enjoy

Games People Play by Owen Mullen

Watching The Bodies by Graham Smith

Acknowledgements

I want to thank all those who have made this book possible – My family Karen, Gemma, Holly and Maureen for their blunt, painful feedback and endless patience. To my band of loyal proofreaders Yvonne, Lesley, Christine, Penny, Christine, Austin, Nicki, Laura, Jackie, Alex, Anne, Frazer and Simon who didn't hold back either and finally my talented editor, Helen Fazal, who kept me sane when I needed it and without whom this work would be devoid of punctuation, grammar and syntax.

Printed in Great Britain
by Amazon